BUSHWHACKED

A Jake Lydon Mystery

BUSHWHACKED

A Jake Lydon Mystery

JOHN OWENS

OTTAWA
PRESS AND
PUBLISHING

OTTAWA PRESS AND PUBLISHING

ottawapressandpublishing.com

ISBN (pbk.)   978-1-988437-46-0
ISBN (MOBI)   978-1-988437-48-4
ISBN (EPUB)   978-1-988437-47-7

Cover and page design: Glenn Torresan
Cover photograph: Glenn Torresan

For my Shannon

Certain individuals
aren't sticking with the plan
- Warren Zevon

I don't expect to be treated like a fool no more
I don't expect to sleep through the night
- Paul Simon

They found Maynard Odell—or what was left of him—on May 5th. He'd been dead about three days, maybe four. Dr. Shaw, our local coroner, couldn't exactly be sure. I was to learn a bit later that, judging by the state of decomposition and the types of insects on the corpse and on the bloodied sides of the woodchopper that had consumed him up to about mid-thigh, Shaw figured most likely three days, with an outside chance it had been four.

A lot of ink and pixels are spent on the dangers of city living. While smog, insane motorists, and drive-by shootings aren't too common out here, there is a bunch of crazy fatal things that happen in the country. Drownings, freezings, hunting accidents, chainsaw kickbacks, and, yes, murderous wood chippers.

There was surprisingly little surprise at Maynard's death—even though it was the very definition of untimely. At least it wasn't a shocker around the tables at the Angler's Arms the next day. I'm not guessing at any of this; I heard the comments. When I'm with Carl, I'm granted entry into his occasional lunch-time klatch of locals, as opposed to the lakeside cottage and homeowners who—even if they've owned on the lake for twenty years as I had—are still regarded as outsiders, interlopers.

These five lads—all middle-aged or over—had the skinny on what had actually happened. They compared notes and offered up bits of gossip to build the 'just the facts, ma'am' story. Maynard was back up on his woodlot, way off the lake on the east side. He had invested in an industrial-sized wood chipper for his expanding mulch business and he was using it to stockpile ground-up brush and small cedars for the spring gardening rush of us Johnny-come-latelys who pathologically must garden.

Their names haven't been omitted to protect their identities; I just don't know them.

"Christ, what a painful way to go!"

"Musta' been screaming like crazy."

"Nobody'd hear up that far. Blue jays maybe."

"Didn't scream for long, thank gawd. I figure he'd bleed out pretty quick."

"Didn't find him for three days?"

"I heard four."

"Lived alone; nobody'd miss him and go lookin'."

"Goddamn shame."

"Good fella."

"Whaddya mean good fella?" Carl interjected, speaking for the first time. "He was a prick."

Wait a minute. Let's back up, shall we? Back a few weeks to the start of the twisting trail that led to the wood chipper and dastardly points beyond.

CHAPTER 1

I get profiled at customs checkpoints all the time. Maybe it's something about my aging ex-hippie look—the long hair, half-assed beard, Hawaiian shirt, shorts, and flip-flops. Or perhaps, after spending months in the Caribbean, it's something in the way I move—with just my shitty laptop and trusty bowling bag—that attracts them like no other. In either event, they're convinced that I'm absolutely loaded to what gunwales I have with drugs or blood diamonds or Disney merch knock-offs. So me, my shitty laptop, and my trusty bowling bag are escorted to small windowless rooms where we are all routinely searched by armed guards who can't re-pack worth shit.

I had believed that the Dominican customs officials decided some years ago that I was an odd but harmless part-time expatriate, whereas I automatically expect the once-over at Pearson International in Toronto. There, I've been torn apart four times and by the same humourless customs guys. I'm a little hurt that we're not on a first-name basis yet. I wanted to ask them about their winter in the Toronto icy cold and slush but figured it might sound as though I were gloating. Like I'd ever do that.

I had believed that the Dominican customs officials decided some years ago that I was an odd but harmless part-time expatriate, whereas I automatically expect the once-over at Pearson International in Toronto. There, I've been torn apart four times and by the same humourless customs guys. I'm a little hurt that we're not on a first-name basis yet. I wanted to ask them about their winter in the Toronto icy cold and slush but figured it might sound as though I were gloating. Like I'd ever do that.

But on this most recent trip back north, one of these luggage takedowns happened at both ends of the same goddamned flight. It started at El Catey airport near Las Terrenas in the Dominican Republic where I usually while away my winters mangling Spanish and my brain cells. Two armed guards took me out of the check-in line and hustled me away to one of those aforementioned windowless rooms. I had a *Midnight Express* moment when they were having trouble unzipping my bag. I moved to help and one guard rather abruptly went for his gun. I may have muttered: "Fine. Open it your own fucking self." Which wasn't all that daring because none of the three searchers spoke English.

After running (that's right—me!—running!) through the airport, I barely made my flight. I was so rattled that I actually paid the piratical price for a beer. Seven times. So I was looking and feeling my best when the plane eventually rolled up to the gate at Pearson four hours later and I rolled off the plane.

The lad at the customs booth decided I needed some extra attention. I am willing to concede that perhaps I too vocally disagreed, asking him several times (and loudly) what the fuck he thought I might've done mid-flight following the search in the DR that had come up empty. He apparently wasn't up for a debate and got quite huffy about it. I wound up in yet another one of those aforementioned windowless rooms.

This time, the rubber-gloved searchers took longer than usual because they seemed sure, absolutely, positively certain that they had me this time. So they were pissed off when they didn't find anything more offensive than my laundry and I was pissed off because my beer hum was wearing off and because I knew Carl, my ride, had been circling the terminal like a slow-motion NASCAR driver waiting for me and a parking spot. And because I wanted a cigarette.

But just to demonstrate that I'm a glass half-full kinda guy, I was secretly grateful that they didn't make me undress like the last time. This time, their trained eagle eyes couldn't have missed the not one but two bullet scars decorating my paunch—the one across my gut coming last summer and the second which now decorates one of my love handles, a souvenir of this past winter. That would've raised some eyebrows and questions.

"Sorry, boys," I said as I stuffed the rest of my shit back in the bag. "Maybe next year."

As I finally escape the terminal and frantically light up, I watched for my silver Vibe. I knew Carl wouldn't say anything about the delay, mostly because Carl doesn't say much ever.

Here's one of our longer conversations—reproduced in its entirety. A phone call I made to him just before my return to Toronto from a winter in Las Terrenas.

"Yeah?"

"Carl?"

"Yeah."

"How ya doin'?"

"Good. You?"

"Good."

"When?"

"April 25th. Air Canada 469. Arrive 11 AM."

"See ya then."

Click.

And he's always there. A big calm presence amid the bustle of the busiest airport in Canada. He drives down from the lake in my ageless Pontiac Vibe and looks sort of ridiculous as he unfolds his 6' 5" frame; it's almost like watching the clowns exit their toy cars in Shriner parades.

And as always, we shake hands rather formally, as if we've just been introduced even though he's been a dear friend of mine for twenty years.

I know it's a big deal for him to leave the lake and I've tried to talk him out of it but it's just an inviolate habit with him now, one of many we have together, even though he white-knuckles it in Toronto traffic. He says that's the price he's willing to pay for me putting the NFL and NHL packages on his cable in exchange for him providing taxi service and watching over my lakeside hovel from his island a couple of hundred feet from my shoreline .

It was not until ninety minutes later as we passed through Peterborough and then by Trent University—one of my alma maters—in the north end that he started to relax.

We didn't speak much on the drive but then again we never speak much. Carl can make Keanu Reeves seem like Robin Williams on a manic roll. Except where the NFL is involved. I think I love the game as much as he does, but our approaches are radically different. I go on hunches and baseless hopes and then scramble to justify why they invariably don't work out. Really, my predictions are just a notch above Lisa Simpson's winning pool entries for Homer based on uniform colours. Whereas, Carl is a goddamned computer, the original moneyballer. He memorizes college combine scores, knows completion percentages on rainy days and can honestly tell you how often a quarterback of Polish extraction has been sacked more than three times on Monday Night Football in the modern era. I've learned a lot from him. Mostly I've learned to despise him because he's right a whole lot more often than he's wrong.

We didn't talk again until we went through the small town of Buckhorn, the last outpost of civilization (because it has a liquor store) before we reach the lake.

"See the game?" he asked, referring obviously to the Super Bowl.

"Of course."

"Turned out alright."

"Fuck off."

Carl broadly grinned. Another thing he doesn't do very often; he usually has a slight restrained Mona Lisa-type half-smile of contentment. He now wears this wide shit-eating grin because his one and only e-mail to me over the winter was his Bet on The Game. Which he had won. Again. I think that makes twenty in a row for the big bastard.

We reached the turn-off road for our lake. On the corner of County Road 507 and our elegantly named Fire Route 162, I saw a construction trailer and a billboard showing an up-scale log home and a happy-looking LL Beaned, aging yuppie couple in a canoe. That hadn't been there when I left last fall. The sign said "Coming Soon - Edgewater Estates" with a Toronto phone number.

"Hear about The Development?" Carl asked.

"I did. Read the *Examiner* on-line. Article said the township planning committee had approved it. Whaddya think?"

"Bound to happen sooner or later."

He concentrated on a winding bit of dirt road following the south shore of the lake.

"Just wish it was later," he eventually added.

"The article said east side of the lake, around the corner from us. Where exactly is it?"

"Starts here."

We were passing The Angler Arms, the best cottage country bar in the world™, where all spring and summer Carl and I religiously attend bar service, a ritual we call going to AA.

"What?!"

"Figured you should hear it in person."

"Must be a fuckin' mistake!"

"Takes in this empty lot, then these two houses…," Carl says by way of slow commentary, "and then…"

"…And then my place!"

"And then mine right after."

"Must be a fuckin' mistake," I repeated, my alarm growing.

"Mebbe. Don't think so."

Carl's not a real sugar-coaty kinda guy. I was stunned.

We came to my laneway. The only way you'd know it's mine is my mailbox with The Lydons' painted on it (not The Lydon's, because the apostrophe there is wrong and fuckin' dumb). It has survived twenty winters of snow ploughing along our road. Every so often, I touch up the paint even though it's been about ten years since there has been home mail delivery. Or plural Lydons, for that matter. But I feel obligated to keep it up. Call me an optimist; maybe they'll start delivering again. I saw the black sign with 'Private Property' spelled in fluorescent orange letters was still tacked to the post.

The laneway winds for about two hundred yards after it plunges into the bush by the road. At the end of the driveway the land opens up. After we passed the storage shed I built a couple of years ago, I got the full view and I was gladdened, despite the news of an alleged development.

As expected, the yard looked early spring-pathetic. The wispy lawn was dun-coloured; fallen black skeletal branches littered it and yellowed hosta leaves limply drooped over the low pink granite retaining walls that ring the grounds. I smiled at the only real blight on the landscape: Carl's battered blue F-150 pickup off to the side facing the island he lives on, a couple of hundred feet from my shoreline.

Carl, me, my shitty laptop, and my trusty bowling bag climbed the low stairs to my house. Calling it a house is being excessively charitable. It's a three-season hovel of a log cottage. But it's my house. We walked through the front door and saw nuthin' but lake out back filling the picture window. It was not the image of the lake I routinely recall; the water was greyish white because it was still iced over.

There's always an element of suspense when I return to the place after five or six months south. I completely shut the house down when I fuck off in the fall. It's not a big deal: Turn off the power and the water pump, blow out the lines, toss some antifreeze in the toilet and I'm gone. The house is not even close to airtight so there's always the chance that gangs of squirrels or mice have partied like drunken frat boys in the place while I was away.

Carl doesn't clean up but he re-starts everything before he picks me up. And I am grateful because it's a busy time for him, opening up houses and cottages for at least twenty other returning fellow snow-birds on this lake and two others nearby.

"Beer?" Carl asked after my silent survey.

That's another key part of the ceremony when I return. He had stocked the fridge with Molson Export ale—another thing we have in common besides football and cantankerousness. He snapped a couple open while I changed out of my Caribbean uniform, pulling on a fleecy, sweat pants, and fucking socks. We headed out to the deck and parked ourselves in the pair of Adirondack chairs facing the hardened water. And then we shivered.

Last week of April and it was cold, jeezly cold. About 45 degrees Fahrenheit (even though my country inexplicably went metric over forty years ago, I did not). In the deepening gloom of late afternoon, it was colder still and I bet we'd probably have frost that night. There were still small piles of snow under the pine or spruce or whatever the fuck they're called.

Now we could have just as easily gone inside, fired up my propane-run fireplace, and huddled around it but we didn't. We never do. Carl thinks it's an abomination unto his eyes and we never speak of it, not since I replaced the wood-burning stove a few years back because I got sick of hauling firewood. Carl's a traditionalist, plus he makes part of his meagre living cutting and selling firewood.

"Good winter?" I asked.

"Yup. Spring, not so much. Hadn't counted on moving."

He sounded like the fatalistic Eeyore droning: "Oh, well. Better find a new home," and I was saddened. Carl lives large in the material world around him, completely comfortable in his skin and confident in his outdoorsy element. It's the world of paper and lawyers and officialdom that fucks him up.

Carl stared at the lake. I could see the fear in his eyes. His face is creased and lined by a hard life in the sun, by cigarette smoke, by laughter, and now by anxiety. He tapped his size twelves nervously on the pine needle-strewn deck. I really felt for him, afraid of the idea of finding himself this far down the road—he was somewhere in his mid-70s—being displaced.

I actually patted one of his giant paws splayed out on the wide armrest.

"Carl, don't worry, buddy. Who gives a shit about their plans? It's our fuckin' land. It's real simple. If I own something and you want it and I don't want to sell it then too bad, so sad for you; that's the end of it."

"Ya figure?"

"Yeah, I figure. We'll just tell them to go fuck themselves. Right? We agree?"

"Yup."

We shook hands *and* clinked beer bottle necks. As far as I'm concerned, that's about as iron-clad a contract as you can get.

Carl drained his beer but declined another one.

"Better get goin.' Gettin' dark," said Eeyore on the move.

That time of year, the ice is treacherous. Not quite thick enough to walk on, but too thick for a vessel. Carl has devised an ingenious way to travel back and forth from his island. He rigged up an iron hook—something like a shepherd's crook—on a proverbial 10-foot pole and he either sinks the hook into the ice in front of his canoe to drag it or reaches back to push himself forward. He does all this while standing up, displaying Wallenda-type balance. He looks, for all the world, like a giant ice-bound gondolier.

I went inside, turned on some lights and was at least psychologically warmed by the glow of the honey-coloured log walls. Actual body heat came about half an hour after I flicked the switch on the gas fireplace.

I walked from room to room which didn't take very long. The whole shebang is about twelve hundred square feet not counting the screened-in porch. About the same size as the two-bedroom condo I bought in Las Terrenas three winters ago. Size matters up here more than it does down there because up here I will mostly be confined indoors for the next four or five weeks while Canada takes its own sweet time to warm the fuck up. And I will be antsy until then, an extended version of pacing the kitchen waiting for a slow toaster to pop. This hump period of weather-enforced house arrest is not an issue in the Dominican Republic where you're always outside and your three choices for temperature settings are warm, hot, and hot-hot.

I shuffled around the kitchen, opening drawers to find the reminders of a mouse infestation—small black granules that look like multiple pepper mills had exploded. I was bagged from the travel and decided that the producers of that excrement would live to shit another night and that I'd set the trap line the next day. Last year, I almost caught enough of the little bastards to make a bomber jacket.

I heated up a can of soup, retrieved another, beer and grabbed the stacks of mail that Carl had neatly placed on the table in two piles marked by little signs that I made in that artsy-crafty way I have: "Shit" and "More Shit."

In front of the fake, blue-tinged flames, I rummaged through the paper. There wasn't much. Carl had my permission to junk all the junk mail including any light brown envelopes from the Canada Revenue Agency. I thought I'd phone them in a couple of days to renew our feud—letters can be so impersonal, can't they?

Prominent in the pile was a large envelope from Lakeshore Developments Inc. I ripped it open.

There was a cover letter that looked more like a brochure—lots of white space, bolded sentences, and a couple of outdoorsy photos.

"Dear Landowner (at least they spelled my name right) [the letter began],

Lakeshore Developments Inc. is pleased to announce the launch of Edgewater Estates, the new **gold standard in leisure living**.

Edgewater Estates is a unique opportunity for everybody to win!

First off, **you'll win**. I think you'll find that we are prepared to make **very generous offers** to existing landowners as we pursue our dream of a prestige community in West Kawartha.

Your community will win with this anchor development as it will create **hundreds of jobs** for your neighbours and not just during construction but for years to come. At the same time, **everybody's land value will increase**, while generating substantial

new tax dollars to improve your township's services.

The environment will win by hosting our sustainable, totally "green," locally-sourced natural building materials and advanced construction techniques respectful of the natural landscape.

Very shortly, I'll be getting in touch with you individually to more completely describe our vision and just **how much you'll benefit**. At the same time, we can discuss an **exciting investment opportunity** that will **richly reward** you for years to come.

In the meantime, please take a look at the enclosed general plan for Edgewater Estates to get just a taste of the **exciting things** we want to do on the Mississauga Lake property you so very **wisely invested** in.

And please do not hesitate to call me **personally** with any questions.

Sincerely

Stuart "Stewie" Woodson"

Except for the "do not hesitate to etc." bit, (who the fuck has ever hesitated?), a few too many adverbs, and the superfluous use of "very" in front of "unique", oh, and the "personally" (as very few people ask to be called impersonally), I had to concede it was a pretty good letter which pissed me off more. It had punched all the right buttons—appeal to personal greed, appeal to community, and there was even a vigorous nod to tree huggery.

I unfolded the glossy plan and spread it out on the coffee table. It was one of those stylized maps, all jagged and colourful, mid-blue lake, mid-green land. Around the outside of the map were inset photos and drawings depicting an idyllic and wealthy lifestyle. Quality stock shots of attractive people playing golf, tennis, and canoeing, their attractive kids swimming near a dock, a fucking attractive loon or two. I decided that every photo had been doctored because the real-life omnipresent clouds of horse/ black/deer flies had obviously been airbrushed—I mean Photoshopped—out.

I snorted at the artist's rendering of giant log mansions where all these attractive people would find shelter. "Locally sourced?" Sure, buddy. Unless they had been cultivating a secret woodlot of BC firs for the last hundred years or so, there wasn't a goddamned chance in hell they'd find logs that thick around these parts. And by these parts, I mean every square inch of Canada not named British Columbia.

The vast majority of the development took up the uninhabited eastern shore of our lake right around the corner from my place on the south shore of the squarish lake. All in, the map said, Edgewater Estates was to be about four square miles of rock and bush bounded on the west by the shoreline of Mississauga Lake and on the north and east butting up against 145 square miles of wilderness that is Kawartha Highlands Provincial Park. Then there's narrow strip leaking around to the south shore. Identifiable on that narrow strip was my little thumb of a land (Carl calls it a middle finger) jutting into the lake near his island. There were two unmarked purple rectangles spreading across my land and the empty lot beside me in front of Carl's island. Then two more smaller rectangles representing the houses already there, a break for another empty lot, and then AA. Dominating the map in the main body of the development was a golf course outlined with houses sprinkled around it and inside it.

Another beer and I was ready to turn in. I just couldn't seem to nod off even though I'd been away from my mighty comfortable sleepin' couch for almost six months. When you're married—as I once was—you're told to not go to bed angry. Same's true for single guys. I was working myself up into a recumbent lather over the arrogance of these fucks who just pick a piece of property and decide that's where they want to make a piss-pot while driving out or complicating the lives of the humans who currently live there.

I'll deal with the mouse turds tomorrow, I thought. Oh, and the droppings in my kitchen drawers as well.

CHAPTER 2

Tomorrow came—as it tends to do—and I decided to let my real estate issues slide as I took care of more pressing matters—like feeding myself and re-stocking my diabetes drug supply. It was odd to be behind the wheel of my soon-to-be-classic car because I hadn't driven for six months. Coming back from Peterborough with a laden Vibe, I felt like a pioneer settler after a-goin' inta town to lay in provisions—only with a car and a debit card.

I was happy on that drive home. Despite the niggling notion of a big development going in near me, I was looking forward to a summer of nothingness, happy to settle in and not move. Unlike the previous summer that saw me shuttling around the lake, Boston, Toronto and San Francisco and all points in between, largely in a committed pursuit to stay alive.

Things hadn't been any more restive this past winter when a bunch of very bad things happened to some very good people and almost to me.

A few days later, as I was picking up and sweeping away the detritus of winter from the front yard, I heard the crunch of tires on my gravel road and turned to watch a silver Mercedes pull up to the house. It brought with it the cloud of dust that you get when you drive too fast on an unpaved driveway.

"See the Private Property sign?" I asked the guy getting out of the car.

He was a big lad, but trim. And he was a sharp-dressed man—beige slacks with knife-edge creases, powder blue shirt cut to fit, set off by a tasteful but conservative dark blue tie, a tight-fitting leather bomber jacket. He was carrying one of those slender soft briefcases. A handsome maybe forty-year old face was topped by curly dark hair so perfectly coiffed he should've been drinking a pina colada at Trader Vic's. Close up, his blue eyes bored as he studied me studying him.

"That sign is exactly why I'm here," he said. [Good segue, I thought] "I'm Stewie Woodson, from Edgewater Estates, Mr. Lydon," he said, thrusting out his hand.

"Not interested," I said as I shake. [Christ, this man had a good handshake].

"You haven't heard my offer."

"Not interested."

"I think you'll see that we're being more than gen—"

"—Look, would it help if I said it louder and slower?" I asked.

"You're not interested in four hundred thousand dollars?"

I stopped—maybe for the nanosecond it took for my greedy self to point out to my defiant self that the amount he'd just tossed out represented a 500% profit over what I paid for the place two decades ago.

He was a pro at this and knew I was doing some calculating. He seized upon this pause as a wedge to start his spiel.

"You should at least hear all the details, get all the information. Where's the harm in that?" [Smart, I thought. End with a question you can't be negative about].

I said nothing but crossed my arms. About the only way I could have made plainer my resistance was if I had held up a poster reading "Shutup!Shutup!Shutup!" But I didn't say it out loud which he took as permission to plough onwards.

"Edgewater Estates is a unique opportunity for everybody to win," he began.

"Say, I've heard that before."

He ignored me and went into an enraptured description of Edgewater designed, I gathered, to draw me into his sublime vision. The only thing missing were swelling violins.

"There will be nothing like it in Ontario," he continued. "The best of amenities, elegant but casual. Comfortable. Assured. A community of peers who have earned their reward. And to ensure we get the right kind of people, our marketing has been designed to be understated and discrete, adding to the panache of the development."

"Well, this is really weird," I said, "because just the other day I was saying: Do you know what we really need around here? We need us some fuckin' panache. In fact, we need a shit-ton of panache. With maybe a touch of élan and perhaps a soupçon of de rigueur."

Stewie must have realized that hyperbole wasn't the way to my heart—or wallet. He pivoted.

"But it's the investment side that may be more attractive to you," he said. "You can take the 400K cash. Or you use it buy 400k in units of our private REIT—are you familiar with Real Estate Income Trusts?"

"Yeah."

"Good. We pay you an annual dividend based on the increasing value of the land."

"How much?"

"Glad you asked [I immediately wished I hadn't]. This is the absolutely best part. For you. 9%! You can't get that anywhere!"

Again I made with the ciphering. That's a nice chunk of annual change, I was forced to admit to myself.

"And I have to move?" I asked and almost smacked myself. [Idiot! My question kept the conversation going].

"Only when we start developing."

"When's that?" [Moron!]

"This section of lakefront? Maybe two years. We're starting with the golf course subdivision first. Meanwhile, we'll pay your mortgage for you."

"Don't have one." [Imbecile!]

"Alright then, tell you what, we'll pay your taxes, utilities, the works. And you get 9% return on your money annually. And you preserve the capital."

I'm naturally inclined towards skepticism, oh hell, let's call it unbridled, raging suspicion with everything having to do with money and today's commerce. My simple rule: With the exception of KFC's Double Down, if something sounds too good to be true, it probably isn't.

"Can I opt out, take the cash and leave?" [Cretin!]

"Of course but we think you'll find—if you talk to *any* financial advisor—that it'd be much more lucrative to stay in."

"I see," was my phenomenally astute comment.

"Why don't you go over this Memorandum of Offering, and I'll follow up?"

He withdrew a sheaf of papers from his brief case and touched me lightly on the arm with it, as though it were a subpoena.

"I'll take it but do not, under any circumstances, think I'm interested," I moronically said.

"Fair enough, but you should know that your neighbors are."

That kind of me-tooism might work with some people. I am not one of those people.

"Can you tell me—precisely—why whatever the fuck they decide to do ought to interest me in the slightest fucking bit?"

He instantly knew he'd made a mistake in his sales patter and pivoted again. Guy could have been an NBA point guard.

"Would you like to know what we've planned for this stretch of shoreline?" he asked, gliding over my terminal misanthropy.

"No. If I sell, then I'm gone, so why would I care?"

[Dolt!]I had said "If I sell."

"Think about it, won't you?" he said giving me his business card. "I'm a patient man."

"Turns out, I'm not, so I believe we're done here. And please, ease off the gas leaving. There might be slow children playing."

After the silver Mercedes left—slowly—I walked back to the house cursing myself for letting the conversation go on as long as it did. But I had to grudgingly admire Stewie; he was a pro. Or I was a sap.

I was mulling over our conversation when Carl showed up.

"That city fella offer you a bunch of money?" he asked.

"Yup."

"Did me too."

"Wanna beer?"

"Yup."

I fished two pints out of my fridge.

"And?" I asked as I turned a frosty over to him.

"Don't be an arsehole. Remember? We shook on it."

"*And* clinked bottles."

"And clinked bottles. Besides, where am I gonna go?"

"Why thee fuck would he want your rock anyway?"

"Showed me the new plans. He wants to put a bridge over to it. Some kind of fool sanctuary for birds and animals."

"Like the Red-faced Drunken Old Coot?"

"Arsehole. By the way, there's a doozy of a pretty parking lot they got planned about there," he says, waving down my laneway.

"Saw it on the map. A parking lot for what?"

"He didn't tell you?"

"Didn't get that far."

"Old folks home. Christ, we could both move in there with the money we'd get!"

"Gee, Carl, do you think it's one of those new places that'll let you keep your guns and smoke like a fuckin' chimney? Cuz I'm betting it's not."

"They got rules like that?"

"And a lot more."

"Well, piss on that idea. You interested in buying in the new place?"

"I think I'd rather burst my—or someone else's—hemorrhoids than live in one of those boxes."

Nosy little fucker that I am, I had to ask the inevitable:

"How much?"

"400K," he answered. "You?"

"Same."

"You understand this shit?" Carl asked, holding up his Offering Memorandum.

"Some."

"Good deal/bad deal?"

"No fuckin' idea. On paper it looks OK."

"He told me to talk to my investment advisor."

"You have an investment advisor?"

"Sure do. You."

"Then you're fucked, buddy."

"Mebbe. But I know where you live…for now anyways."

"OK, so I did the math. According to them, you'd get $36,000 the first year. Bunch more each year after that without touching the original 400K."

Carl took one of his long, thoughtful pauses.

"Thirty-six thousand?" he said. "That's twice what I make for busting my hump."

"So you just want to get fat and lazy?"

He paused yet again.

"Lookin' at it that way, mebbe I could give it a whirl."

As per usual with Carl, I couldn't tell if he was being serious or just yanking my chain. But his hesitation stopped me. So *I* wanted to stay in *my* place? So fucking what? Where do I get off leaning on a guy who's worked like a dog all his life?

"Carl, if you want to take it easy, then you should take it easy. Christ knows, you've earned it," I said and I meant it.

He looked at me, all surprised and suspicious.

"You tellin' me if I sell, you'd be OK about it?"

"Yes."

"Even though we shook?"

"Yes."

"And clinked bottles?"

"Yes."

"Serious?"

"Yes."

"Straight up?

"Yes."

"No bullshit?"

"For fuck's sake, buddy. YES!"

He thought for a while, looking at me sideways a couple of times.

"In that case," he finally said, "I'm stayin'."

There might be a whole bunch of landowners and business people who wanted this thing to happen. But I had Carl on my side. I liked our chances.

Just because I'm outlandishly considerate by nature, I thought I'd give Stewie a heads-up about our irrevocable decision so he could change his plans accordingly.

He didn't thank me and he didn't go into a more frenetic sales pitch. In a flat tone, he just said: "You should reconsider." And he hung up.

I have this reflex reaction, like what happens when a doctor taps your knee cap with a rubber hammer. It instantly occurs when someone tells me I "should" do anything. I guess they'd call it a trigger word today. A little bloom of rage suddenly appears in my gut whenever I *should*.

No matter, I decided. We'd put an end to Edgewater Estates' covetous designs on our properties and, as far as I was concerned, that was that.

CHAPTER 3

I had a life beyond being vexed by the plans of a hoity-toity developer lusting after my land. OK, OK, I managed to fill my days. But—and this is critical—I filled them with *exactly* the ingredients I wanted to in *exactly* the right dosages as I wished.

I have no bucket list. I had a sort of retroactive one, but abandoned it when it finally and painfully dawned on me that I wasn't ever going to co-found the Rolling Stones or play nets for the Toronto Maple Leafs.

At 61, and more than semi-retired from the PR and communications biz, I had a shockingly short list of hobbies and pursuits. Once or twice a week I drive to Peterborough to get the snot beaten out of me at a ratty old gym where I indulge in—I won't call it a passion— a mild interest in amateur boxing. I ache more and I bruise more easily than I used to but I still enjoy it. Raises a sweat, raises the ol' heartbeat, and raises a few welts.

Occasionally I play tennis but that's dwindling. I'm at the age where doubles is the only real chance to have a decent game. And because little Jake-y doesn't play well with others, I don't play doubles. Then there's something new called pickleball which is slow-motion tennis for gummers using paddles and a dead wiffle-type ball. I just can't bring myself to do it. I first came upon this recreational monstrosity the one winter I spent in Florida. I invite you to stand near a pickleball court, close your eyes, and try to identify the sound. Spoiler alert: it sounds like a bunch of coked-up woodsmen hacking away at a forest with dull axes. Because the court's so small and the ball so dead, the players hardly ever miss so the grating pop-pop-popping sound is continuous. Add that to the fact that, because the invariably paunchy and slow-moving athletes are close to each other on a court about half the size of the tennis version, it means they talk and laugh and screech as if they're sitting across from each other at a lively house party.

Despite my adoration for the Rolling Stones, I do like doing quiet things. I love gardening. Just because I like having a hand in stuff growing. Beth always claimed that the real reason I rooted around in the earth was because I love getting dirty in honour of my favourite cartoon character, Pig Pen. As I get older, the bendy parts about gardening—and there are a lot of bendy parts—are starting to take a toll on my knee joints and back, but I am undeterred. To be clear: I achieve no Zen-like state when I'm gardening and the closest I've ever come to talking to my plants is yelling: "Grow, you lazy motherfuckers!"

Most mornings I can found—if anyone's looking—sitting at my shitty laptop, tap-tap-tapping away at a novel or two. I had one published a few years back. That may impress some. I know it did me, even after I had to kick in some money to cover things like proofreading and editing. My small publisher—well, the actual guy—Frank McCann—wasn't small, about 6-2—but the press he ran was. It featured titles like *Kawartha Lakes – Beauty and Beasts* and *The Engineering Marvel of the Peterborough Lift Locks*. Frank said he was taking a chance on my trans-Canadian fiction set during the Great Depression, particularly because the word "Kawartha" did not appear once.

I sold something just over 500 copies, got my money back plus a couple of hundred bucks. And some local exposure. There was an article in the *Examiner*—on-line edition only—that was, charitable. Oh let's call it undeservedly rhapsodic.

Publisher Frank had arranged signings at the two independent bookstores in Peterborough. There were no line-ups outside and around the block of new acolytes clutching their copies of my book, feverishly hopeful over maybe getting an autograph. Rather, Frank told me that I couldn't just sit there the whole time beside the stack of books but was expected to "get out and meet the people," as he put it. I wanted to sit there with a stupid grin of my face. Consequently, I alternated between feeling like an Amsterdam hooker being appraised by bookish johns and a carny barker browbeating passersby.

Oh, and then there was that ill-fated appearance at a local book club where I discovered that the exclusively female seniors group didn't mind obscenity in its printed form but were clearly uncomfortable with my frequent verbal use of it.

As the chemicals in my wee brain dictate, I had to figure out my hourly wage for my literary effort. Three years spent more or less continuously researching and writing the thing and then add another two collecting polite fuck-off letters from big-time agents and publishers. It worked out to about .003 cents an hour, I reckoned. And that's not counting the time spent imagining what sort of Mexican villa I'd buy when the movie rights were auctioned.

I'd sent Frank a few chapters of what I was working on at the time, and still—the story of a drunken flamenco guitarist getting really messed up by the Nazis.

He sent me a polite fuck-off letter.

All indications are I should give up this e-scribbling but I know I won't. Some combination of raging ego and a few kind notes from people who claimed to have read the book fuels my dream, one that's also sustained by real animus towards all the editors and agents who rejected it. I truly want every one of those tasteless fucks to feel like the Decca Records execs who passed on the Beatles before they went to Capitol.

I usually pack in the tap-tap-tapping around noon and then consider the raft of things I want to or have to do to keep the place from passing through the neglected stage to full-blown ruins. I take some time going over this mental list because I'm usually hoping that Carl will show up and off we'll go to AA instead. Most times we'll eat and drink alone but sometimes we'll be joined by a group of middle-aged local lads who have known Carl for decades.

That's what happened on the early May day just after Maynard Odell's partially ground-up body was found. It hadn't taken long for the impromptu wake—sorry, I meant celebration of life—to switch to a nasty assessment of the dearly departed. Carl kicked things off.

"Whaddya mean good fella?" Carl interjected. "He was a prick."

"Well, yeah. But you can't speak ill of the dead."

"Why not? He ain't gettin' more dead," Carl countered.

"He sure liked his drink," someone offered; (that's the country code phrase for raging alcoholic).

Another said: "Heard he had a bit of a heavy hand." (Country code phrase for violent domestic abuser).

"Shame his boy and him hadn't made peace."

"Wife left him with the kid ten years ago. Maybe twelve. You remember that kid? Blaine, was it?"

"Blair. Smart kid."

"Yeah, Blair. Told me back then he was going to be lawyer."

"And he upped and done it too. That's what I heard, anyways."

"And I heard his mom died a couple of years ago."

"And I heard she never divorced Maynard."

"Well, at least Blair come back for the funeral, I heard."

"It's true; I think I seen him in Buckhorn yesterday. Sharp-lookin' kid."

"He's goin' to be about the only audience at the graveyard."

"And Elsie, 'a course. She won't miss a good funeral."

"You know what? Just can't figure how Maynard died."

"Must've been trying to kick away a jam."

"While the chipper was runnin'?"

"Dumb shit."

"Don't forget, Maynard was always either drunk or dreaming around."

"Surprised it didn't happen sooner. What with The Development stuff goin' on, probably didn't have his eye on the ball."

Ah, yes, The Development. Capital 'T', capital 'D'. I assumed it had been The (capital 'T' again) topic of conversation for months.

The senior Odell was likely more distracted than most with The Development owing to his position on the seven-person council that governed the local affairs of West Kawartha Township, the municipality that included our Mississauga Lake and a bunch of others.

Given the less than laudatory barroom eulogy, it must've been a water-into-wine-type miracle how he ever got elected. But as we've seen over and over again, people will rally around distasteful candidates if they feel anything like kinship for him or her, and/or animosity towards any challenger.

"So he had a lot to do with making the development happen?" I asked, my first contribution to the post-mortem.

"Not really. He just had to vote."

"So why would he be distracted?"

"Probably figuring out what to do with his millions."

"Millions?" I said.

"He must've owned five hundred acres of that bush where the development's goin' in."

"Yup, Ol' Maynard's passing just made the vote pretty interesting."

"How so?" I asked.

Together, the lads looked at me as if I had somehow confirmed their low opinion of people "not from around these parts." Carl looked embarrassed.

"'Cause it's a tie again, that's why."

"Oh, yeah...*that*," I said, bluffing exactly no one.

I shut the fuck up after that and focused on my beer until, by general although not spoken agreement, our group busted up. Carl and I—the tipsy pair of us—left the deck and made our way to my excessively tipsy canoe. We paddled—well, he paddled and I thrashed—back to his dock.

"Why did he say the vote would be a tie *again*?" I asked.

"We lost another councilor a while back. You were south."

"Who?"

"Greta Hill. That Toronto doctor."

"What happened?"

"Dunno. She took sick in the city."

"So she was against it?"

"Yup. And everybody knew Maynard was for it. Christ, that woodlot where he got found is smack dab in the middle of The Development."

"Wait a minute," I said, applying my keen insight into voting procedures in municipal politics. "How can you have a tie on a seven person—now a five-person—council?"

"Elsie don't like to vote."

Elsie McQuaig had once been a long-time local school teacher and was now the twelve-term mayor of West Kawartha (and avid funeral-goer). I had met her a few times. She was somewhere between, I'd say, 88 and 113 years old.

There was nothing prim or schoolmarmish about her. Tiny, wrinkled, wiry, and spry, she'd hang out at AA every election year, drinking and smoking and cussing with her congregated constituents. We got along like a house on fire. But then again, Elsie got along with everybody which is why she'd been mayor since Christ was a cowboy.

Besides turning up for every event—funerals, Legion dinners, family reunions, even the proverbial letter opening—another way she remained popular was not to publicly take a stand on anything. Ever. That way, she never offended anyone.

Even I knew that as Mayor, she always had the tie-breaking vote on stuff council had to decide but she would do anything to avoid having to use that vote. Instead, she secretly strong-armed one or two councilors behind closed doors to vote the way she wanted the issue to turn out without actually having to declare herself. Thus do the wheels of democracy turn, albeit a little wobbly. Like old grocery store shopping carts.

But the rest of the council? I didn't really have much of a clue about them.

"I guess I should get my head out of my ass, pay attention a bit more," I admitted in a rare episode of public self-recrimination.

"I guess you should. Hill was our neighbor."

"No way! The asshole next door's got that Volvo, gives me shit about my recycling. Nice wife but I know she's not a doctor."

"Not that place; the one beside it."

"Big house with the grey siding, fancy black gate?"

"That'd be the one."

"Never met her."

"And you won't now."

As I—eventually—crossed the two hundred feet of water to my place, there was some more self-chiding going on as I considered just how out of touch I was with shit going on around me.

I determined it was time to brush up on all things Township of West Kawartha-related.

And dead Toronto doctor-related.

CHAPTER 4

Facing a bunch of chilly, dreary, showery mid-May days, I settled into the workstation I set up inside the screened-in porch. By workstation, I mean a small card table with just enough surface area for my shitty laptop, a mouse pad, pack of smokes, an ashtray, and either a coffee or a beer depending on the time of day. My kind of ergonomics.

When I'm not being a yard ape or a drunk, I spend a stupid amount of time in front of my shitty laptop. I could do all this computer stuff inside in relative comfort but I don't. OCD rules. I could smoke in my house if I wanted to but I don't. Beth never liked it.

I took a deep breath and e-dove in. And it felt great to be back doing one of the few things I'm really good at: messing with the Interwebs. Lots of people spend their working days laboriously hunting or idly wandering around the Internet; I do it voluntarily and with laser-like purpose. Hours, fucking days can pass if I'm on one my Quixotic quests to learn as much as possible about something without actually speaking to humans.

I started with Dr. Greta Hill. There were several brief archived news articles. Dr. Greta Hill, 56, of Toronto had died, according to police, of an accidental drug overdose in her Cabbagetown condo two months earlier. Foul play was not suspected.

She was also mentioned in a longer magazine piece on drug abuse within the health care industry. I then found her obituary. No surviving husband or children were listed. The obit didn't mention the overdose but whoever had placed the notice had asked that donations to be made to Felicity House which, I quickly found out, was an addiction recovery centre.

I didn't doubt that with a semi-high-profile death like this, there would have been some kind of official investigation to see if there'd been anything odd about the doctor's demise besides the fact that it happened at all.

So I sent a note to Halley, my daughter, asking her if there was anything strange about Hill's death. Halley's a Detective in the Homicide Squad of the Toronto Police Service, having overcome gender and youth bias—as well as having the father she has—to rise quickly through the ranks.

Returning to the Google pages, I found bits on Dr. Hill's speeches delivered at conferences and descriptions of her foreign aid work in Honduras concerned with maternal and child health. She was also included in a slew of tables in which her marathon finishing times were listed.

There were also numerous older local articles on *PTBO.com, my Kawartha.com*, the *Examiner* and *Peterborough This Week*, including an in-depth profile of her. In it, she spoke about splitting her time between Mississauga Lake and downtown Toronto, of how she was spending more and more time up here and was leaning towards eventually chucking her ob-gyn practice in the big city for the more relaxed and friendlier environment of West Kawartha. She also made it plain that her goin' up the country did not mean she was slowing down. She spoke of how much she was enjoying her first term on Council, of her plans to establish an outreach program for pregnant teen-agers, and of her passion for long-distance running.

It clicked that I had occasionally seen her running when I ventured out from behind my wall of bush. Clipped silverish hair, tight expression, slender but muscled, and a graceful stride. But I was sure that had been years ago. And equally sure I'd seen the same person several times last summer on our road but she had been walking.

At the end of that meander through her former life, I considered what I had on Dr. Greta Hill. A dedicated, unmarried, high-energy professional who somewhat incongruously had a prescription drug habit more usually found in your less affluent citizenry who are often less affluent because they spend most of their money and time getting chemically fucked up.

Put that together with the death of a fellow councilor and you've got an intriguing fact. I'm no statistician, but the odds of 28.6% of an elected municipal body becoming unnaturally dead in the space of a couple of months must be pretty steep, right up there with probability of the US ever adopting the metric system or Donald Trump getting a buzz cut.

I turned my attention to the area where I live. I had never spent much time actually researching West Kawartha. When Beth and I bought up here we weren't any more scientific than aimlessly driving back roads in widening circles around Peterborough until we found this lake and this place.

Mississauga Lake is about forty-five winding minutes north of Peterborough and two and a half hours—and a universe—away from Toronto where I was born and raised. The lake and a bunch of others sit in the Township of West Kawartha, which according to their website, occupies 327 square miles. It's home to about 2,500 permanent residents and almost 10,000 'transients,' i.e. summer squatters like me.

It's cottage country, that giant swath of North America not a city that stretches from about Minnesota to the Atlantic, south to Georgia and the Carolinas and north to the livable bits of central and eastern Canada. It's dotted with hundreds of thousands big and small lakes to which millions of people flee for parts of their summer vacations along twisty roads, past seasonally-operated restaurants, stores, and marinas. To fish, to chill, to vainly attempt to amuse kids on rainy days.

All cottage areas within this land mass about the size of Europe aren't created equal. About the same distance from Toronto but with better highway access, the Muskokas (note: residents of this area go apeshit when you say "the Muskokas" instead of "Muskoka" which, of course, is a real good reason to do it) had for years been recording

Manhattan-type real estate prices. Some Hollywood types and stars in the NHL had places up there. In the Kawarthas, we get regional theatre lighting directors and NHL fourth liners, back-up goaltenders and aging defencemen. But let's keep in mind, even those hockey guys have a higher base pay than a Canadian Prime Minister or a US president.

Anyway, since the 1960s, the series of interconnected lakes (Chemong, Pigeon, Stony, Clear, and Buckhorn) minutes north of Peterborough had seen the vast majority of development. Much more recently, the creeping urban exodus has spread farther north to our neck of the woods. That ooze northward was about to turn into a torrent with the proposed development.

On the township website—quite pro-looking I noted—there was a separate button marked 'Edgewater Estates.'

There I found a chronology of events, the timeline stretching back to mid-November of last year when Lakeshore Developments first made their proposal for Edgewater Estates to the township that had then been referred to the business development and planning sub-committee. The seven-person council then approved the original request in principle, subject to a bunch of conditions. That happened by Christmas last year while I was in the DR.

Those conditions involved the production of a slew of consultants' reports to address all sorts of possible effects of carving something out of the bush nothingness. And they were all available in their multi-page glory on the township website: a stormwater management report, hydro-geological report, planning report, traffic impact report, environmental report, economic impact report, a lake capacity report, and a report on the number of reports.

Lakeshore Developments had obviously anticipated the demand for these studies and started working on them long before the conditions were set because they'd been completed, submitted, and approved real quickly.

Bullet holes in my doughy body aside, do you wanna hint about what kind of exciting life I lead? I read every fucking one of them.

Peterborough County was also involved. They had filed no objection, agreed to add a turn lane and stop light at the main road, County Road 507, and our road around the lake. They had already approved a name change for the road leading to the new houses. I had to admit that Edgewater Lane sounded a little bit classier than Fire Route 162.

So lots of people had been busy-busy over the winter while I was unsuccessfully pursing my dream of becoming a drunken but really well-tanned slacker in the Caribbean.

The real trove—to me anyway—was the collection of the minutes from all the official meetings. Even though these sorts of things are usually terse and sanitized, you can get a true sense of who said what about the issues, who voted which way and, incidentally, you wind up with some knowledge about the characters and the human dynamics behind the scrubbed clean facts.

There was the standard tension between new and old residents that usually exists when times they are a-changin.' Long-time residents had a memory of how things always were while the recent arrivals had a hope of the way things would be. These imaginings are not ever the same.

And that might lead you to suspect that the old timers on council would be opposed while the newcomers would favour bringing a progressive touch of class to the 'hood. But you'd be dead wrong. It was the opposite in West Kawartha. The newcomers wanted to freeze the region exactly as they had found it (it was, after all, the reason they had bought here in the first place), while the lifers were lining up on the pro side.

I didn't know Maynard Odell although I probably should have been a mulch client of his. But I stay away from the natural mulch that looks great when you first put it on but then lightens and turns grey in less than a summer. I prefer driving to a big box store in Peterborough and loading up on bags of dyed-brown cedar chips—even though tree trunks are never brown.

I had a passing acquaintance with the other two pro-development councilors.

Preston Peterson together with his three sons had cornered the local market on machinery. They rented out and/or operated all the heavy equipment—bulldozers, backhoes, dump trucks —you could need to ravage wilderness. I first met the enterprising Preston and his lads years ago because they did snow removal in the winter and I had used them before I started going south and leaving a snow barrier across the driveway. I still hired him once a year in the fall to bring the 'honey wagon' to my place to pump out my septic holding tank (now illegal).

You've got some time on your hands when you're having your septic tank pumped out, so Preston and I would stand around and shoot the shit, as it were. Over the course of our annual encounters I found out that we had diabetes in common so we'd resurrect our shared medical condition and talk about that. He was on the spike so I wanted to know what daily insulin injections were like as I figured that was in my near future. How many units was he taking, how often, did he cut back on the metformin and so on. Innocuous as hell, right? Not exactly. Preston led it slip that he hadn't been to a doctor in fifteen years. Nosy fucker that I am, I wanted to know why not.

"Cuz then it's Big Brother, right? They got you in their microscope," he whispered, his eyes darting around as though the medical police were lurking in the bushes.

I thought he was a pretty good lad, of the kind with whom you can have pleasant incidental contact. But this kind of paranoia added an odd new dimension.

So I had to ask how he got the insulin and the other meds he was taking if no one was writing prescriptions for him. He wouldn't answer that one.

All three of his boys were maniacally hard workers, always polite but not exactly sparkling conversationalists. And all three were following in their dad's footsteps in both the business and body shape. Years of sitting in hard seats operating big machines while eating shit food had turned them into four burly bordering on obese men, any one of whom could collapse your rib cage in a bear hug if he so chose.

The other pro-development councilor was Bradley Dugald. I knew Bradley too. Excuse me, P. Bradley Dugald, the star of Kawartha Publishing's stable of writers. His travelogue/local history books were sold up and down the 250-mile Trent-Severn Waterway to recreational boaters who use the canals, locks, and connected rivers and lakes to get from Lake Ontario up to Lake Huron without going anywhere near Toronto.

Frank McCann, our publisher overlord, had gathered us altogether to staff a booth at the Peterborough Ex, the city's annual mostly agricultural fair. We were expected to hawk our wares in the Food Building, mercifully a distance from the goat and chicken enclosures and happily right across from the beer tent. Resplendent in altogether too much corduroy, Bradley got the crowds (and sales) while I got a hernia lugging unsold boxes of my weighty tome.

According to the township website bio, Councilor P. Bradley Dugald's family had lived in this part of Canada since before there was a Canada. He himself had not. As a young man, he had departed for the bright lights big city and an engineering degree that had led to a career in the BC forestry business. He had retired a few years ago and returned to the 'hood from Vancouver—specifically, to his family's barely subsistent farm west of the highway from Mississauga Lake where he had become something of an unofficial historian for West Kawartha. He wrote a column in the *West Kawartha Komet*, a township newsletter whose main content sought to nostalgically recreate life in West Kawartha when the timber industry was a big deal and there was nary a pickleball court to be found.

Combing through the minutes, an oddity had emerged. Bradley was the only councilor who had switched sides. In the meetings of early winter he was pretty vocal about how Edgewater Estates would cause the lumbermen of yesterday to spin in their graves faster than they ever log-rolled when they were on water and not underground. But by the end of January of this year, he was decrying the lack of vision displayed by any council member opposed to the development.

There was no explanation for the ol' switcheroo. But I found a couple of his columns he'd written after he converted to favouring the development wherein he admitted to being uniformed about the project in the early days but his subsequent education had led him to believe that that Edgewater Estates would be "harmonious with the bold spirit of our early pioneers" and "an absolutely authentic expression of their vision of prosperity."

Post-it note to self: find out if there's another other reason for his about-face beyond what he called "seeing the light" in one of those columns.

While not very public in her support, I classed Mayor Elsie McQuaig as probably the loudest "yes" vote for the development. I doubt there's a mayor in the world who doesn't want to get their hands on gobs more tax money.

Opposed to Edgewater were the newcomers to council. Standing alongside Greta Hill was her fellow ex-Torontonian, Phil Vogel. Phil was the newest arrival, having bought on the lake two years ago. He was an easy going guy, instantly identifiable by a mighty impressive handlebar moustache and a booming voice. Phil was in semi-retirement and he told me (and inadvertently everyone else on the patio at the Angler Arms) that he'd sold his city insurance business and moved up here with his wife to "fish and get old." But he—unlike me—had become instantly bored and so hung out his shingle, more or less to keep busy. He had an uphill battle because the locals were fiercely loyal—bless them—to local businesses and most residents were clients of one of two brokers in the area who both had been here for generations. I like underdogs, so I switched my house and car insurance to him…just because.

Mary Ellen Conway rounded out the anti-development team. I'd never met her but knew what she looked like and what she did by the 'For Sale' signs in the area which advertised her real estate company. Mary Ellen had likely attended a marketing seminar advising her to stand out in her promotional efforts. So her portrait on the signs always had her wearing a huge white hat festooned with black feathers that might be considered gaudy by Kentucky Derby attendees.

On the surface, her opposition to the development struck me as counter-intuitive. More houses in the 'hood meant a steady inventory of more houses to re-sell. But, she reminded us on her website, she was opposed to the development, even though this stance would cost her money personally. That's how dearly she wanted she said to protect the quality of life in West Kawartha. Maybe for space reasons, her website neglected to mention that, in the short term, Stewie had the exclusive right to sell the development so she wasn't going to get any slice of that action anyway. I presumed she was busily signing up listings of everybody anywhere near Edgewater Estates who were anticipating a bonanza once the development was approved.

Judging by their procedural wrangling as noted in the minutes, the trio of nays had obviously brushed up on their Robert's Rules of Order. They also had an idea of what conflict of interest meant.

The anti-development group had made it a point to point out at least once a meeting that all three of the official yeasayers, Odell, Dugald, and Peterson—as well as the Mayor herself—owned a bunch of land within the targeted area. And because this Gang of Four stood to make out if not like bandits then grifting politicos, they should have nothing to do with the deliberations.

This allegation of conflicted interest would have been a bombshell in a city. Apparently not up here and I could guess why. Rural municipal politicians tend to concern themselves with practical things, garbage collection, road repair, and snow removal being the biggies. They didn't run for election to these low-paying, long-hour jobs to get rich and everybody knew that. The electorate thinks that as long as they stick to these pragmatic topics, there's no need for outrage. So a few of them would profit from this out-of-left-field development, so exactly what?

The only recorded response to the charge of betraying public trust came from the Mayor. Isn't that convenient, she lectured, that the "no" bloc was demanding that the "yes's" recuse themselves? If they were to do so, there wouldn't be quorum and so nothing would happen. And who did that benefit, the Mayor wanted to know. Only the "Johnny-come-latelys and Negative Nellies," as she characterized them, who would selfishly stop the development on a technicality. How fair was that to the long-time landowners who were no doubt hoping to final-ly see some value for their stone farms and acres of evergreen scrub bush? And how fair was that to the local businesses and to the voting public who appeared to be pretty supportive of the enterprise?

There was a small and unelected opposition voicing their disapproval at public meetings over the winter and spring. When I say small, I mean two people. The loudest was Sarah Ruth Evans, whose occupa-tion she noted was as a 'business owner, community activist and envi-ronmentalist.' She owned a stained glass shop in Buckhorn (located between the bait and tackle shop and the hunting outfitter and across from the hardware store—which made for an eclectic mixture of New Age and Stone Age).

Up here, community activism meant you volunteered to coach pee-wee soccer or help decorate the Lions Club float in the Christmas parade so she wasn't terribly busy on that front. But she was coming into her own as an environmentalist because she was loudly cham-pioning the cause of the Blanding's turtles who would be displaced by the development and forced to move—albeit slowly—on to other wilds.

At several public meetings she had insisted that all her remarks be recorded. So they dutifully were, always with the descriptor that read: "Ms. Sarah Ruth Evans, turtle proponent, claimed…etc."

Backing her up at these meetings was Drew Bregg—my Volvo-driving, recycling-obsessed next door neighbor. Leastwise in the meeting minutes, Bregg's contribution seemed to be limited to different forms of "what she said," following one of Sarah Ruth's declarations.

So there it was. Not a lot of people were involved in deciding the fate of a multi-million dollar project. I discounted the effect of Sarah Ruth Evans' and my obnoxious neighbour's protests; they obviously hadn't drummed up much in the way of support. The whole development hung on the yay/nay of a seven-person council.

Oh, and two of those seven were otherwise occupied being dead.

CHAPTER 5

As I was finishing up my research, Carl swam over to my place as he is wont to do, starting at the end of May when the water is about a half a degree above freezing.

"Go ahead," I told him. "Ask me anything about council. Anything."

"Want to go to a wedding?" he asked instead, ignoring me as he toweled off as calmly as if he'd just stepped out of a hot shower.

"Carl! Congratulations, you old hound! Didn't even know you were seeing someone."

"Not mine, arsehole. My granddaughter's."

"Granddaughter! I didn't even know you had kids."

"Kid. One. A son. Jordy."

"I've never seen him."

"I haven't either for more'n twenty years."

"Why not?"

"Long story."

But, because Carl never tells long stories, I knew I wasn't about to hear why.

"So your son wants to patch things up?" I said. "That's great."

"Doubt it. Allison sent me the invite."

"So how come I get to go?"

"Invite said 'plus 1.' Didn't say man or woman."

"Meaning you'll turn up looking like the gay old grandpappy—not that there's anything wrong with that."

"Arsehole. Meaning I'll turn up with someone I know there."

"I'm back-up? Sure I'll be your wing man. You old hound."

Show me a dead horse and I'll flog it. When I get like that, Carl gets like this: he walks away.

He plunged back into the lake. I tossed some pine cones at him as he swam. Missed him but not by that much.

Standing on the rocks on his island, he turned to yell at me.

"Arsehole!"

I went back inside and did something I rarely do: I considered Carl. It struck me as kinda odd that someone who spends every waking moment think-think-thinking about something or other—usually dumb shit—had taken so little time to examine something that I truly treasured: our friendship.

And maybe that was the point. I presumed he didn't consider me. So we're even. We had—and continue to have—a friendship built on apparent disinterest, constant sarcasm, and complete equality.

As I've said before, I know squat about his backstory. I believe he grew up and spent his whole life in and around the lake area. I don't know that for a fact and he's neither confirmed nor denied it. Just like he's neither confirmed nor denied if he's ever been married, ever had kids, ever went to school past grade eight. He was here when I got here; he'll likely be here when I'm gone—even though he's at least fifteen years older than me. I can't be exactly sure of that either.

He has never shown the slightest interest in my history even though I've known him for two decades, so we're square. The closest he ever got to personal was after Beth, my wife, died.

Carl has something of an edge through exposure to the people I have cherished. He knew Beth for the ten years we were weekending it up here as a couple before she died. He's known Halley for—now that I think of it—double that amount of time. I may have fueled my daughter's inquisitive nature through book larnin' but it was Carl who taught her (and me) about the real world stuff during the summers she spent up here. What side of the tree moss usually grows on. Where Orion was in a mid-summer sky. What wild berries or mushrooms you can safely eat, best way to gut and clean a fish, how to make a snare for rabbits, you know, the important stuff for a life in the woods.

At the root of this friendship, I find the same basis for the marriage I had, and roughly the same foundation for the relationship I have with my daughter. And with Alexandra, as it was turning out. No expectation, no obligation, only choice to act a certain way or not. Only the intent to enjoy and laugh.

Is that a fucked up way to conduct my life? Who knows? I don't. And for sure you don't. What I do know is that I'm a model of consistency. I have not spent—nor will I ever spend—a single goddamned second trying to improve myself. Why fuck with the hard-won mediocrity I've spent decades perfecting?

I am secretly delighted that deep existential questions of any sort do not trouble me in the least. Why am I here? Why is there evil? Is there a god? Do I want to know a secret? Do I promise not to tell? I owe my sturdy defence of this blithe ignorance to a single line in a shattering movie I saw in a theatre forty years ago. It's the scene in *Deer Hunter* when De Niro is sitting on the hood of Axel's Caddy as the boys shed their wedding tuxes for hunting clothes. He holds up a bullet and like a heavily-armed Buddhist says: "See this? This is this. This ain't something else. This is *this*. From now on you're on your own."

A couple of days later, Carl and I were drinking beer on the deck of Angler Arms. It had been a hard morning for both of us. Carl had caught and cleaned some rainbow trout, checked his trapline in the provincial park and split a couple of cords of dry maple. I had written an involved scenario for a crisis communications workshop run by the giant PR firm that hired me from time to time to keep me in cigarette money. I didn't know about him, but I was whipped.

The great thing—one of many great things—about a small local bar is that you pretty well know everybody. Everyone's not all buddy-buddy, but we at least recognize each other and maybe nod from time to time or ask: "How's it goin,' eh?"

It may be that different groups don't sit together but there are no utter strangers here and we get along. Familiarity breeds tolerance, as they should say.

At least, we all got along until that day.

There was a table of twenty-somethings at the other end of the deck. Three pretty rustic lads I sort of recognized including one of Preston Peterson's boys and a well-dressed guy I didn't. One of the locals was staring rather intently at me. The very sight of me was apparently enough to incite him to finally get up and approach me.

"You're fuckin' lucky *he's* here," the guy said to me indicating my large pal. "Otherwise I'd pour this beer on you, you selfish prick."

"Pretend I ain't here," Carl, the big bastard, said, presumably because he wanted to see my beer-soaked noggin.

The kid couldn't extend his imagination that far and instead half-heartedly kicked my white plastic chair.

That brief boot to the chair leg was like a wild barroom brawl to Carla, the head server—OK, the only server at AA. She was on the guy pretty fast because Carla doesn't like any problems in the bar. She turns into a furious five-foot buzz saw ball of hate when that happens. In no time, the guy, who was a whole lot bigger than her, was through the bar and out the front door with Carla trailing after him and yelling, stopping just short of twisting his ear and leading him out, presumably because she couldn't reach that high. Jimmy, the owner, made a rare appearance from the kitchen. He saw Carla had the situation well in hand and retreated back through the swinging door.

"Who was that?" I asked Carl of the low-down, no-good chair kicker.

"Derek Collins, Mel's boy. Just an arsehole. Him, not Mel. Mel's a dead arsehole."

"What the fuck is his problem?"

"I s'pose word got out about us not sellin'."

"So?"

"Mel—well, Derek now—Mel died a while back—owns some land up the east side."

"But," I protested, "it doesn't matter to him—or to anybody else who owns up there—what I do or you do. A fucking retirement home ain't a housing development. All they have to do is drop it from the plans or move it….You tell anyone we weren't going to sell?"

"Nope. You?"

"Nope."

"So that means ol' Stewie must've leaked it," Carl said.

"Doesn't exactly help his case, advertising the hold-outs."

"Mebbe. Or mebbe it does, 'cause it sets off little shows like Derek's just now."

"Who are those guys he was with?" I asked, indicating the table from whence the recently departed Mr. Collins originated.

"Bert Chesley's one of the others, the other's Billy Peterson. I don't know the spiffy lad."

Just then, the well-dressed guy from the table got up and came over to us. Late 20's, casually but expensively dressed in slacks, top-siders, and a tasteful and tailored Tommy Bahama Hawaiian shirt that costs more than twenty of mine. I braced myself for another confrontation.

"Excuse me," he said. "I'm Blair Odell. Please forgive my friend; he's a bit emotional. I don't know if you've heard but Lakeshore Developments contacted our group of landowners and informed us that they were putting their offers on hold pending negotiations with you two gentlemen."

"Well, Mr. Odell," I said, "first off, my condolences about your father" (Odell the Younger nodded briefly) "But I'm afraid there won't be much in the way of negotiations. We're both pretty sure we'll be staying, aren't we Carl?"

Carl nodded.

"Gentlemen," Odell said, looking not the least bit perturbed, "In my experience, there isn't much that can't be negotiated as long as the parties remain reasonable."

"You should know that I don't get accused of being reasonable very often," I said.

"Maybe you'll see the light," Blair Odell said, taking a business card from his wallet. "When you do, give me a call; my cell number's there. There's every possibility that the other landowners would be willing to sweeten your incentive to sell."

I quickly read the card before pocketing it: M. Blair Odell, Associate, Wilson, Scharf, Arpell, Barristers & Solicitors.

"We better get goin'," Carl said after Blair Odell left us.

"Where are we going?" I asked, not at all inclined to disrupt this bucolic—and beercolic—scene.

"The wedding."

"It's today?!"

"Yup."

"Thanks for the warning!"

"Got something else on your schedule?" Carl asked.

I quickly packed my trusty bowling bag, figuring I'd go formal Hawaiian with quite an understated black number and met Carl by our vehicles.

"Truck makes more sense," Carl pronounced, throwing an old suit-case in the back. "Roads are real shitty."

"Road trip!" I yelled, snapping open a beer.

Our voyage was far, far from the ideal of screaming down a four-lane in a vintage Mustang convertible with the top down and the Stones blasting. Rather, we rattled and clattered along on a two-hour drive where not a lot of ground got covered. Eighty miles maybe, north-east into the sparsely populated Kawartha Highlands. It had started raining which slowed us. The roads turned to dirt—well, mud in the rain—soon after we left which slowed us some more and Carl was working from memory as to where his son's place even was.

A few generations before moneyed people started fleeing the cities and humanity to build permanent homes in the wilderness, there were waves of poor Scottish and Irish fleeing the cities across the Atlantic. Hardy and fiercely self-sufficient, they eked out a living on land where the main crop was granite and the main activity was eking. The remnants of those families were still there as evidenced by the same names on strings of mail boxes we passed.

Jordy (and Carl) were from "around here" I found out. In the country, "around here" is probably anything within a fifty-mile radius. That'd be like someone from Danbury, Connecticut, claiming they had a close neighbour living in the Bronx.

I realized that it'd been almost an hour since we'd seen a car on the ever-narrowing, ever-shittier roads. This lack of vehicular presence made the traffic in our little community on Mississauga Lake look like downtown Bangkok at rush hour.

Carl was visibly nervous as we pulled into the driveway marked with a big red paper heart. He had barely got out of the truck when a pretty young brunette dashed out of a cottage and flung herself into his arms. I could see the young woman crying as they spun around and then immediately Carl started crying. And, the bastard almost made me cry to see such overwhelming emotion sweep over the big man.

The screen door to the cottage opened then whapped shut and a tall man strode up to Carl.

"Dad," he said.

"Jordy."

There in the constant drizzle, they shook hands briefly which changed to hugs and more tears and, right there on the spot, that was that for family schisms.

They pulled away awkwardly, trying the disguise their show of affection the way John Candy and Steve Martin gloss over their accidental contact in bed. "See the Bears game this week?"

We were ushered through the cottage and onto the back deck, ideally built overlooking a sharp bend in the river. Other than the (now illegal) footbridge and the string of lanterns above it up, the scene looked for all the world like the shallow origins of the Cahulawassee River in *Deliverance*, as it was busily doing two of the only things small rivers/large creeks do: rilling and burbling, along the sand and stone.

Jordy's wife's family owned large parcels of land on both sides of the budding river, joined by that solid-looking footbridge. A total of four cottages sprang up over a half century to accommodate grown children and then grown grandchildren. Not quite Hyannis Port but a true compound.

Not surprisingly, I was one of the elderly who were quarantined on this side of the river in an actual cottage while the youth, the ones with limitless energy and tolerance, camped out in tents and trailers and their cars in an open area on the other side that had been christened Young Town.

I trooped along behind Jordy and Carl across the narrow footbridge to the other side to see how the preparations were going. A huge white canvas tent sheltered the rows of tables and chairs. A band was setting up under the roof of a permanent-looking stage nearby and the caterers rather sullenly were firing up a string of gas barbeques in the light rain.

Prominent—to me anyway—were two giant metal tubs filled with ice and beer. Risking hypothermia, I fished around all the heinous bottles of light beer to find two ales. Carl and I stood under the tent, a steady run-off of rain providing something of a curtain as we surveyed the scene.

Nobody seemed to care about the rain and so, eventually, neither did we. Back on the old fart side of the river, we had some more beer. While Carl gussied himself up for the wedding, Jordy invited me to see his new lawn tractor. You don't turn down an invite like that. I followed him and a couple of his buddies to the equipment shed and we stood around admiring the machine—a 24 hp, 48-inch blade John

Deere with hydrostatic tranny—for a bit until the real reason for my invitation appeared.

The joints came out and were lit, a large spliff being handed to yours truly. I declined as I had for the last forty years, amused that yet again, my long hair was a siren call to folks wanting to get me high. Not that I have anything against weed—I spent much of my high school and university careers under a stultifying cloud of it, until I finally realized I liked the herb waaaay too much.

It's legal now in Canada so, theoretically, Jordy could've sparked one up at the patio table. But smoking pot and being furtive always went hand in hand.

Looking around the shed at a hardware store worth of tools, it was evident that Jordy, like his old man, was a master of trades. You had to be up here because shit breaks. Even if you had the money—and it didn't look like these people did—you couldn't find a repair service. So you plumbed, wired, and carpentered and fixed big and small engines yourself. Put another way, useless tits such as myself would last about a week in these parts.

The newly-benign smiles and I returned to the back deck just as Carl was making his runway appearance. He looked like a septuagenarian version of a five-year old made to dress up for church. Shiny blue dress pants, checked shirt with striped tie, brown sports jacket and his unruly grey mop of hair slicked down. We all hooted and whistled our appreciation of his very much put-together ensemble.

He looked uncomfortable and nervous as we made our way back across the narrow footbridge spanning the nascent river towards the white canvas tent.

I'd say 95% of the crowd were young city dwellers—friends rather than relatives—largely from Toronto where Allison and groom-to-be Connor worked. All of whom seemed to be having a swell time. I had seen some of them earlier, discarding their hipster clothes to plunge into the deeper pools in the river, a-whooping and a-hollering and showing not the slightest trace of irony.

Not being a regular attendee at nuptials I found the wedding itself to be a refreshing evolution from the churchy formalities I saw—and participated in—when I was younger. They had a non-sectarian minister, self-written vows, lots of music, and home-made decorations and gifts. All in all, it was simple, heart-felt, and affecting, punctuated by wise-ass comments being shouted at the couple as they recited their vows.

After dinner, Allison and her new husband didn't go anywhere except to the roaring bonfire (probably illegal) that had been started to spite the dampness. Amid roasting marshmallows, boisterous good will, and a prodigious amount of beer, the band started up.

It drizzled off and on all evening and night and not a person's spirit seem dampened.

Carl and I packed it in early—although late for us—around midnight. Being a tad drunky pants, our trip across the footbridge was a bit of an adventure. I scored one couch; Carl got the other one, although it looked more like a loveseat as it tried to accommodate his Royal Lankiness.

"That was nice," Carl said in the dark before his snorefest started. I lay awake for a bit and listened to the band across the river pumping the tunes, the crowd having moved from boisterous to somewhere in between rowdy and raucous.

I woke up early Sunday morning. The light was grey and feeble as I rummaged around in the unfamiliar kitchen, finding then making a vital—perhaps life-saving—pot of coffee.

There wasn't a hint of blue in the sky, just balls of dark low hanging clouds, as I sat outside, drank my coffee, and slowly came back to life.

Briefly, the sun shot through a break in the clouds and lit up the spruce boughs overhanging the river in front of the deck. The needles were heavy from last night's rain and illuminated themselves like millions of crystals, like gaudy chandeliers—or a sparkling coating of freezing rain I recalled, even though I hadn't seen freezing rain in five years.

Eventually, Carl and Jordy straggled out and I figured they wanted some father and son time so, mug in hand, I crossed the footbridge back to the wedding scene.

I helped clean up alongside a few of the least hung-over kids, all I discovered classmates of Allison's from Dalhousie University. We stacked wet chairs, harvested a vast crop of empties, and had slight arguments about the biodegradability of marshmallows. Everything was sodden.

Back at the cottage, everyone was packing up. In minutes, we were assembled by the cars. Hugs and handshakes and more tears.

We didn't say much on our drive back. For almost all the time I've known him, Carl wears a perpetual Mona Lisa-type smile of contentment. But I could see something was on his mind.

"What?" I asked.

"Nuthin'."

"Bullshit. What?" I repeated because it always requires two 'whats?' before Carl answers a probing question.

"Well…Jordy said there was a fella up around his place a few days ago asking about me."

"About you? What about you?"

"Nuthin'.….Hell of a wedding wasn't it?"

"Sure was. Allie looked fantastic."

But even that indirect compliment didn't make the giant Mona Lisa in plaid re-emerge.

CHAPTER 6

The following Tuesday was the township council meeting where all residents and us transients were going to get the big "pree-sent" as Carl called it and the council would likely give its final approval for Edgewater Estates. I figured I couldn't just sit back and watch all this happen without being able to kid myself that I had at least tried to stop it.

Time for a one-man lobbying effort. Modifying this whole process to delete my land from the plans hung on changing the vote of one or both the surviving councilors who favoured the development.

I figured Mayor McQuaig was steadfast, so first up was Preston Peterson. His yard was a sprawling mess of big machines everywhere, a grader, two backhoes, a larger high hoe, two bulldozers, piles of top soil, sand, and crushed stone, and two old dump trucks that may have been used in *Sorcerer* ferrying dynamite across the Andes.

Preston came out of his shed to greet me. To no particular effect, he was wiping engine grease with a filthy rag off his gnarled hands.

"You come here to change my vote?" he asked straight off.

"No…I mean yes. Sort of. I want you to make Edgewater leave me alone."

"Mayor called. Said that's what you'd probably do. She said that even that one change could delay things for months."

"She's full of shit."

"You want to be the one to tell her?"

I flashed to an ugly confrontation with Elsie that concluded with my face being re-arranged by the meeting gavel she so adroitly wielded.

"Point," I said. "So that's it?"

"Yup. I'm afraid so. No sense in beating around the bush."

"Alrighty then," I said, turning to leave. I stopped, deciding I'd collect some background.

"Tell me, Preston: do you have any doubts about the Edgewater people, especially that Stewie?" I asked.

"He's a slick one, I'll give you that. Bullshit artist, if you want the truth. But his money's good. He paid me big and upfront to get goin' on the land when they start up. Swore they'd send all the heavy equipment work my way."

"And you believe him?"

"He promised—in front of people—that they wouldn't bring in a fancy Toronto outfit. Maybe because I told him that would be a dumber than fuck move. Any out-of-towners would've never worked this kind of land."

"That's great for you. And then there's the land you got up there too."

"Never mind the land sale. That's gravy. The big thing is we got real steady work, for years maybe. That's what matters. The work. It's gonna be all the wife can do to keep up with the bookkeeping."

Preston was glancing around his yard. Various sons were attending to the machinery. I could hear them laughing and mocking each other as their father stared at them.

"You know something?" Preston said, now facing me. "All their lives my boys got shit. I give 'em all I had and what I had was shit. At Christmas, their birthdays, school clothes, everything. All they got was shit. They're grown men and they stayed. And they still bust their asses every day we got work. One—Billy over there—he loves his pa's business, loves the machines. He wants the company when I'm done. I don't have the heart to tell him that without the development I likely got to fold it. He's twenty-seven; this is all he's ever done. Now what the fuck's he supposed do?"

"I don't know," I said, watching young William apply a giant wrench to a tractor tire lug nut. He twisted it off as easily as a beer cap.

"Why shouldn't they have a chance?" Preston asked. "Go back to school if they want. Dress nice. Provide for their families. Travel. Do the things their old man was too dumb to ever have the wherewithal to give them."

"They absolutely should."

"So then lemme ask you something. You always seemed like a good fella. Why would you fuck your neighbours like that instead of doing the right thing by people?"

"I don't want to fuck you people. I really don't. I just want them to change the plans."

"I get it. But Elsie said that's like being half pregnant; either you are or you aren't. We gotta get this started because otherwise we'll keep goin' back and forth and meanwhile fuck-all gets done. Fish or cut bait."

"Shit or get off the pot?" I added.

"And speakin' of. You better find someone else to pump your tank, OK?"

I was chastened and I was angry as I drove away. Up close and personal, I had just witnessed how much Edgewater Estates could impact the lives of people around here, people I knew.

But I was also mad over the fear being mongered that my refusal to sell my piddly four acres had endangered the whole project. Fear that had no doubt been invented by Stewie and stoked by the mayor.

While it was another long shot, I reasoned that Councilor Dugald, the only politician who had switched his vote, might be switched back. Carl pointed me in the direction of the Dugald place as he had with Peterson's.

The white wooden farmhouse was at the end of a long laneway off Regional Road 507 just north of our road, near a small sleepy four corners-type of village called Catchacoma where I thought that's exactly what would happen to kids growing up there.

Bradley's place was impossible to miss. The scrub bush flanking the highway just stopped on the left side and opened up to acres of what had once been farmland, and now was a green field of short grass. His spread was immaculate and actually quite grand in that rolling-hilled-Virginia-horse-farm-mown-lawns-white-fenced-giant-willows kinda way. I tried to imagine the years of machine-less work the Dugald clan would've spent clearing and de-stumping the land to get it this way. And the much more recent work to fence it and produce perfect lawns.

Dugald greeted me at the front door of the large farmhouse. "Hail, fellow scribe!" he said and ushered me into a new-looking solarium overlooking the back yard. Passing through the house, it was obvious that a bunch of money had been sunk into it. Designer kitchen with high-end appliances, lots of crown molding, burnished wide-plank oak floors. Triple-glazed windows with inset California shutters. I imagined the original family farm house had been gutted and that there was just as much money inside the new walls in plumbing, wiring, and heating as there was put into the interior decoration.

"Beautiful place you've got here," I said as we sat down in tasteful white whicker arm chairs.

"Thank you, kind sir. The missus and I do rather enjoy it," he said waving out the floor-to-ceiling glass at I assumed the missus under a Tilley hat weeding away in their rose garden.

We chatted about writing for a bit. Well, he chatted while I listened to him talking about of his book sales numbers.

"To what do I owe the pleasure…?" he abruptly asked.

"I wanted to talk to you about Edgewater Estates."

"Of course you do, of course you do. I fear you may have frittered away your time by journeying here. Your opposition to this economic boon is—to be frank—unconscionable."

"I'm not opposed to it!" I protested. "I just want to keep my home."

"Well, that doesn't seem quite feasible, does it?"

"Of course it is! All council has to do is stipulate that the retirement home be moved."

"There is not a chance of that happening. The public consultation period concluded months ago."

"I wasn't here."

"However you choose to spend your winters is of no concern to me or to the business of council and we believe work must begin posthaste."

"Aww, for fuck's sake, Bradley."

"Profanity is the effort of a feeble brain to express itself forcibly," he cited some arsehole.

"How's about I express myself forcibly to the authorities over your obvious conflict of interest?"

P. Bradley Dugald got amped up over that line.

"I resent the implication that I have capitulated to base mercantile interests. Let me assure you, I have no pressing need for the money. Forty-five years in the forestry industry have been more than generous to me. I purchased that land forty years ago. At that time, I contemplated building a place in which to retire. But I'm 72 and I simply do not have an exhausting project like that left in me. Instead I renovated this home. Do you seriously think that I would jeopardize my reputation for something as sordid as the profit motive?"

"Then why did you change your mind?"

"Because I thought about it, that's why. In a moment of startling clarity, I saw the vast benefits accruing to my constituency. I shall do nothing to impede those benefits. Now, if you'll excuse me…," he said rising.

Sometimes, I honestly don't know why I do or say the things I do, but at the door I couldn't stop myself.

"Can I ask you one more question?" I said.

"Yes?"

"The 'P' in P. Bradley Dugald. What's it stand for?"

"Parker."

"Oh. I would've bet Pompous."

So I was 0 for 2 at the lobbying plate. I won't say my effort had been half-hearted but I do understand I couldn't sell shit to a fly. I just about always take 'no' for an answer.

However, even with the looming council approval, I still wasn't all that concerned. Let them build whatever they wanted to. For sure, it was going to be without my land and Carl's island. Unless they intended to do it at gunpoint, there wasn't a fucking way in the world they could force me—or Carl—to sell.

CHAPTER 7

Meeting night arrived and Carl and I sat at the back of the packed Council Chambers. Out of habit I suspect, Carl always sits at the back wherever he goes because otherwise he'd obscure the view of everyone sitting behind him.

Lining the walls of the meeting room were large foam core-backed presentation boards on easels which even at a distance I saw were representations of Edgewater Estates.

Mayor McQuaig brought the throng to order. She introduced Stewie who got a big hand from the crowd, then a bubbly saleslady identified as a Marketing Representative named Theresa Wright who waved happily and one other guy, Jerry Glavin, who, we were told, was in charge of site preparation. Jerry was a fireplug of a guy, sort of like Bob Hoskins on 'roids. He looked uncomfortable and stood off to the side, barely acknowledging the crowd's polite applause,

I suppose they had to look all sharp and rich. Imagine if they'd turned up in plaid shirts and John Deere ball caps to the council meetings. First off, you wouldn't be able to tell them apart from the regular citizens of West Kawartha Township and, secondly, you wouldn't give them any credit at being able to pull off a multi-million dollar luxury development. Not very enlightened of me, I know, but true nonetheless.

I'm not thinking Stewie was as slick and greedy as conman Lyle Lanley and that we were as dumb and greedy as the town of Springfield when they bought the monorail. But not too far off.

Boy, was he polished. Starting with his shoes which had a shine on them that I never trust.

"Folks, now I know you might have a lot of questions," Stewie began. "I'll try to answer them all but I ask you save them until the end and I'll get to them one by one."

Smart, I thought. Why take questions out in front of everybody if they might create misgivings? Well fuck that, I thought in that not quite endearing, pouty way I have.

"Since we first met with you good folks about six months ago, a lot has changed," he continued. "Before Council votes, we wanted to bring you up to date on all the new and exciting things that've happened, to go along with all the old, exciting things."

There were a few more chuckles, you know the sort: the mystifying little laughs in a crowd that make you wonder what kind of person finds shockingly lame jokes even remotely funny.

Stewie then ran through what sounded like a tightly-scripted info-mercial as a video played behind him. The video was a combination of dissolving stills from the promo material and computer animations that included a fly-over of the proposed golf course, the club house and assorted log McMansions squatting on their one-acre estate lots. Familiar shots appeared and disappeared of hiking trails, bicycle trails, cross–country ski trails, and those fucking loons again. As far as I could tell, there had been new additions to the list of amenities including a yoga platform, a common area set aside for a vegetable garden kinda co-op, a tuck shop, a sauna, a small marina with canoes and paddleboards supplied by the developer.

Every fucking aging boomer "lifestyle" trend you could think of was crammed in the plans and his little speech. I was surprised they hadn't renamed it Arugala Acres or Kale Corner. He hit the mutually exclu-sive buzzwords. "Tranquil" and "serene" juxtaposed with "energetic" and "active." It reminded me of those self-conflicting wine reviews that tell you a Riesling is "bold yet reticent."

I fucking hated to admit it but Edgewater Estates actually looked really swell. But with two-bedroom, two-bath condos starting in the "low 400s"—I assumed there were at least an additional three zeroes implied—it would not be for the faint of heart or wallet.

It struck me that the prices being asked had to be that high to recoup what had to have been a ton o' money sunk into marketing as well as all the consultants' reports.

Stewie then moved on to the retirement home which directly concerned me as it was supposedly to be built on my goddamned land. He was looking at me while he was describing the high-quality care seniors would receiving, first in the self-sufficient retirement block and, as age marched on, how they could transfer to the nursing home next door where round the clock medical attention would be on hand—along with gourmet food, advanced physiotherapy, as well as a library, cooking and woodworking shops, and a sewing room. A new wrinkle, he announced, was the walk-in medical clinic open to all township residents. That brought a few appreciative "ooos" from the largely senior crowd.

A few heads swiveled to look at Carl and me. There was no love in their collective eye.

Stewie then produced a slide of an opinion survey of Peterborough County residents claiming that 84.5% of respondents favoured the development.

"You get a call?" I whispered to Carl.

"Nope. You?"

"No," I said, looking around at some other people evidently asking their neighbours the same thing.

Stewie was doing the big finish, telling us, more or less, that we'd be congenital idiots to pass up this opportunity. People were actually clapping. As the applause turned to a smattering, I piped up, pretty loudly.

"Has anybody done due diligence on your financials? I see you doling out a lot of money. But I don't see how you can pay for the kind of development you're planning."

"Mr. Lydon, is it?" he said, knowing fucking full well what my name was. "Good question. We, *of course*, couldn't begin selling properties up here until we had council's blessing. But we've mentioned it to more than a few high wealth clients and let me say the interest they've shown is very much like the support you good people just showed. Thank you for your question. So folks, I want to thank you for that sup—"

"Can you tell me what the sample size was for your survey?" I asked, interrupting him again.

"Five hundred responses work for a national poll. We used three hundred in the county. You should know that's a big enough sample to be statistically valid. I assume that before you were fired from your last job, you must have done surveys."

There were a few chuckles and a few understated boos directed at me.

"So," said Stewie, obviously feeling the crowd was with him, "if there are no more questions from one of only two people trying to kill this dream, we'll call it a night."

The presentation portion ended. Despite some louder boos, Council agreed to go in camera for final deliberations and a vote. It was promised as a straight up or down, no putting it off.

While that was going on, a bunch of us sort of shuffled around the stations of the presentation boards, examining the various drawings and pie charts. I was studying the graphics as if they were the Dead Sea scrolls to avoid the many glares directed my way.

And then I saw that the Angler Arms—the best cottage country bar in the world™—was to be re-named and re-launched as Bentley's on the Water. Drawings of the proposed bar—inside and out—did not feature one rendering of a patron with either a plaid shirt or a base-ball cap. You didn't need extensive market research to know who your typical customer might be; casual observation would've worked. But the local lads were going to be cut out in favour of the well-heeled Edgewater occupants desperately seeking an impudent yet respectful pinot after a hard day of cycling and tennis and golf and paddling and hiking.

Stewie sought me out.

"Jake, I'm glad you came," he said, looking not at all glad. "I was hop-ing to set up a meeting with you. Discuss the plans."

I played at ignoring him as I moved to the big board where the whole development was mapped out.

"What's this unmarked building near the lake?" I asked, pointing at a dark brown square just around the corner from Carl's island and his thirty-foot wide road access strip on the mainland.

"That's the facilities plant—for the lagoon sewage system for the high-er density properties, water treatment and pumping and so on."

"So what's this over here marked 'facilities plant'?" I asked indicating a second brown square near the club house.

"A sub-plant—mostly a pumping station for the sprinkler system for the golf course."

"And what's this?" I said in that way a toddler ceaselessly asks "why?" after every goddamned sentence you utter.

His eyes flashed anger. He caught himself, composed himself, and leaned into me.

"There are other ways to get you two to play ball," he whispered.

"Such as?"

"Some folks are pretty pissed off so you'll probably find out," he said, his mouth a slit, his words barely audible.

He turned away, broke into a small knot of people looking at the artist's conception of the clubhouse.

"Folks!" he said in a loud and cheery voice. "You do know township residents get a big discount on greens fees."

I was left standing there considering his statement. It wasn't a threat exactly but it was in the same postal code as one. And he sounded ultra-confident. That worried me.

The council returned from their inner chamber and Mayor Elsie McQuaig stepped up to the microphone and the crowd hushed without prompting.

"Ladies and gentlemen," she rasped, "let's skip the suspense, shall we? Let the record show that the Council of West Kawartha Township, by a vote of 3 to 2, has officially approved the plan for Edgewater Estates! Let the work begin!"

The audience cheered, for the result and likely for being present at the historic occasion when Mayor McQuaig actually voted. Councilors Phil Vogel and Mary Ellen Conway, the hold-outs, looked glum. Sarah Ruth Evans shouted "Travesty!" while my neighbour nodded his head in agreement and more than few people around me looked at me with that 'na-na-boo-boo' expression. Stewie wore a Cheshire cat expression that only needed a canary feather caught between his perfect teeth.

"Let's get out of here," Carl said. "Not in the mood to be a human sacrifice."

So we skedaddled out of there, passing through a gauntlet of glares.

Carl drove; I fumed. Not about the vote; that was foregone conclusion. But because Stewie had handled me like a bouncer giving the bum's rush to a drunk, (I know what that feels like). That was bad enough. Worse still, he had obviously been nosing around in my past, such as it was.

"You were pretty smooth in there, boss," Carl said.

"Fuck off."

"Yup, you really showed the knife."

"Carl…" I warned.

"Yessiree, Bob; they know fer sure they ain't playin' with kids."

"Are you done?"

We pulled up to my laneway.

I had had visitors while we'd been at the meeting.

Somebody had played an inning of mailbox baseball. My crumpled metal box lay near the 4 X 4 post now at about a 45 degree angle. Whoever the slugger was, he'd gotten all of that baby.

Shit!

Carl trained the headlights on my newly Leaning Tower of Postal as I examined the damage. I spotted the 'Private Property' sign about twenty yards away where it had landed in a tree after a vandal's Frisbee toss.

Shit!

Carl and I had a nightcap or two in the screened-in porch. I wanted to enjoy just sitting there, warm breeze strained through the screen, waiting for the next loon cry. All I could think of was what a shitty evening I had just had, topped off by what was way too coincidental to have been a random shitty drunken prank.

In the grand scheme of things, it was just a fucking mailbox—and one long past receiving mail—but it was my fucking mailbox. It was one of the first things I had added to the property after Beth and I bought it. She had wandered down the laneway—looking all summery and beautiful—to mock me while I was trying to gouge a posthole into the Canadian Shield.

How can someone take shit or break shit that isn't theirs? What crosses their minds—if anything—the split second before they do it? What sense of entitlement, what twisted justification, what moral vacuum allows these trespasses that should not ever be forgiven?

Well, wasn't I being the self-righteous, morally pure little snot? Especially when I had stolen. Once. A candy bar—Turkish Delight as it turns out—lifted from the corner store when I was seven or eight. I walked around for a couple of hours in the summer sun with the bar in my pocket, my heart pounding as furiously as when I first jacked the bar. Imagining the thumping I was in for if the old man ever found out, imagining the rage from the Greek shopkeeper whose store I had ripped off. Imagining my life behind bars. So I returned to the store and put the sticky, half-melted blob back. And of course I got caught doing that and everybody yelled at me anyway.

That was it for my criminal career. Unless you count some of the shit I did last summer. And I don't.

Carl intruded on my felonious remembrance.

"Best let it go, boss."

"How? How can you let crap like that go?"

"Cuz there's likely worse comin'."

CHAPTER 8

For the next week or so, I hunkered down, initially because sticking my head in sand is often my preferred way of dealing with shit but soon after because I had time to fill and the desire not to have humans—even Carl—help me to fill it. I went on a writing jag.

Used to be reading was the refuge I sought, made-up worlds that begged me to enter. Now, there were DIY made-up worlds that I got to build. During that week, I was in post-war Buenos Aries, laying out, decorating, and populating the Gypsy *barrio* of San Telmo.

Carl—bless him—knows to stay away, not because he's intuitive but because we've agreed on a signaling system, a small Canadian flag stuck in a plant pot facing his island. If the cheap flag is a-flyin', he doesn't come a-knockin'.

It did strike me as odd that on a couple of days I forgot to hoist the colours and Carl still hadn't come over.

Stewie, however, didn't get the memo and he just showed up one day.

"Shame about your mailbox," he said by way of greeting.

"Well, I really, *really* appreciate your sincere, heart-felt sympathy."

"Look, Jake, we need to have an open and honest discussion."

"No, we don't. There's nothing to discuss. I'm not selling."

"We can go to five hundred thousand. Not a penny more."

This time there was no pause for calculatin'.

"I really don't care what you can or cannot do," I said. "The answer's still no. Same for Carl."

"Really?" was his answer that took me aback. "I don't think so. Didn't you hear? We raised his offer to 500K too and he had a change of heart, came to his senses. Ask him," he said with only the slightest of smug grins.

I assumed that I looked the way I felt: dumbfounded, gobsmacked, flummoxed.

Stewie's grin widened a bit as he watched his news sink in. All I could think of is I wanted to either land a haymaker in the middle of that self-satisfied smile or have him instantly disappear. Something visceral, primal happens when someone I don't want there, steps onto my four acres and acts like a dick. It's my four acres. Not yours. Mine. No dicks allowed* (*except the owner). I can't explain it and I don't try to understand it. You know the look in Clint's eyes when he growls out "Get off my lawn?" That pretty well captures it.

Apparently my body language wasn't too convincing.

"Don't make me say it," I said.

"Say what?"

"Get off my lawn."

"Or what?"

Shit! No one ever asked "or what?" of Mr. Eastwood.

"Or…or Carl will punch you soft."

"You mean Carl, my new client?"

Shit again!

So we stood there for a few moments, him obviously lolling around in his victory, me on the verge of apoplexy.

"I'll go now but if I were you I'd take this a little more seriously," Stewie said.

"And if I were you, I'd climb into a burlap sack and drown myself as a civic duty."

"Oh," Stewie said ignoring me, "are you coming to the official opening next week? We'd *love* to see you there."

As he pulled away quickly, kicking up a cloud of dust, I realized Stewie *had* to be telling the truth. I mean, it was a ridiculous thing to say otherwise, accomplishing nothing and easily disproven.

I sat down, shaking.

"That fella botherin' you again?" Carl asked as I turned to see him trudging up from the shore.

"Carl," I said as he stepped onto the deck, "ol' Stewie's been spreading lies about you. Says you sold out. Like a two-dollar whore."

"He ain't lyin', but I guess you figured that."

"Carl, we had a deal. We shook and everything. What the fuck happened?"

"Ran into Stewie at the hardware store a couple of days ago while you were jerkin' off at the computer. Buddy upped his bid to 500,000."

"Isn't that fucking wonderful? I want to know why the Christ you're selling *at all!*"

"Something to give my granddaughter. I don't have anything else.

Look, I'm sorry."

And he was. You could see the remorse. Maybe I shouldn't have said anything. Maybe I should have realized that if my friend had changed his mind, he must have had a good reason, and just leave it at that.

But I couldn't.

"You know you at least owe me an explanation," I said. "I am involved."

"Sorry," was all he said before he turned, got into his canoe, and paddled back to the island.

I was still shaking as I stared after him.

Humiliated for sure by the way Stewie had suckered me into the news. And angry, for sure, but more than anything, I was absolutely rocked by the fork in the road that my friendship with Carl had abruptly just reached. It didn't take a goddamned chess grandmaster to see ahead and imagine what it all looked like. How were we now supposed to deal with each other? Just act as if nothing had happened? We could try to do that. I presumed he'd stay in the 'hood. There are telephones. There is the NFL. There is beer. Most friends don't live beside each other. But what if we didn't treat it is a non-event? How would it even be physically possible to avoid each other before he moved? Do I make him remove his truck from my land and onto the less convenient narrow lake access he always had? Do we now keep all our sports chats to ourselves? Do I help him pack?

And what did we just lose? I had never quantified our dealings with each other, but here we were, on the verge of losing a lot. Sitting on the deck, I played through some the scenes that could very well have just come to an end: spending at least seven hours every Sunday parked in front of my big screen from the first Opening Sunday kick-off until mid-season when I left for points south for the winter. Drinking at the AA, pretending to fish while not pretending to get loaded.

The thing about rituals is that they're rituals. They exist because they feel as though they've always existed and as though you expect them to always exist unless something disruptive, something cataclysmic happens. Like somebody dies. Or for no good reason Carl had switched to a light beer.

Or this.

Very briefly, I even tried to be philosophic. As philosophic as a good line from a movie will let you be. This from *Tequila Sunrise*: "Maybe friends are like tires. Maybe they just wear out."

Bullshit! I thought. Our twenty years as buddies didn't wear out; it blew up. And over what? Carl wanting to sell *his* land? On one hand, so what? It's his land; he can do whatever the fuck he wants to with it. But on the other, we had a deal. Made just days ago.

I think of another line, this from TV's *Kung Fu*. The earnestly Shaolin Buddhist David Carradine—just before he slow-motion kicks the shit out of the town baddie for doing something or other exploitive—asks in his halting whisper: "You do this…for money?"

Bullshit! I think to myself again. $400,000 and he wouldn't sell, but for five hundred he would? That made no sense at all. And just so he could bequeath the cash to his recently recovered granddaughter? She was young; he was not. She'd soon be getting the island when he kicked. It'd be even more valuable by then.

Carl isn't exactly the flexible type. Turns out, neither am I. You could easily see the pack ice setting in, a prideful wall being erected. And then where'd we be?

Something had to give. There was no choice. It would have to be me.

I rowed over to the island—with about one tenth the grace and ability with which Carl makes the crossing.

He was sitting at his kitchen table rolling his next day's supply of cigarettes. Well, not exactly. All the fixings were around him but he was just staring out at the lake. I startled him.

"Carl, what the fuck's up?"

"With what?"

"You selling."

"Told you. For my granddaughter."

"You're full of shit."

"Nice. You comin' over here to call me liar."

"Let's see here now: you're not telling the truth. So that would make you…oh, I don't know…a liar."

I don't know if he was debating about whether or not to get up and beat the shit out of me for calling him out—something he most likely could accomplish while in a semi-coma—but he took an extra-long time responding.

"Alright," he finally said. "Something came up."

"What?"

"Can't say."

"We're friends, aren't we?"

"Mebbe."

"Arsehole. Just tell me."

The next bit of Carl's conversation should, strictly speaking, be contained in a single paragraph. But that wouldn't capture what actually happened. There were long silences between each short sentence or phrase. They gave Carl enough time to peer up and down the lake, to work his toothpick, roll a cigarette. I could see he was about to tell a story and I knew I just had to wait and let it play out.

"Told you about that guy askin' around…up by Jordy's….

"….Well, buddy found out something….

"…It's bad….

"…From a while back….

"….Twenty years or so."

"Carl, it can't be that terrible," I said, working to pry an answer out of him that normally feels like trying to open a sardine can with an overripe banana. "Look, I'll tell you something bad and we'll be even. That's the way we play, isn't it? All square."

He looked intrigued. And while he was looking intrigued I was think-think-thinking.

"OK, here goes…," I began. "…I fucked a chicken once."

For a second, Carl looked stunned and then disgusted. And then he broke out laughing.

"No, you didn't!" he said.

No, I didn't but my job at that moment was to convince Carl that I had. A drunk stranger in a bar in Freeport had actually confessed that bit of fowl bestiality to me; I have zero idea what possessed him to do that, other than I may look like somebody you tell shit like that to. I was light on details after the guy said that because that's just not the kind of revelation that begs for follow-up questions. So I improvised a story.

"On my uncle's farm outside of Ottawa," I told Carl. "I was maybe thirteen. Working in the coop."

I could see Carl imagining the scene. He turned to me looking deadly serious.

"Leghorn or Rhode Island Red?" he asked.

"I don't know! Why's that matter?"

"Well, you don't want an ugly one."

We laughed and the joke seemed to lighten things, made them feel like the way we normally are. I don't know if he believed my revolting story or not but he looked like a man wanting to unburden.

"What, Carl?"

Yet another pause.

"What?" I repeated.

"I killed a man…. Didn't mean to but I did."

"What happened?" I asked, surprised and trying hard to imagine how this archetypal gentle giant could take a life.

"Jordy," he began. "He was gettin' in with the wrong fellas when he was a kid. You know, drugs and shit. I wanted to have a chat with one of them. I knew he was fishing on the Irondale near the Gooderham Dam so I followed him up there. Pretty heavy spring run-off, so's the water was poundin' down the sluices. Punk told me to fuck off. I snapped and went for him. He slipped. Rocks were wet from the spray. In he went. River picked him up, smashed him into some rocks. Nothing I could do."

"That's it? It was an accident, for Christ's sake!"

Carl ignored me.

"I guess you could say I panicked," he continued. "I didn't call the police. Didn't tell no one. But Jordy, he knew. Knew something had happened. Never forgave me."

"Until the wedding. I saw it. You guys are OK now."

"That's not the goddamned point!" he insisted, his voice uncharacteristically rising. "Even if that guy was a shit, he had parents, friends. They didn't find his body for two days."

"It was an accident," I repeated.

Carl stared at me, even and direct.

"It's real simple, Jake. If I don't go up to the dam that day, he doesn't die."

"Well, he did. Now here we all are."

"Here we all are."

"So what happened to bring it up?"

"Fella came by here. Not Stewie. Another lad. He was that beefy guy at the town meeting. Glavin? Must be the same guy Jordy told me about. Buddy says they're going to re-open the investigation. Gonna be lots of questions. Said the family could sue me, take everything. Never mind what the cops find."

"Must've talked to Jordy."

"I dunno. Jordy says no, so more'n likely someone else. Up there, people talk."

"C'mon, Carl! People talk everywhere. So exactly what? Twenty-year old rumours, you never laid a hand on him. Zero proof, zero witnesses. It's just: he said, she said."

"Ya figure?"

"Yeah, I figure. Plus, that guy Glavin is extorting you. Today. Cops would find that even more interesting."

"You are an arsehole but you may be right."

"You sign anything with Stewie?"

"Nope."

"So are you gonna call the real arsehole in all this?"

"Already did. While you were sittin' over there, fumin' like a…like a wet hen."

"I was *not* fuming."

"I seen ya. Beer?"

We didn't say much as we sat and drank.

"What'd ol' Stewie say when you told him?"

"He yelled a bit about suing me?"

"A bit?"

"Might've been a lot, but I hung up. Can he do that?"

"What?"

"Sue."

"He could try, I suppose, but there's nothing in writing. You're clear."

Carl didn't look all the convinced about the legal advice I was dispensing. He went silent again.

"Why'd you change your mind?" I finally asked.

"Nuthin' to do with you, if that's what you're askin.' Like I said, you're an arsehole."

"Then why?"

"It didn't feel right. I just couldn't go through with it. This is my home."

Sure, I was glad about Carl's decision. But I was worried too. All this was getting a good distance beyond a business deal being attempted. There was deliberate vandalism, someone other than Stewie digging into Carl's past, and attempted blackmail.

This was hard ball.

CHAPTER 9

No doubt The Development deserved its capital letters. This was going to be big. The biggest thing that happened to this area ever. A doubling of the permanent population almost overnight. And with the dollar spillover all the way down to Peterborough that came with it. Stores, restaurants, events, doctors, everything that always accompanies a tribe of monied, old people descending on a place like reverse locusts. Roads would be improved. Copycat housing developments. There'd be millions of dollars floating around and for decades.

I knew there was no goddamned reason in the world that I could be held responsible for stopping all this prosperity and I was pissed that I was being accused of exactly that.

Halley got back to me later in the day.

"Dad, we found out Hill was a serious marathoner," she started off. Not big on chit-chat, that one.

"I knew that."

"Listen, will ya? She blew out her knee a couple of years ago. Wrecked all the cartilage, ACL, MCL, the works. She needed a series of surgeries to rebuild it. That's when, we're guessing, she became addicted to opiates. It was risky but she did have access. We found a bunch of pills—Oxy, Vicodin, Percocet. We traced the batches to St. Mark's Hospital where she had privileges. An anesthesiologist copped to supplying her after her legal scrips ran out."

"A solid gone addict with that kinda job?" I asked. "Plus, she was a town councilor up here?"

"By all accounts, Dr. Hill was fully functioning, quite able to separate her work from getting wrecked."

"So, bottom line, an accident?"

"Reading the file, it seems textbook OD. Fentanyl is nasty shit—fifty times more potent than pharmacy-grade heroin; a hundred times stronger than morphine. You gotta know what you're doing with this stuff and most people don't."

"Would Dr. Hill?"

"Probably. There is one thing that's kinda odd."

"Which is?"

"Fentanyl doesn't show up until the night she was found. There was no Fentanyl in her stash. Her supplier at the hospital swears he never gave her any. He was already busted so he doesn't have a lot of reason to lie."

"So why'd she step up?"

"I don't know. Addicts do that, dad. Lookin' for a bigger high."

"Was it pills or liquid or a patch?" I thought to ask.

"Pill. Still traces in the autopsy."

"Well, I'm no pharmacologist, but a fluid would be how you'd get it in a hospital to control the doses during operations or patches from a doctor later during recovery. It's pure. A pill you get from basement labs. You don't have a fucking clue what's in it. That's a huge risk."

"True."

"Does Dr. Hill fit the profile of a reckless gambler?"

"No."

"There's something there, Halley."

"I was already thinking that. I'll keep you posted," she said and hung up.

A suspicious end for one councilor. Why not for the other? There had to be more details about the fatal mangling of Maynard Odell.

I called Detective Sergeant Les Macgregor, a buddy of mine at the OPP detachment in Peterborough. He had hired me a few times in the past—a couple of days each time—to review some puzzling cold cases because, as he put it, I "don't look at things like a normal person."

For a fee of fuck-all, I volunteered to take a look at Maynard's death. He told me to get stuffed.

"You can't be anywhere near this, Jake," he told me. "You know that. You're involved. The land and all."

"Heard about that, did you?"

"Who hasn't?"

"Odell's death. Not a little bit suspicious to you?"

"No. We were all over it. The way it plays is he climbed up the side of the chipper, and tried to kick away a blockage. When he did, the motor re-engaged, the vibration shook his other foot loose. He slipped and down the chute he went. It's like a funnel. Case closed."

"What if someone fed him into it?"

"Yeah, he'd just stand there and let somebody pick up all 220 pounds of him, hoist him five feet in the air so he could go in feet first."

"What if he was unconscious?"

"No head bruise, no drugs in his system."

"Booze?"

"Yup. More than double 08. We found at least ten empty beer cans."

"So he nods off."

"He might've been shitfaced but his blood alcohol level wasn't high enough to make him pass out. And even if he did, passing out doesn't levitate him into the chipper."

"Any fingerprints identifiable?"

"His and a Derek Collins."

"Derek?"

"Yeah. We had him on file for a juvie rap years ago. We talked to him. Said he'd been helping Maynard a week earlier. We've got three witnesses saw him and Odell at the Angler Arms before driving past your place to his woodlot. But nobody saw Collins with Odell on the day he died, and Derek has two buddies who swore they were fishing with him all day on Chrystal Lake, miles away. And there's no way Derek lifts over 200 pounds."

"So, accident?"

"A really dumb, drunken accident but, yes, an accident."

Something occurred to me.

"Was there gas in the tank?" I asked.

I could hear papers being shuffled. Then shuffled again, only more frantically.

"Shit! Nothing in the report…Looks like no one checked."

He paused.

"But that doesn't prove anything," he said. "Maybe the engine stalled when Odell's body jammed it."

"Maybe. But why didn't it stall earlier with the wood blockage that Odell was supposedly kicking away at?"

"I…don't know."

"Just check the chipper."

"Can't. We were done with it, so we hosed it down and we turned it over."

"To who?"

"The kid. Blair Odell."

"A Toronto lawyer needs a wood chipper?"

"Apparently not. He had already sold it to somebody named Peterson. Says here the guy showed up with a bill of sale so we released it."

CHAPTER 10

There are those among us who claim that dependence on caffeine is psychological. Those misguided souls ought not to ever make those claims while standing between me and my coffee machine first thing in the morning. I am completely without the power of speech or even the capacity for thought. I am a marginally ambulatory zombie as I shuffle to the kitchen, and, by rote, take the cut-rate coffee can out of the cupboard, plunk enough ground beans into the filter for eight strong cups. Then head to the sink to fill the pot.

On this particular morning, I turned on the tap and to my awakening horror I saw no water come out, heard nothing but that angry hissing sound of empty pipes.

Fuck!

The sun had just risen and there I was: wriggling on my belly like a reptile on the dirt floor of the enclosed crawlspace under the cabin to check the water pump. In addition to the normal funky basement smell there was the unmistakable odour of burnt something. Time to deploy my vast arsenal of technical skills. I unplugged the pump then I plugged it back in. Nada.

By the shore, I fished out the stiff plastic pipe through which comes the lake water. It extends five or six feet into the lake. The pipe is heavy because there's a foot valve at the end that screens for debris and prevents water from washing back into the lake. It was there alright. But wrapped in a plastic garbage bag cinched at the pipe with a small bungee cord. The pump had run dry and burnt out.

Fuckers!

I asked Carl to take a look after I described to him what had happened.

"No point, chief. It's calved. I'll help put in the new one. You want at least ¾ horse. Gas back-up would be good."

So that was a day shot. As well as six hundred bucks.

And a big fucking dark cloud over my normally sunny disposition.

I got even less sunnier after I called Phil Vogel, my insurance guy, who sounded genuinely pained when he pointed out that I had a $1000 deductible on my policy.

He did commiserate with me as I whined about the development. After all, he had opposed Edgewater Estates in his other job as a township councilor.

"Well, it's a shame. We made our stand and we lost," he said.

"Why were you against it, anyway?" I asked.

"It was politically dumb. Obviously it had a lot of support right from the start but I just wanted this to be a place that didn't change. Christ, that's all I saw in Toronto. I loved it up here; that's why we moved. I suppose I should have switched but what the hell…"

"What about Dr. Hill?"

There was a pause.

"Why do you ask?"

"No big deal. I was wondering."

"I'm pretty sure she had the same reason I did."

After I hung up, I chose being perplexed as my next activity. Phil's answer to my question—or rather his vagueness and hesitation—did not make a lot of sense. How could one of the two councilors united against the development not have known *exactly* why the other was opposed? They would have had lots of discussions—public and private—about the basis for their resistance.

Note to self: find out what the hell was going on with that.

As Carl lay on his side hooking up the pump I'd bought in Peterborough and I occasionally handed him requested tools for the job, I thought about where we were at in this shit show. A bunch of citizens of West Kawartha pissed off at me—with Derek Collins being the only one who had directly confronted me—and a couple of way too coincidental bits of property destruction. Oh, and two dead councilors with, to me anyway, suspicious causes of death.

Beyond that, somebody had been digging into Carl's past and mine, obviously looking for something to leverage, some incident, some indiscretion to use as blackmail material. It of course all pointed to Stewie as the puppeteer. Stewie knew I had been fired, and presumably through Jerry Glavin, now knew about Carl's event twenty years ago.

I thought back to the public meeting and that 'Ooooo, did you hear: he was *fired*' reaction I got from the crowd. Even though it happens to a lot of people and had happened to me fifteen fucking years ago, the subtext is always: what kind of an incompetent degenerate gets his ass fired?

So what else could he find and use? I had had a life of excess and indiscretion but nothing indictable. That's not counting the occasional half-mile of drunk driving from AA to my place. When we decide not to walk or paddle there, Carl and I take turns driving and are scrupulous about not exceeding 10 miles an hour. If we were unsafe at any speed, the only thing we could possibly hit was bush.

Other than that, about my only official crime had been an assault charge. But A) I was sixteen and drunk at a party where the other guy smoked me first, and B) I got a whole six months probation and C) the record had been sealed and then expunged.

Those facts don't matter much anymore as people crave a shorthand on other people so they can make quick, nasty—always nasty—assessments and then move on to slag somebody else. Newspapers do it a lot, usually with athletes or entertainers. When a paragraph begins: "This is not the first time (insert name here) has run into trouble with the law" you know they're about to string together the current issue with, say, a minor bust for pot possession twenty years earlier so the reader can plainly see that the subject of the story is a loathsome career criminal unworthy of our adulation. The media does the same thing when they want to prove you shouldn't go to Mexico without sporting Kevlar beach wear. Subtract *los gringos norte* who, chock full of testosterone and hubris, go to Mexico believing they can teach the locals how to sell and smuggle drugs, and you actually don't have a lot of wrongful deaths. But attach a list of tourists who've died over the last ten years to your article and it's a wonder everybody hasn't given up tacos and tried to ban mariachi music.

One defence against these brutal simplifications is to have led an absolutely exemplary life which rules out everybody except Tom Hanks and maybe a few popes. The other way to go is to have outlandish behaviour expected of you. What possibly could come to light about Keith Richards that would shock us?

Maybe it was because I was lying in the fucking dirt under my cottage at the time, but it came to me that if Stewie was digging, I'd better grab a shovel too. I mean, who was this guy anyway? All we knew about him was that he was a "Toronto developer" as if that's all we ought to or needed to go on.

Once I had running water again, I went on an e-hunt. I started with Stewie's website where I was a little surprised to see his primary job was as an independent residential real estate agent. He didn't have a ton of listings but then again he didn't need to because he was high-end all the way. Nothing being "offered" at less than two million. 2½ to 5% commission on a few of those babies a year would help pay the bills. And the way house prices were going insane in Toronto, those two million dollar piles were now fetching three mill almost overnight.

There was a section on his site called My Philosophy which was a platform from which he could launch a bunch of warm and fuzzies about his tireless efforts to "connect people with their perfect homes." He got to work in pictures of his perfect family and action shots of his perfect performance in amateur triathlons all over Ontario and the US North-east. Apparently you can prove professional integrity by being good at cycling and swimming, and running.

I stopped.

Running.

Greta Hill was a runner.

I had to find out if there was any way Stewie's athletic path had crossed Hill's, (Yeah, yeah, I know; they're different sports; get off my back, will ya?), but just maybe they dabbled in the other's prime interest.

Somewhat eerily, given that she'd been deceased for months, Greta Hill's Facebook page was still up. As a retail politician, she had an Open setting on it. There I found info that she belonged to the Toronto Olympic Club headquartered in the centre west of Toronto. Flipping over to Stewie's site, I saw that he competed for the Iron Canucks out of Burlington, way southwest of the city. Dr. Hill's Olympic Club was strictly devoted to distance running while the Iron Canucks were triathlon only. Both club sites had reams and reams of race results probably dating as far back as when Thog was hotfooting it away from a sabre-toothed tiger.

Near as I could tell there was no overlap in pursuit of their respective hobbies. And at the end of my search I knew far more than I ever wanted to about the pretending you're bringing bad news to an ancient Greek king or chasing prehistoric game across the African veldt. Sure, it was the only form of locomotion at one time but then we went and invented the car so you can cover their distances the way you're supposed to: in minutes, and without breaking a sweat.

On his Facebook page, Stewie had praised a sports medicine doctor by name so I tracked him down. Again, the medical guy was in Hamilton, forty or fifty miles southwest of Toronto. His listing with the Ontario Medical Association showed no contact with St. Mark's Hospital, Hill's home base in centre town Toronto.

OK, could Dr. Hill have been a real estate client of Stewie's? At least recently, the answer was no. I scrolled through all the properties he had sold within the last six months. He had no listings in centre town. All his previous sales were houses in the deep west end while Dr. Hill's place, according to Halley, was a condo in Cabbagetown in the heart of centre east. So how about vice versa? Could Stewie's perfect children have been delivered by an ob-gyn named Greta Hill? I bet a guy like him has birth announcements which I found. Dr. Hill and the staff of St. Mark's were not praised but two other doctors and one Mississauga hospital were. Alrighty then, what about Mrs. Stewie being a patient of Hill's for woman things? Doubtful, again, because of the distances that'd be involved for someone who appeared to be a stay-at-home mom.

So, the way it looked was that Stewie probably first met Dr. Hill up here just before or at the council meeting last winter when he first started pitching the development. By then she was out of running. But that didn't mean Stewie couldn't have gotten close to her through their shared interest in covering large distances on foot. It's something he would've latched onto and encouraged as all great shmoozers would do. Note to self. Ask around. See if they were chummy.

I then concentrated on Stewie's business. His development work was underwhelming or, at best, whelming. Near as I could tell, he had put together three residential subdivisions, all small, no more than thirty houses each, all just west of Toronto. I looked up the trio by name—all bland real-estate-y type names. Same for their street names on the Google maps. Evidently, it was compulsory to use some combination of a tree name or an animal's name and/or a geographic feature. Take, for example, Stewie's Sable Ridge Oaks Corporation. A stroll through the 'hood on Google street view featured neither sable nor ridge nor oak trees among its giant executive homes. Squatting on tiny lots, the houses looked like clones with slight mutations. After only a couple of pints, I could see myself pulling into the wrong driveway.

All three subdivisions were incorporated as separate companies which, I knew, was standard practice to limit liability and enforce covenants on the buyers—like they *had* to have three-car garages and the exterior *had* to be some shade of boring beige brick.

The developments were pretty close to each other, all built on flat featureless land without any hint of forest. Judging by the surrounding parcels on Google Earth, the subdivisions sat on former farmers' fields. So he'd have zero experience dealing with the sort of bush and rock offered by West Kawartha.

There was a separate site button for Edgewater Estates. On the landing page for it were these words: "Sorry, folks! This section under construction. Check back."

Overall, I was puzzled. Here's a far west-end city guy who has no apparent connection to anything up here more than two hours northeast of Toronto and who's never done anything this big on this kind of terrain now trying to pull off something of a megaproject.

I don't know if he thought he'd find it real easy to deal with us because we were all just a bunch of dumbass country rubes. But that couldn't be; he'd bought (or said he'd bought) the two big houses near me. They'd been owned by not unsophisticated urban folk—Dr. Hill being one, my annoying neighbor, Drew Bregg, being the other. I assumed Stewie would have found them to be pretty sharp people. True, he would've had exposure to officialdom, getting approvals and such for his housing projects, but nothing like the hoops he was jumping through to get Edgewater Estates off the ground.

More bewildering was the fact that the biggest project of his life wasn't being crowed about on his own goddamned website. Maybe he was reluctant to mention it until he got West Kawartha approval but that also didn't make a lot of sense. Christ, there was more hype on the township website plus he'd already produced publicly-available marketing stuff that would travel easily to his website.

I hit the section on his site called Partnerships. There I found descriptions of four commercial projects he claimed involvement in, one in the west end of Toronto and three downtown. Now these really were big, two I had even heard about. I switched over to the news hunters and gatherers. Up popped five years worth of stories about them, some of them chock full of hyperbole about "Transforming the skyline, revolutionizing urban living, creating retail meccas" and some of them looking at the other side of the coin, detailing parking problems, traffic problems and ugliness problems. But none of the stories starred Stuart "Stewie" Woodson beyond a couple of brief mentions of his appearances at business associations and city subcommittee meetings.

So, yes, he had had a role in some pretty big deals but he wasn't driving the bus. Probably then, he'd been hired as a front man. He was smart-looking, smooth, well-spoken, and he'd no doubt spent his waking life radiating supreme confidence. More than likely, he had some skin in the game with a minor equity investment, maybe some fraction of a percentage point but that had to be about it.

At this point, I had to conclude that Stewie just wasn't up to pulling off something like Edgewater Estates. And that meant either he was crammed with enough hubris to spectacularly fail on his own or somebody else had the brains and deep pockets to get'er done.

As much as he annoyed me, I didn't figure Stewie was that dumb and so went looking for a potential senior partner.

I started with the developments he'd crowed about. They involved a who's who of Toronto commercial real estate and literally hundreds of contractors and sub-contractors. I looked for any connection, any pattern but couldn't see one and couldn't find any useful mention of Stewie. It took me about four fucking hours to reach a complete dead end, leaving me with the same desperate feeling of shrieking existential nothingness that washed over me the one and only time I watched the Grammys.

The only tangible reward for my web hunt was a raft of yellow sticky post-its decorating my screened-in porch. When I'm powering through web pages, I have this deathly fear of forgetting anything remotely germane so I'll scribble a note to myself. I've done it for years, probably kept 3M in business. Yes, I could cut and paste the bits into one big research Word document but I don't because I have this questionable habit—one of many—that I can't or won't break.

You may have guessed that I'm not somebody you'd call a team player. Even though my efforts in support of pretty much anything athletic can best be graded from mediocre to buffoonish on the competency scale, I like to do things badly, but all by myself. Same goes for the rest of my life. Nobody ever said: "That Jake, what a consensus builder!"

In this case, I persuaded myself to seek help in seeing all there was to see about Edgewater Estates. I sent a note to Steve Golding—one of my few friends—OK, OK, the *only* friend—I wouldn't mind seeing more often.

Steve is one of the best business and crime journalists in the country—to hear him tell it. Our dealings stretched back to more than twenty years ago when I was gainfully and improbably employed as the PR slut for a very large computer services company and he was an all-star business reporter for the *Globe & Mail* whose only reason for existence I thought was to make my life a living hell. But he was always fair and we more than got along because of two mutual interests: smoking and spending considerable time inside the now-extinct dive bars that used to lie between his offices and mine in downtown Toronto.

Our friendship fizzled away when I got fired, my wife died, I retreated up here and blah, blah but was re-awakened during the international shitshow that went on last summer.

Steve had gained a bunch of notoriety and moo-la over the last year. His book—*Deadly Web*—based on I want to say my exploits but really it was my stumbling and careening around a global conspiracy to rig all manner of computer systems. The book came out in early January and had him on the talk-show circuit and best seller lists for the last five months. Rumour had it that DiCaprio was attached to the movie project, despite my insistence that the role of me was perfect for Wilford Brimley until he—sadly—became unavailable.

While he had switched from financial reporting to the crime beat some years ago, I reckoned his knowledge of the corporate world could be helpful so I e-mailed him, asking how companies are typically structured around big real estate developments and how he used to unravel their connections.

He's a busy boy now so I was pleased to get an answer the next morning.

Usually there's a bunch of numbered companies. It's always the players, not the companies. Ignore the companies. You want to look for common names among the officers and shareholders, similar addresses. Now fuck off and leave me alone! Hugs, Steve."

Time to switch gears and focus solely on Lakeshore Developments, the actual incorporated company that created and owned Edgewater Estates. So who was behind this project? Who really was behind it?

That's when my hunt got even more boring and more time-consuming. It started out promising after a few minutes when I found the numbered Ontario company 12567802—doing biz as Lakeshore Developments Inc.—because they had to register a prospectus for the Real Estate Income Trust Stewie had originally dangled in front of me.

I then searched any way I could think of to see if there were any subsidiaries or connections to other companies. Anything that mentioned Mississauga Lake. Anything that had Kawartha in it or Edgewater or companies with numbers adjacent to 12567802.

Eventually, I found the company registrations for all the various arms of what appeared to be the mother corp. Among them were Mississauga Engineering, Lakeshore Construction and Go Kawartha Inc. But there were others: Edgewater Property Management, EE Condo Corporation, Edgewater Golf and Country Club and a bunch more.

The corporate organization chart started to resemble the Tudor monarchy's family tree with at least eleven different companies under Lakeshore Developments Holdings. They all had three directors and they all listed Lakeshore (Caymans) PLC as their 100% owner. There was also a 51% ownership in a company called Shield Security.

Remembering what Steve had told me—to look for repeating names and addresses—I put together a list of the players. James Traynor was a director or an officer on six of them. A Howard Veitch showed up in seven, five of them in common with Traynor's. Stewie made an appearance as director for Edgewater Marketing. Only one name— 'M. Stavros'—was on all twelve registrations.

George Town was home to Lakeshore (Caymans) PLC. Six of the remaining eleven listed 10 Mercer Street in Toronto as their corporate headquarters. The other five had an address on Front Street West, I assumed near my beloved Royal York Hotel. LinkedIn and Google searches yielded the connection between Traynor and Veitch. They were partners in a law firm called...wait for it, wait for it... Traynor-Veitch.

Their name combo immediately reminded me of Trevor Veitch, the Canadian-born guitarist who toured and recorded with 60s folk icon Tom Rush. But beyond that arcane word association, what did I have—other than blurry eyesight? It wasn't too surprising lawyers were involved in all these corporate set-ups; you'd have to know your way around the law to build the octopus of companies.

What the hell? Try Facebook. I typed in 'M. Stavros Toronto' and seven hits popped up. Melanie, two Marys, a Marcus, Margaret, Myrna, and a Magdalena. Six of the seven had open settings so I rooted around in their pages for a while.

I eliminated Melanie as she devoted all her postings to photos of Mr. Boo-Boo, her perpetually dormant, perhaps deceased cat. Margaret and one Mary were off the list as they both looked to be about nineteen years old and both appeared to me to be too involved in selfie posting to run a giant real estate company. I dropped the second Mary as a possibility as the 'Fuck the 1%!' banner on her profile page with the inset picture of her wearing an 'Eat the Rich' t-shirt slyly hinted at her not being a high-powered business exec. From his profile picture, Marcus Stavros appeared to be about twelve years old while Myrna must've been 80 and heavily into competitive quilting.

The one remaining M. Stavros had a completely private setting. Of course. But I could see her landing page photos—a giant sprawling mansion ran side to side with an inset photo of a bunch of kids. In the six photos of friends I could see, four of them were one Stavros or another. So not much there except the house photo indicated she lived pretty well and she had a lot of family as friends which I always think is kinda sad.

I switched over to Google maps and entered 10 Mercer Street. The street was a whole block long in downtown Toronto, a narrow little pipeline between the financial and theatre districts lined by rows of old three- or four-story brick buildings that had been either re-conditioned into hipness or were real dilapidated and begging to be reduced to rubble. 10 Mercer was in the former category with a re-faced brick exterior, ground floor walls of smoked glass windows and doors flanked with understated brass signage.

I then entered the Front Street address listed as the HQ for the other half of Lakeshore's subsidiaries. It was the UPS office about a block and half from the law offices of Traynor-Veitch on Mercer.

So after frittering away many hours of my life that I'd never get back, I had built a multi-branched corporate tree with absolutely no background or insight as to who or what they were.

The phone rang. 508 area code. I answer those. It was Alexandra.

We chit-chatted for a bit, nothing of consequence except it allowed me to enjoy her sweet voice tinged with just a hint of "pack the ca in the yad at Havad" New Englandness.

"Are you coming south this summer?" she asked.

"I can't, sweetie. I'm sorry, but there's a bunch of serious things going on with the place that I have to fix. September at the earliest. And even then…"

She didn't press for details and I didn't supply any. There was a pause and I mentally kicked myself for causing even momentary hurt in this wonderful woman.

"So do you mind if I come north?" she said.

"Mind? You crazy? I'd love you to see me again in my natural habitat. When?"

"I'm thinking July."

"July the what?"

"All of July."

"Woman make heart soar like eagle!"

"Should I bring my skis?"

"Of course."

The prospect of spending a month with her had me almost giddy. Finally, some good could be coming from this summer.

CHAPTER 11

The e-mail from Halley was short and to the point. *Fentanyl that killed Hill came from a batch responsible for 3 other ODs. Are you ready? 2 fatal in Peterborough, 1 death in Lindsay in the last 9 months. No arrests up there.*

So, Dr. Hill bought her deadly dose up here. But from whom? I called my Peterborough police buddy, Les Macgregor.

"What?" he demanded, proving the cops had finally paid the two bucks a month and gotten Call Display instead of employing an electronic surveillance team to laboriously trace calls.

"I'm fine, Les. And thanks for asking," I said.

"C'mon, Jake, what is it?"

"Those three fentanyl deaths this year…"

"Three? There've been eight."

"Holy shit."

"Holy shit is right. Twenty-two last year. This is bad."

"You had three from the same lab, one of them in Lindsay."

"I remember. Somebody named Lydon in Toronto Homicide asked for copies of all the cases. She found a batch that killed some poor moron in TO."

"Did you get the lab that made it?"

"No. If the cook has a bunch of street sellers, it's not easy to connect the dots. Who knows who, who lives where, that's how we nail them. We got nothing here so far."

"I can narrow it down for you. The lab's definitely up here. Lindsay's north of you, the moron who died in Toronto was Greta Hill, formerly of the West Kawartha township council."

"No kidding? That helps. I owe you,"

"Well now that you mention it..."

"It's a figure of speech," Macgregor said and hung up.

I heard a knock on my front door. There's hardly ever a knock on my front door. Well, there were a couple of erstwhile Jehovah Witnesses a few years back. They don't come around here no more. And don't any of you fucking start with me. Just because someone claims to have been told to go door-to-door pushing an alleged faith and a shrill magazine doesn't obligate me to spend one goddamned second of my dwindling life forgiving the trespasser standing in front of me at some ungodly hour. Would it have cost me anything to have been civil? No. Did it cost me anything to have been antagonistically lippy? No again. Other than they think I'm the devil incarnate and probably won't be back. So, on the whole, I'm ahead. And they are too, because I saved them time to go after more likely prospects for eternal salvation.

Let's be clear here: I don't give a good goddamn what you believe as long as you don't tell me about it. And you don't hurt anyone because of it.

"Mr. Lydon?" the middle-aged woman asked through the screen door.

"That's what's on the mail box."

"What mailbox?" she asked.

"Can I help you?" I more or less demanded of Sarah Ruth Evans.

"Is this a bad time?"

"Yup. Bad time for sure. It started around 1992. No sign of letting up."

She stood there fidgeting and I relented the way you do with an old and gentle Labrador.

I led her through the house and into the screened-in porch.

"Beer?" I ask.

"No, thank you. Tea, perhaps?"

"Perhaps. Lemme check."

I rummaged around the kitchen, found the mouse-proof tin with tea bags of indeterminate age, got the water going.

"How do you take it?" I shouted.

"Honey and a bit of lemon."

"What about lime and maple syrup?"

"Plain's just fine."

We settled back and I asked her to account for her visit.

"Jake, I just want you to know that you and Mr. Breedlove—"

"Who?"

"Carl. [Damn, I had forgotten his family name!]. You and Carl are not alone in fighting this development."

"Ruth..."

"Sarah."

"OK. Sarah…"

"No, Ruth Sarah."

"OK, Ms. Evans. To be clear: I'm not fighting this development. Just them taking my house and land."

She looked saddened at first, then seemed to grow pissed off.

"Oh, so NIMBY, is it?" she more or less demanded.

"Exactly! Although technically, it's NIMFY. Not In My *Front* Yard. My back yard is the lake."

"Short-sighted, isn't it?"

"Yes again! I really, *really* have no problem with building houses. Especially in a country that's as big and as regulated as Canada. Invariably, yes, some trees die, some animals have to move on. We got lots of both. People—even rich people—gotta live somewhere."

"They don't have to live like that," she pronounced.

And I was off.

"Excuse me, but who the fuck are you to decide how people should live?" I asked. "It makes me dumb how the latest thing is that we're all supposed to live small in tiny houses the size of my garden shed. Grow kale on our roofs, put up windmills and, in general, live like fucking 19th century Keebler elves in the second largest country by land mass in the world. A-hewin' wood, a-drawin' water, and a-churnin' butter."

"We have to do our bit."

"Why?"

"So…so we can be a global leader, a country worth copying."

"Like anybody anywhere wakes up and thinks: "Gosh, I wonder what the heck Canada is up to today"."

"It's the right thing to do," she insisted.

"Why? In sympathy with Hong Kong? Tough noogies to Hong Kong. The math is agin them. I know; I've actually done it. After you subtract the 95% of Canada I consider uninhabitable—even though there are tens of thousands of hardier stock than me who think it is—you still get five and half *square miles* per person. With that kind of landholding ratio, there'd be seventy-seven and a half people in Hong Kong, not the seven million who live there now. We may have been fucked in the decent climate sweepstakes but we lucked out in the cosmic lottery for available land."

This was one of those conversations which you absolutely know right from its outset there is no point in having because of the intractability of one or both of the talkers. But sometimes they're fun. Especially when you can recall facts you learned, as I had when recently I spent a half of a day looking at charts and graphs and lists. Of course every major issue is a whole lot more complex than a few pie charts. I know that. But in a minutes-long discussion, you ain't getting close to the heart of the matter anyway.

It didn't take much investigating to reveal that Ruth Sarah was all for putting on the brakes on everything. And then reversing all the way back to pre-industrial days so as to save Canada's whopping 2% contribution to the world's greenhouse gas emissions. And for what?

"What's wrong with protesting, with taking a stand, making people think before they do something?" Sarah Ruth asked.

"Not a goddamned thing. I'm all for it. What's wrong is you don't think. You get to a point where it's just No! Whatever it is that has to do with oil. No! Ruin Alberta's economy, put tens of thousands of people out of work? We're good with that. Let my various governments piss away billions by wildly overpaying for wind and solar? Yup. But in the meantime, keep buying mid-East oil as they continue to treat women like shit while they blow the fuck out of each other? Fine. Oh, and let's ignore all that air and water pollution from refining it and using ships to bring the oil here. Look, I know oil's doomed. And it should be. But, Jesus, not tomorrow."

"Tomorrow's too late. The problem's today."

"Right again! Then go after the biggest polluters. China, India, the States, that's half the ball of gas right there. Toss in the EU and you've got your work cut out for you."

"There doing some wonderful things over there. Germany particularly."

"Good for them. I mean that. But right now as we speak, Germany's burning seven times as much coal as we are."

"But per capita we're right up there."

"What a bullshit standard! Who cares how many people in each nation are doing it? The planet doesn't. It's the total output by country that matters."

"How about we agree to disagree?" Sarah Ruth asked, not because she was absolutely and thoroughly convinced by the brilliance of my harangue. More likely because she'd heard it all before and, like me, wasn't giving a goddamned inch.

"Deal."

"I can't persuade you to become more active in stopping this travesty?"

"Nope."

I guess Sarah Ruth didn't much care for either the tea or my lack of sympathy because she beetled it out of there pretty quick.

It, of course, didn't mean a goddamned thing to go on a rant but it sure was distracting.

It was also a tad invigorating. In a rare display of self-discipline I willed myself away from my shitty lap-top and outside.

Well, this theory that I have…that is to say, which is mine…is mine… is that we ought to spend as much time as possible outside. And you can't do that in central Ontario without either a thick outer coating of DEET or more clothing than a mummy for a while—say five months— to ward off some combination of mosquitoes and deer flies and black flies and horse flies that exist in clouds hanging around, waiting to pounce and draw blood. Unless you have a screened-in porch, like the one I built—and quite shoddily may I add—to keep the hordes at bay.

An extension of my shockingly original theory is: be on or near big water, if you're as goddamned lucky as I've been. Facing mostly west, I get sunsets like the sunsets I can see through the tall palms from my apartment balcony in the DR. Despite all her kvetching and moaning about the drive, Beth knew and I knew the second we stood on the rocks above the shoreline that this was the place where we could get old and all drooly.

It was early evening and I sat for a bit on my big deck which juts out over the water (now illegal). It's perched on 6X6s resting on a big rock shelf that hasn't moved since before dinosaurs were in charge of things.

Of late, my contemplation of said sunsets, shoreline, and big water was being ruined by the harsh sounds of machinery in the distance coming from the east side of the lake. Louder was the rumbling of trucks past my place. I couldn't see them from the Hovel but they clattered heavily on the ribbed dirt road. The noises weren't constant but you focused on them because they were foreign and annoying.

I was looking around for something safe to go all medieval on when there was another fucking knock at my front door. All these visitors (at least four in two months and, no, Carl doesn't count) were not helping my mood.

"What?" I demanded of the guy in the pale yellow short-sleeved shirt.

"Mr. Lydon?" he asked, looking nervous and pushing his wire-rim glasses up the bridge of his nose.

"Yes. What?" I ask.

"There's been a complaint."

"Whoa! Back up. Who the Christ are you?"

"Kenneth Larsen, Municipality of West Kawartha, Public Works Department," he said, handing me a business card that read—none too surprisingly—'Kenneth Larsen, Municipality of West Kawartha, Public Works Department.'

"Alright. Now. What was this complaint about?" I asked. "Was it about fucking credit card interest rates? Gas price gouging? I should hope so. You can sign me up for both."

"No, sir. Someone's complained about you."

"Me? What about me?"

"Your storage shed."

"My storage shed? What the fuck is wrong with my storage shed?"

"You built it in front of your house," he said turning to point at it as though I might need a hint about where it was located.

"Where was I supposed to build it?" I asked.

"By-law says on the side or at the back. But not in front of."

"Could you look around? This house is on a point of land. Water on three sides. If I did that, it'd be in the fuckin' lake. And then it wouldn't be a shed anymore; it'd be a boat house."

"Perhaps…but—"

"—Why?" I asked, changing tack.

"Why what?"

"Why do I have to, why does anyone have to?"

"Because…it's unsightly."

"Unsightly to whom? First off, you can't even see the goddamned thing from the road. And even if you could, most people would drive by and think: what a magnificent goddamned shed!"

"It doesn't matter. It's the law."

"What law?"

He quoted me a subsection of a subsection of the municipal building code.

"How old is this law?"

"Passed about five years ago."

"Hah! I put this up six years ago. Grandfathered," I said, using the term that gives all by-law enforcement officers the night sweats.

"I'm sorry, sir, but you built this less than three years ago."

"Says who?"

"Can't say."

"They're lying!"

"And I've got an aerial survey from four years ago showing nothing here which says they're not."

"But, Mr....what was your name again?"

"Larsen, Kenneth Larsen."

"Kenny, why is it the law? All laws are supposed to have a reason. What possible reason could there be?"

"I don't know. Unsightly, like I said."

"This shed's unsightly? It's fucking beautiful! Who complained?"

"Can't say."

"What's the downside here, Ken?"

"Downside?"

"What are you going to do if I tell you I'm not touching it?"

"Well...there's a warning. That's what this is. We give you thirty days to tear it down or move it. If you don't, then there's a fine."

"How much?"

"$200. And you get another thirty days. And then there's another fine; that one's double. Then another thirty days goes by. If you don't move it by then, we come and tear it down. And charge you for the demolition."

"You know the easiest thing to do here, don't you? Go back to the office and say the complainer was full of shit."

"But that would be lying."

"So here's your dilemma—a harmless fib or fining a 20-year taxpayer hundreds of dollars for violating an inexplicable law on the say-so of a cowardly anonymous complainer."

"I can't lie."

"Look, Ken, take the rest of the day off; you've done your job. You explained the law, the consequences. But until you can give me the rationale for that law and you recognize my right to confront my accusers, you should probably be fucking off right about now."

Which he did.

That left me alone and fuming. I went on a silent rant, the nub of it being that we're getting dinkered to death—a combination of tinkered with and dicked by various levels of government.

It starts with the politicians who set forth every three or four years to keep their jobs. They don't just want to but *have* to be seen to be doing good to us, taking action, governing. They reckon that governing has to mean new rules and regulations which always mean bigger by-law departments. Their budget requests get approved, the department grows and then it needs to find something to do. These departments—and I don't care at what level of government—blow through their budgets before year-end to ensure they get the same money plus at least inflation the next year and the whole thing becomes normal and beyond question. Annually, it blossoms like those giant ocean algae blooms the size of Greenland that regularly coat Chinese beaches. Or maybe more accurately, the burgeoning floating island state of plastic garbage in the Pacific.

These departments have an acute sense of self-survival. Once they exist, they don't want to not exist. So they cast around to see where else they can poke their governmental fingers because they have to find things to do.

Take a personal beef of mine. Anti-smoking campaigns. I can almost hear at least three quarters of you rolling your eyes. I get it: smoking inside bad. But after that, the yearly assault with new rules to chip away at us morons is just piling on. Plain packaging, having to stand on the sidewalk on the other side of a patio railing while passing cars, buses, and trucks spew hydrocarbons on everybody or not lighting up in a hundred-acre public park.

And none of these departments exist in isolation; they stay in touch with each other, huddling up in national and international forums. It's a race. Who's got the tougher laws? Who's working on something even more draconian? They hand out awards to each other and use other jurisdictions to prove they should get tougher on their own citizens in that bullshit leapfrogging tactic. "Oh, yeah? Well, we can be nastier."

As though they've never heard of the law of diminishing returns, as though they can't imagine a steady state where they all look at each other in a meeting room one day and say out loud: "You know what? We've done all we can do. There isn't a person on the planet who doesn't know it's bad for them. Let's leave that small percentage of poor hopelessly addicted bastards who pay our salaries alone for a while. And then let's take the billions they give us and get serious about finding a cure for all cancers, or heart disease."

Even without an audience, these rants of mine serve only one purpose: they make me smug in my curmudgeonlyness.

CHAPTER 12

"Jake, I can't serve you," Carla said, her eyes darting everywhere but at mine.

Now, I've had that sentence said to me a significant number times in my life. But always towards the end of an evening. Here it was just after mid-day and an apologetic Carla on the deck of the Angler Arms, the best cottage country etc., was telling me I was cut off.

"Carl, yes, but not you. Sorry," she added.

I didn't have the heart to squeal on Carl and tell her about his changed position.

"Jimmy's orders?" I asked.

"Yes."

I was half-expecting this. As a point of principle, it made sense. I was the arsehole neighbour standing in the way of the restaurant owner's windfall. As a point of alcoholic thirst, I was pissed off.

"I should talk to him," I said.

"Probably not a good idea," she said.

So of course, I left my chair and made my way back to Jimmy's kitchen kingdom.

Jimmy's this Lebanese guy who's been on the lake running AA for longer than I've been coming up here. How he left Beirut and wound up in the middle of the Ontario bush is an intriguing international mystery, made more mysterious because Jimmy won't say a goddamned word about his journey. "Who care?" he has shrugged.

He's not a glad-handing natural at the bar biz. He doesn't ever mingle with his patrons; instead, he perpetually confines himself to the kitchen where he fixes up good and cheap meals. He wasn't the type of owner to ever comp a beer for his regulars. And yet still Carl and I showed up.

He was sitting and glowering at the little card table he kept near the deep fryer. I have seen him sitting there hundreds of times because he's briefly visible as the door to the kitchen swings open. Every time, he's been playing solitaire. He plays the game old school, with actual cards, when he's not covering food in hot grease.

I didn't take much notice of his pissed-off expression because Jimmy always glowered. I presumed that's why he always stayed out of sight, as a public service.

"Jimmy, can we talk?"

"Why? You sell?"

"No."

"Nothing to talk."

"For fuck's sake, Jimmy. Doesn't it matter that I've bought enough beer and chicken wings over the last twenty years to put at least one of your kids through medical school?"

The glower lightened a bit but then another bank of dark clouds quickly rolled onto his bushy brows.

"I get money; you get cheap beer. We even-steve. And where else you get drunk?"

Game, set, and match, I thought as I left the kitchen. Well played, sir. I did have grudging respect for Jimmy's refusal to indulge in the irony of serving the man who was costing him tens, maybe hundreds of thousands of dollars.

Carl was quite happy—smug even—at still being able to get bar service while I could not. He made a big show of ordering for me once we established with Carla that he could double his order, give me one, and still not violate Jimmy's ban. Yes, that got me beer which is why we were there in the first place, but it didn't do anything towards lifting my sense of being cut from the drinking herd.

So I left when a friend of Carl's sat down with us. I have to admit feeling a bit lonely and alienated as I walked home. That doesn't happen to me a lot. I cheered myself up a bit by considering all the other people up here—and everywhere—who decide to exist without much humanity around them.

There are lots of people who don't want to be found, who like the idea of living in seclusion. I'm one of them, but there's a bunch more up here far less sociable than me. You'd be driving along a back road— well, they're all back roads—and there'd be a hole in the forest, a laneway, and maybe you'd catch sight of a massive woodpile or the corner of a Tyvek-wrapped bungalow. Maybe an abandoned pick-up.

Some of these people are bug fuck crazy survivoralists, some are gentle and harmless back-to-the-landers, and some are anti-social introverts like myself. And there's some people who decided decades ago that what they'd like to do with their time on the planet was buy a remote plot of land, plant dope fields, get high, deal a little weed, plant dope fields, get high, deal a little weed, and repeat and repeat for fucking ever.

And some just like privacy so they can do illegal shit on a grander scale. I'm pretty sure there are more than a few grow ops, chop shops, meth labs, and pill factories up here.

But one thing needs to be clear here: despite some appearances to the contrary, this ain't no *Deliverance* scenario. Regardless of their remoteness and regardless of the stereotype, people here are not isolated hicks. This is not some kind of cultural sideshow that middle-class urban white folks get to snicker at. Our citizenry drives to Toronto to see, buy and eat things, Most go south on holidays, a lot of their kids go away to college or university and everybody has electronic access to the planet.

Yes, there are mostly poor folks. Some like it that way, content with the lives they've fashioned. And some don't and are continuously bitter at their hard-scrabble existence.

Generally, those who have stayed, wanted to because they prefer small towns or no towns and those that went away and came back wanted to for the same reason. Most liked their extended families and wanted to live near them. By the same token, other than me, all the ex-urbanites aren't pretentious, helpless idiot savants in the wilderness. They also simply prefer to live in small towns or no towns after their cities have exhausted and drained them.

These were the people I was now at odds with. On the one hand, I stood in the way of normally decent people getting their hands on more money for their land than they likely ever thought possible. On the other hand is my irresistible urge to say fuck 'em. This is my home and I love it. My daughter was mostly raised here, my friend is here. My wife's ashes are here.

Just fuck 'em, I thought as I started down my driveway.

I usually don't get into my place through the front door. I automatically head down the side nearest the driveway then two steps up to the deck and go in via the screened-in porch at the back. This time, as I was following my habitual route, I glanced at the front door. An unusual splash of red caught my eye.

From thirty feet away, I could see a big axe embedded in the middle of the dark wooden door.

"Fuck!"I yelled.

The axe wasn't one of those small hatchets that weekend warriors use to hack away at slender branches and feel like Paul fucking Bunyan. This was a long-handled pro model. Its big head was painted red. What you could see of it. Whoever had swung it put a lot of force into it. Most the blade was sunk into the wood, such that I imagined it had been driven right through the door.

Just as I was trying to extract the thing, I heard a voice.

"Lose your keys?" Carl asked.

Together, we pried and jiggled and eventually freed it.

Carl examined it.

"Three-foot, hickory handle. Five, maybe six pounds total. Tempered alloy steel, inch and half of blade," he almost crooned. "This is your lucky day."

"What?"

"It's a beaut. Must be worth two hundred bucks. Not every day, you get a free axe."

"I think you're missing the point," I said.

"Well, whaddya goin' to do?"

"Oh, I don't know, maybe track down the motherfucker who did this," I suggested.

"How? By finding out who around here bought one of these?"

"That'd be a good place to start."

"Forget it, son. Someone took care of this baby. Feel the linseed on the handle. And the oiled head. But she ain't new. Look at the nicks up high on the handle where he leaned too far into it. Gotta be years old," he said as he handed it to me.

"Maybe it's rare."

"Nope. Upper end at Canadian Tire. Must've sold hundreds."

"Congratulations, neighbour. By pissing on my parade and crushing all hope, you just won yourself a brand new old axe!" I said, handing it back.

"Serious?"

"As a big axe buried in a front door."

"By rights, it's yours. You might need it."

"For what? I can hire you. Take the goddamned thing."

Thank you, son."

Carl was genuinely tickled. So that was a good thing.

The bad thing, of course, was the fact that someone had come a-knockin' at my door with the means to achieve a pretty high degree of lethality.

CHAPTER 13

I tried to forget about the door chopper. It wasn't easy because I imagined him—from several camera angles—hoisting the axe, straining up on his tiptoes with the thing fully extended over his head and then whipping down, using the force of his back and hips to sink the blade with a loud resonating 'thock!'

I weighed that single arresting image against what had caused it. Me being blamed for standing in the way of the development and the millions of dollars flowing from it. It struck me as almost surreal. Things had been the way they'd been for the twenty years I had owned up here and then abruptly they had changed. Same piece of water, same trees, same rocks had a new value ascribed them, an abstract notion of what they were now worth that caused emotions to roil, hearts to beat faster, and minds to race ahead to sudden imagined wealth.

The meter had been turned on as everyone signed on their particular dotted line. Politicians, land sellers, REIT owners, consultants had coalesced into this mass of inevitability that made my resistance seem puny and fucking futile.

The money was staggering. Not Wall Street staggering where a 5 *billion dollar* Facebook fine by the FCC translates to their stock price rising, but huge by our area's standard. Millions going out with the expectation that many more millions would soon be coming in.

The entire land assembly including the two houses and AA on the other side of me might be costing them, I wildly guessed, somewhere between ten and fifteen million smackeroos. Never mind the building costs, and never mind that within the year all the REIT owners would be looking for their healthy 9% return.

So, all this had to happen quickly for Edgewater to start recouping its outlay. And that's what was bothering me. I could see how Stewie et al. wanted shit to get moving jack snap. I could see why the elected politicians were jumping on board as if it was the last available lifeboat from the Titanic, and I understand why all the possible trades, men like Preston Pearson wanted to get working.

What struck me as highly improbable was the speed with which all the government bureaucracies had give their collective thumbs up. Their usually rusting, grinding wheels were now carrying a runaway train.

Time is relative. There's time the way most of us see it and then there's government time.

My old—and now dead—former boss once told me that "*everything takes longer than you think it should.*" And he was talking about the *real* world. In government, any government, there is no incentive to do anything quickly. Issuing permits, producing results of inquiries, studying traffic, fixing roads, anything—if it doesn't happen today, oh well, it might happen tomorrow. There is no clock on anything. In fact, it's the opposite. If you really work hard and fast then your 'file' ends, along with all the paperwork you were aiming to generate. You'd also be missing your pals in all the meetings you planned to fill your days.

And yet. For this project, the ol' concurrent canards had been lined up pretty quickly.

Could it be that simple that someone greased someone to giddyup with the favourable paperwork? Or simpler still, could it be that everybody just did their goddamned jobs?

Yes, the West Kawartha Township council had given Edgewater Estates the green light. But it couldn't have done so without the crucial stamp of approval from the Ministry of Environment.

Luc Dubois was the local Environment guy. The joke around AA was that we oughtta rename *all* the lakes around here Lac Dubois in honour of the French-Canadian's famous vigilance in protecting the water and shorelines. He's the guy who had the one-man vote on what people did around water, how their septic systems were designed, tree-cutting within fifty feet of the shoreline, the size of boat docks and on and on. He would intrude whenever and wherever he thought "his" lakes were being threatened.

He lived with his wife, Gisele, on the far shore from me in a cabin that made my heap look like Frank Lloyd Wright's crowning achievement.

I knew him. Everybody around the lake knew him because he had made it a point ten years ago when he was first stationed here to pop in to conduct environmental spot checks. As *Bull Durham* has it: "He announced his presence with authority," pissing off a lot of people in the bargain by writing out tickets for clearing brush or having an unlicensed fire pit or improperly installed docks and on and on. What angered them more was the discovery that there was absolutely no appeal process, no one to complain to about any of his decisions.

When he paddled up to my dinky dock I turned the tables on him by pissing him off. Everything that I rely on has been "grandfathered" in because I bought before all the environmental laws came to pass and there wasn't a goddamned thing he could do about it. I've got a holding tank (now illegal) instead of a septic system, I draw water from the lake and have no well (now illegal). And I'm allowed to have a lawn and cut my grass right to the water's edge (now illegal).

What bothered him the most was his inability to enforce the new law prohibiting land owners from touching the shoreline or any tree within fifty feet of it except for a fifteen-foot swath to use as access to the water. The rest had to stay as pristine as when Sammy of Champlain wandered around here four hundred years ago. My place has a broad vista on all sides of the point I'm on because its previous owner understood that the simple reason you buy goddamned lakefront is to see the goddamned lake.

Some years ago Luc was paddling close to my place. I was on the deck and I invited him over for a drink. To this day, I'm not exactly sure why I did that. Beth had died a couple of months earlier so maybe I was looking for a little variety from my routine of being more manic depressive and surlier than normal while drinking myself stupid alone.

Gin and tonic, as it turned out, was his weapon of choice and more than one, as it turned out. He made it clear that he normally didn't drink but he thought he should be sociable.

Unaccustomed as his smallish body was to excessive alcohol intake, he was shit-faced in no time, puffing away on my cigarettes and telling me why his Canadiens were going to kick Maple Leaf ass the next season. As he slurped the Tanqueray with a sparkle in his eye, something told me he was getting back to an old friend and I felt a little badly for re-corrupting him. But he was already loaded and I hadn't used a gun to get him so. And I wasn't about to pump his stomach so: barn door open, horse gone.

By philosophy and personality, Luc is the kinda guy who's never entirely off the clock and he couldn't resist quizzing me on my living habits while he was pounding the juniper as they say—well, nobody says that.

I'm never in a hurry to justify myself to anyone but it didn't take much of an interrogation by him to see that I didn't have much of a foot-print. One guy living a hermetic life for half a year up here, who rarely does laundry, has no dishwasher, hardly ever drives, doesn't fish or hunt and who generates next to no garbage isn't a threat to anybody or anything. Ever. Except to himself. OK, there's the mountain of cig-arette butts I send to the local dump. But other than that.

Once he completed his environmental assessment of me, it was my turn to ask the questions. Most people will tell you just about any-thing about themselves as long as you listen to their answers. The ones to avoid are those who don't need prompting.

Luc spoke lovingly of his time in the Laurentian Mountains north of Montreal. I've been there and it truly is a magical place, chock full of gorgeous scenery, superb restaurants, and uniformly warm people. He'd met Gisele there, explored the backwoods and lakes in summer and winter and built a simple and solid life.

So how do you *not* ask why he chucked it all to come here, the heart of English Canada?

He explained that his fierce love of the whole country led him to hate the decades-long political to-ing and fro-ing between independence for his province and staying inside Canada. So he left St. Sauveur and Ste. Agathe, St. Jerome, St. Hippolyte (my personal favourite—the patron saint of dieting river hogs?) and all the other holy places and moved to Ontario.

"And how was Gisele with all this?" I asked.

Apparently not good. More than a decade away from family, friends, and culture had diminished her *joie de vivre* whose English translation—tellingly—is joie de vivre.

He told me about his—their—new compromise dream of heading to more temperate zones—in particular Chile. They planned to both work in a vineyard in a drier place where the lack of humidity wouldn't be so punishing on his muscles and joints.

As he was unsteadily leaving my place, Luc christened me his "bad English friend," a nickname I've lived up to whenever he occasionally drops in. I never mind being the asterisk to someone's record of otherwise upstanding behavior, Plus, watching a drunk guy paddle a canoe always amuses the fuck out of me.

I make a point of watching for him when he's out on one of his canoe patrols just so I can retrieve my lawnmower from my magnificent shed, fire it up, and take it to the edge of the lake (now illegal) right up to my boulder retaining wall (now illegal) and wave at him (still legal). Drives him nuts.

Yes, he was a hard ass when it came to the environmental laws but after a few gin sessions, it was pretty clear that he was also a good guy. And there's nothing wrong with good guys who have jobs that they take real seriously.

It was exactly because of this reputation for toughness, for saying 'no' a lot, that I found his speedy approval of Edgewater Estates a tad odd and I wanted to speak to him about it.

I knew he didn't keep office hours because he didn't keep an office. I wasn't in a hurry to get scowled at by Gisele if I showed up at his place so I had to watch for him on the water.

He was easy to spot out there because other than Carl whose hulking form is a foot higher than his, Luc was the only guy paddling who knew what he was doing. In a rare burst of energy, I was at the water's edge, flipping over my beached canoe and then paddling like a bat out of a watery hell to intercept him.

"Heave to and prepare to boarded!" I shouted in between laboured breaths.

We stretched to grab each other's gunwales (I know that sounds salacious) and pulled our canoes together. He winced in pain.

"*Ce va*?" I said, alarmed a bit at his pain and pretty much exhausting my knowledge of French greetings.

"I'm not too good me," he said, rubbing his elbow. "Too much in the canoe. Twenty year. Back, arms, knees, *tout le gang*. I don't know how *les voyageurs* do that," he added, referencing the French explorers who had ridden the lakes and rivers of Eastern Canada from Montreal all the way to Detroit and, for shits and giggles, straight down the Mississippi River to the Gulf of Mexico.

"Those guys all died by thirty," I pointed out.

"Pffttt!" he said, flicking out his hand in that dismissive Gallic way. "Jack, you come here for the exercise or to talk about my healths?"

"Luc, I gotta ask you: how come the project over there got your approval so fast? I mean, Jesus, you blocked that boathouse down the shore from me for four years."

He stiffened up and it wasn't from his blooming arthritis. Questioning a man with imperial authority normally has that effect. He rattled off his justification as though he had rehearsed it.

"It was not so fast," he told me. "Four month. They did their homeworks. Everything by the books. None of their house along the lake is permitted a dock. Common marina in Big Rock Bay. You can't hurt those stone. They will not cut trees along the shore. No chemical—'erbicide, pesticide—nothing allowed for houses or golf course. The plans for water treatment, for waste treatment, all 100 per cent. And they don't take much water from the lake. Enough to water the golf course, provide for about tree hundred house. Better than drilling into the aquifer."

"How much?"

"Their *permi* is for 650,000 litres per daily."

"That's not much?" I asked after my instant visualization of what kinda stockpile of beer cases that volume would represent—every 24 hours.

"Not for a golf course. Below average. But no problem for the lakes."

"Even drawing for the houses too?"

"House take only another about tousand litre a day per each."

"So nothing there was a problem for you?"

"You know I like a fight, me."

"Yeah, I know."

"But there was nothing to fight. But you. You fight."

"Me, I fight."

Our canoes were rocking but his gaze was steady.

"Maybe you give up soon? That is *un bonne idée*, I think," he said dead seriously.

"See you, Luc," I said as I pushed off, turned, and paddled home. Slowly.

Along the way, I didn't really enjoy the scenery. I couldn't get Luc's good idea for me to quit out of my head. I figured that when the environment guy tells you—however gently—that you should stop opposing something that would change the environment, there are only two possible scenarios. One: I was yet again being a misguided asshole. The other: something not quite legit was up.

CHAPTER 14

I don't routinely hang around people who look like they're pretty comfy with violence. Maybe Donny Simpson in the third grade, but his schoolyard thuggery doesn't seem that big a deal anymore, although I assume he went on to bigger and nastier things. And yes, this past winter in the DR and the summer before, I ran into a passel of bad guys with murderous intent. But generally, my acquaintances think it's a good thing when they collar the criminal at the 29-minute mark of *Law & Order*.

Which is why I surprised myself—and later Carl when I told him— that I had decided to visit Derek Collins.

"What the hell are you thinking?" Carl asked, "That boy ain't right."

"Look, he's probably the guy that's been busting up my shit, right?"

"Probably."

"Well, I need to him convince to stop. I need to persuade him to take his beef to Stewie. Get him to change the plans, move the old folks home off my land, and everybody wins."

"You're gonna be the voice of reason?"

"Arsehole."

"You really think you can get him to back off?"

"Can't hurt to try."

"Well, yes it could. Want me to come along?" he asked.

"Nah. I think you scare him."

"That'd be the point."

"I'll be fine."

Saying that didn't convince Carl—or me—but I figured I had to at least give it a shot.

Following Carl's directions, I found Stevens Road and eventually a break in the bush that marked #53. I hesitated, reading and re-reading the large "No Trespassing" sign nailed to a tree. Fuck it, I thought. I'm here.

The gravel driveway quickly bent around and ended in front of boxy, non-descript bungalow. Even though the house was less than a hundred feet from the road it had been invisible behind the screen of poplar, spruce and maple. The only domestic plant I recognized was by the front window—an old, gnarled lilac bush, planted, I presumed, by a previous owner.

There was no yard to speak of; mostly, it was a parking lot for man toys—a giant white Dodge Ram pick-up, several muddied-up all terrain vehicles whose original paint colour was, I think, army cammo. For contrast, there were two neon-painted dirt bike rockets—one mostly lime green, the other an electric red. And behind them, a rusted metal trailer carrying, side by side, twin metallic blue Sea-Doos. And next to that trailer was another one, cradling a sleek and powerful-looking cabin cruiser whose brethren were likely running dope into Florida from the Bahamas. Oh, did I mention the gleaming black Harley? I'm no multi-vehicle assessment officer, but there was a shit-ton worth of transportation sitting there, at least triple the value of the house.

Behind the bungalow up a bit of a hill was a large industrial-looking silver Quonset hut with a lot more square footage than the house. I bet myself that a fleet of snowmobiles huddled there.

Derek Collins hadn't exactly thrown out the welcome mat, unless you count the 'BeFUCKINGware of the Dog' sign in the curtained window of the side door as an invitation.

I knocked on the door. Instead of hearing the knob turn in response, I heard, in order, the furious loud and deep barking of a giant dog inside and then a sharp 'click' behind me. I turned to face Derek and a shotgun.

"Can't read?" he asked.

"I wasn't trespassing!" I protested. "I have business with you."

"Well, I got none with you so that must mean you came to play with my dog. Wait a second and I'll let him out."

"No, no!"

Derek smiled at my panic-stricken reaction.

"Then what the fuck do you want?" he asked as my hyperactive heart and breathing slowed.

I sat down on the step before I collapsed; Derek lowered his gun and leaned against the box of the truck.

"I just want to keep my house."

"No matter who it fucks over."

"Look, if…if ten of your neighbours showed up here and threatened to kick your ass if you didn't leave, what would you do?"

"I'd fight. I'd fuck 'em up."

"Same for me…without the fucking up part."

His anger seemed to subside a bit. He stood the gun up against the truck fender beside him, a sort of nonchalant sentry. He lit a cigarette; I lit a cigarette. We regarded each other. I don't know what he was thinking although he might have been somewhat amused by my bravery—or stupidity —in even setting foot on his property.

He struck me as a man capable of bad things. There are guys who buy *Guns & Ammo* and then there are guys who buy guns and ammo. Derek was in the latter category. He would not ever back down from a fight that he had probably caused. Outdoorsy but not in any way Thoreau would recognize. Nature was Derek Collins' stage upon which he could roar around in loud and expensive machines making his deafening mark. And woe to anyone who attempted to silence his particular idea of individual freedom.

"There's a way out of this," I said.

"Talk."

Without ever accusing him of the vandalism, I explained how I thought he—as a major landholder—should be leaning on Stewie to get the plans changed; it would be a simple matter. He'd get full pop for his land right away, I'd keep my house, and everybody would be happy, or at the very least, marginally amused.

He was considering the logic of it, no doubt weighing it against the pleasure he derived from breaking other people's stuff.

"I'll think about it."

"Maybe talk to Blair. He might be on side."

"I said I'll think about it. In the meantime, you might want to be getting out here. Time to feed the dog."

I could hear Derek laugh as I scrambled into the Vibe just as Cujo's bigger brother came bounding out, his eye full of business. Even though I was in the car at this point, I was grateful Derek had grabbed the giant hell hound by its spiked collar. I was pretty sure that if the beast decided to charge me, he'd stove in the side of the Vibe the way rhinos collapse Range Rovers on safari.

I drove away thinking that maybe there was a slight chance something might come out of my plea to Derek. But then again, I reminded myself, for close to fifty years I thought the Maple Leafs might put a decent team on the ice.

A big chunk of my past professional life had been spent imagining the worst case and advising clients what to do and say to journalists when the *merde* frapped the ol' fan. My doomsday view of things stretched back a whole lot farther—to my student days when I imagined failing every exam I ever wrote, being cut from every team I tried out for, and getting nothing but a lump of coal every Christmas. I tell you this by way of explaining my growing but shapeless view that something nasty was going on with Edgewater Estates. To give it form, I figured I'd bounce my suspicions off someone whose stock and trade was criminality.

I didn't expect to reach Steve on the first try. And I didn't. But he did call back a couple of hours later.

"Steve, are you still lying around eating bon-bons or are you actually working again?"

"What's it to ya?"

"I'm betting your publisher wants to find out if you're a one-trick pony. Hell, I wouldn't mind knowing either if you've got another book in you."

"It's come up. Whaddya got?"

"I think I got a real fishy housing development, political malfeasance up the wazoo, deliberate vandalism, oh, and a couple of bodies —four things that might fascinate your readers."

"Is there mayhem? I gotta get me some mayhem."

"There's mayhem. Quiet Canadian mayhem, but mayhem nonetheless."

"So what's up?"

I laid out the story so far, starting with the untimely deaths of Councilors Hill and Odell. It took a while as I tend to cram every fucking detail I can remember into even the simplest of tales. Put it this way: whenever I start a sentence with "Long story short...," it ain't.

"Wood chipper?" Steve said after I'd finished.

"Figured that'd get your attention. But before we get to that, we need to unravel some corporate shenanigans."

"Talk about bait and switch."

I went through what I thought I had found. The apparent company structure, the holdings, the offshore mother corp, Stewie's lack of experience.

"This all sounds remarkably boring," Steve said. "Who are the other players?"

"There's a Stavros shows up pretty regularly."

"Holy shit!" Steve said, becoming instantly enthused. "Guy Stavros?"

"Documents say M. Stavros."

"It's gotta be him! Maybe his wife or a kid is the 'M'."

"You know him?"

"Looks like nobody *knows* him. I know *of* him."

"And?"

"Developer, big time for a while. On the west coast. He got busted a few years ago."

"Land scam?"

"Close. He was pimping a stock offering on a luxury project north of Victoria that went bust. He got a big fine, but no jail. Booted from trading on the Vancouver Exchange. Just disappeared. Been quiet since then."

"Well, it looks like he's making noise again."

"Is he the bad guy here?"

"I dunno, but it might be worth finding out."

"You'd have to find him first."

"Yeah, you're right. I wouldn't know where to start. Why, I bet even a big shot author with a background in business and crime journalism couldn't track him down…"

"Quit with the fuckin' Tom Sawyer-whitewashing-the-fence bullshit, will ya? I'll look around."

"Might make it worth your while, big boy."

"Yeah, yeah, you love me long time."

"I'm serious, bud. This could be your follow-up"

"We'd have to negotiate a realistic price on this one."

"How so?"

"Lemme see. You got handsomely rewarded for my last book—if I recall correctly, 200K which, by the way, you promptly pissed away—"

"—Buying a fire truck for Las Terrenas," I pointed out.

"Who am I to judge people's addictions?"

"So?"

"So that book was about a world-wide attempt to hijack every major network and government computer system. Along the way there were a bunch of corpses, gunfire, and billions of dollars at stake. Now you want me to investigate a small land scam in the Ontario hinterlands. My publisher might see a difference."

"Alright, alright."

"Seventeen bucks…Canadian," he said.

"You're forgetting the wood chipper."

"Oh, right. In that case…twenty three ninety five. Take it or leave it."

"US dollars."

"Deal!"

I then decided to stop jerking him around.

"Oh I forgot to mention." I said, "You might want to start looking for him at 10 Mercer Street. That's the address on the documents."

"Arsehole."

Not that I'm the collaborative type, but it felt good to know Steve was on the case. He was smart and relentless. If there was anything nefarious going on, he'd find it.

CHAPTER 15

I don't get a lot of physical stuff sent to me. Pizza and Chinese food don't get delivered up here. Christmas cards or gifts of any kind don't come my way anymore. Slowly but surely, I'd switched to getting e-bills. So it was an oddity to see a courier van in the driveway.

I signed for the bulky package then ripped open the plastic envelope, briefly imagining it to be the galleys of my new best-seller which was, I forced myself to admit, a bit improbable because I hadn't finished writing anything.

Instead, it was a thick manila envelope with the black Government of Ontario crest in the top left, the Ministry of Health and Long Term Care printed below it.

Unless it's a passport renewal, governments are not in the habit of sending good news to the governed.

The covering letter was headlined 'Notice of Intent to Expropriate'.

Fuck!

There were a lot of whereas and wherefores but essentially the government had decided that the public good would be served by a retirement/nursing home facility on Lot #45089-parcel # 6117, AKA my goddamned house and my goddamned land. The owner of said Lot #45089-parcel # 6117 was to receive "a fair market value" of $400,000 from the Ministry which would in turn lease it to Lakeshore Developments for 99 years for a dollar a year provided the company built the nursing home.

They were going to invoke the Canadian equivalent of eminent domain. And not even at the higher price Stewie had offered!

Fuckers!

Accompanying the two-page letter was a sheaf of supporting documents, some official (a preliminary environmental assessment indicating no damage would be done by putting up a 200-bed facility. And more Ministry of Health reports on the urgent need for nursing care facilities, the township's passed resolution to proceed, the county's approval, and then a bunch of "evidence"—demographics on aging populations, letters of support from residents, all written within the last six months and all sounding real similar.

Except the last letter. It was dated 16 years ago. It was a rather forceful, elegant, and quite persuasive three-pager asking for, nay, *demanding* that long-term care be approved in this neck of the woods as the growing cottager population was also aging which meant A) they needed a place to be humanely warehoused when they could no longer cottage (note: 'cottage' is a verb in Ontario) or do much of anything else and B) it should be nearby because they obviously enjoyed the woodsy 'hood and should be allowed to stare at it while their synapses stopped firing.

I thought that if I could just get my hands on the arsehole letter writer I'd strangle him, other than the fact that I only vaguely remembered writing the thing when my mother's brain then body was shutting down.

If I wasn't so fucking angry I would have noted my letter's inclusion was pretty smart in an ironic, hoisted-on-my-own-petard kinda way. Christ, re-reading the letter, I saw that I had even offered up my land for an old age home!

I called Stewie. I tried—as best as I possibly could—to be reasonable.

"What fucking public good?!" I shouted as a gentle conversation starter as soon as he answered.

"Why, whatever are you talking about it?"

"You know goddamned well what I'm talking about! Taking my land."

"Oh, *that*. You might want to talk to your elected councilors and to the Ministry of Health. I believe their names are on the notice. Maybe have a chat with some of the people who wrote letters. Especially that guy from some years ago, a Jake somebody or other."

And he hung up.

Fucker!

I was going to heave the receiver through one of my log walls. I stopped only when I realized that, with my luck these days, the coiled cord would likely send the phone boomeranging back at my head with concussive consequences.

I then called the only lawyer I really knew and trusted. Gordon Wellsley was even older than me, smart and patient, and he loved corny legal jokes and puns. I guessed he tried them all out on his clients before he amused the hell out of his grandchildren. I had used him when Beth and I bought the place two decades earlier and I was thankful he was still in business. He said he'd see me right away because "time was of the essence."

As I was about to swing out onto the highway, I saw a big banner draped over the billboard on the corner proclaiming that the Edgewater Estate Presentation Centre was now open. I couldn't resist checking it out.

The presentation centre was a mobile home that looked permanent with neat white lattice skirting it. There were wide wooden steps up to the door and decorating the sides to hide the vinyl cladding was red, white and blue bunting.

"Care to register?" asked the same young and obviously keen saleslady who'd been introduced at the council meeting. She didn't seem to remember me despite Stewie's singling me out, such is the impression I can make.

"Naw."

"We'd like to send you more information."

"No thanks. I'll drop by to pick it up."

"But we'd really, really would like you to register."

I disengaged the way you sometimes do with sales people on commission. This evasion tactic is easiest to carry out in big furniture stores as you've got all sorts of obstacles and narrow pathways between sofa groupings. To trap you, they almost have to hunt in pairs like those velociraptors in *Jurassic Park*.

But in this tiny playing field of a 40 X 12 gussied-up construction trailer, there was no room to break for daylight. Instead I became utterly transfixed, in a trance really, by the scale model replica of The Development. I'm a sucker for those things anyway. A four-foot by six-foot plexiglass dome covered the scale model. Major bucks had gone into detailing all the facilities, right down to hundreds of tiny trees.

I got all angry again seeing the small but now three-dimensional representation of the nursing home where my house used to be. As the salesperson maneuvered around the table-mounted display, I kept moving out of reach, murmuring how beautiful the model was, scooping up a one-pager of a fact sheet, and skedaddling the fuck out of there.

And I stayed angry sitting in my car, reading the bullet points in the fact sheet.

- 6500 yard championship golf course covering 130 acres
- 100,000-gallon free-form infinity pool overlooking the lake
- Choice of luxury accommodation – condos, retirement suites, single family log executive homes (1200 to 5000 sq. ft.)
- Pick of finishes
- Optional turnkey furniture packages

- Gourmet dining at Bentley's on the Water
- Free membership in the Edgewater Country Club with resort-style amenities
- Free use of tennis, watersports, fitness centre
- 25 miles of hiking trails
- Medical clinic
- Tuck shop
- Assisted living retirement home

Where the fuck, I fumed, do they get off designing the perfect place to retire and get old?

I hold this fuming responsible for not immediately grasping the meaning of the last bullet point. It finally hit me. The sons of bitches had already included the nursing home in their marketing shit as though they owned the land. My land!

I peeled out of the gravel parking lot—well, if you think a twelve year-old Pontiac Vibe can peel out of anywhere—and drove to Peterborough.

Turns out the drive was a good thing because it settled me down. It wasn't as if a Buddhist-like calm descended on me but at least the aggravation subsided a bit. Dare I say, a little perspective appeared. I was still pissed off, mostly because the summer I had envisioned had gone up in flames so far. Two solid months worth of a shitshow and no sign of letting up but whenever it did end, I'd likely be out on the street.

Yeah, yeah, I know: nuthin' but first world problems, Jake. Here's almost a half a million bucks and your woman's coming to spend a month with you at your place on a lake. Gee, you've got a tough life. Buck up, little soldier. But as it turns out, I live in the first world so I don't know what other kind of problems I'd have. And, I'm cursed with enough self-knowledge to understand that I usually resist public opinion. Oh, and I truly hate being told to give up.

I had just crossed the small causeway at Buckhorn when I took another figurative step back and considered the reason why the government said it wanted to expropriate my land in the first place. To do something I thought was a swell thing to do many years ago, the same reason I had actively supported back then.

I have to admit this reason wasn't civic activism but entirely personal as I watched my mother's mind disintegrate with Alzheimer's.

By the by, as I draw ever-nearer to my end, I figure that's the way to go. If my mother is any indicator. That disease is tough on everyone else but easy on you as your brain grid shuts down. Yes, it wasn't much fun for her for a few months when she knew she was losing her mind. But then she lost it and it wasn't ever coming back as she retreated further and further back into her childhood. In her final months she didn't have a fucking clue who I was, but she knew the street her childhood church was on. At the end, emaciated and immobile, she spoke only Ukrainian, her first-taught language.

My mother was officially diagnosed with Alzheimer's when she was relatively young—74—but I knew and she knew long before the medical results were in. Maybe my father knew too but he had fucked off years earlier so I can't be sure about that.

It was a very short while after the diagnosis when the hunt started for a place for her to go where she'd receive the round the clock care she'd need real soon. Phone calls, visits, Internet searches of the privately-owned and publicly-funded nursing homes.

After dear old dad exited and I went off to university, my mother moved to a small and neat apartment in a pleasant enough Scarborough low-rise. She lived happily there for thirty years. During my visits in the later years, she started to display a jarring absentmindedness. Within months, she reached a point when couldn't recall a plain statement made minutes earlier.

That happened in summertime so Beth and I would often pack her up and bring her to the lake. She liked that. At least I think she did. She'd sit on the deck, usually wrapped up in a blanket and stare for hours out at the water. Or at Halley. Always with a half-smile.

Inevitably, she deteriorated, completely unaware of all the waiting lists she was on. As she declined, my anger and frustration grew.

It's the one fucking demographic trend you've been absolutely sure of for, oh, I don't know, the last 10,000 years. People get old and then they die. But before they die, they usually get sick and need care. How much care depends on the number of people aging—a number that's been known for decades.

Instead of being anticipated, this grey-haired population bulge has apparently created a crisis. It's an emergency replete with cries for a 'national strategy' as though it's all a big surprise. The various professional groups involved in the elderly biz hold summits, conferences, forums. They use names like Council, Alliance, Partnership, Coalition. They're all good-willed people who argue about stuff like 'aging in place.' Governments are big on aging in place because the place the government preferred was the old person's home, not a tax-payer funded home or hospital.

That's all well and good as long as there's some capacity to get on. But that slips away and you don't even fucking recognize the place you're aging in. And then what?

The answer is obvious. Build more places like the ones they're waiting for. Right the fuck now. Pick the operation that's popular in the area and copy it over and over again after you've done the math and you can account for everybody who's going to need shelter against the coming storm in their heads. And these places aren't going to empty anytime soon. Because the post-WWII generation went forth and multiplied in astonishing numbers, we products of this population boom are now fast becoming the newest nation of old people who can't remember shit.

Build at least some of them in pleasant surroundings, not in cities. Cities are more convenient for families to visit. Three-quarters of the people in captivity don't remember you anyway. So whether you go or not makes absolutely zero difference to them. But it does for you. Out of obligation or tenderness or making sure you're still in the will or whatever, it's for your benefit.

Maybe I should have seen my mother more often. But why regret that now? I didn't. And unless I was going to pop down to the basement— if I had one—and invent a time machine, it wouldn't ever matter. I don't mark the date she died or even remember it. Nothing makes me think more or less about her.

But I'll admit to remembering the absolutely goddamned adorable things she said and did in her final years. I tried mighty hard to forget the moments when I saw her quiet grief and anger as she slipped away from herself. There were hours, days in which she—and everyone else with dementia—spent understanding they were becoming demented. A slow and inexorable robbery was going on and they couldn't do a goddamned thing about it. That wasn't a pleasant recollection.

But of course it got worse, when her body began to forget to do things. Like eating or breathing. And the concerned but harried doctor took me aside and in low tones explained that my mother's struggle to stay alive was not only futile but cruel. And that's why they were going to stop feeding her through a tube. He gave some medical bullshit about site infections and collapsing veins. But really, they were going to let her die. I saw only compassion. And then I saw my mother's shrunken unrecognizable body. I'd rather not let that final remembrance distort the nothing but sweet and kind and pleasant memories of her over my entire life.

So you focus on the funny or tender things as they're reeling in the years. The goofy grin on her face when she got busted for stealing a hairbrush from another inmate. Or the look of joy on her face when she confided that me that she'd just received a marriage proposal.

"Don't tell your father," she'd whispered. "But I said yes."

By the time we got her into a private care facility, my mother the saint was completely docile and smiley and pretty much only obsessed with her next meal. But some of her fellow inmates had rebellion on what was left of their minds and were focused on making a break for it.

The acute floor featured heavy double doors to which visitors were given a code to punch in both when they entered and when they left. On my way out, some of the elderly would shuffle over to me like old zombies, peering around me to watch me enter the code. They may not have remembered their families but they sure knew what a combination lock was. And they knew that if they only had the numbers, they'd blow this pop stand and be down the road in a cloud of smoke.

One woman, staff told me, was particularly adept at cadging the combinations and crafty enough to wait until she was alone and then 'poof!' she'd be on the lam. Not on a long jaunt, leading to police alerts and distraught offspring. She'd just go down the elevator and out the front door but only as far as the sidewalk in front of the place. Whether she was confused or nervous, no one could say. She'd wait until she was missed and gently retrieved. I had an idea that that was the kind of freedom statement I'd like to make when it's my turn.

In the two years my mother was incarcerated, I found all staff friendly and compassionate with their charges. That's the kind of treatment I was now standing against. Was I being a flaming hypocrite? Of course I was. Ol' Walt Whitman had a line I usually found handy: "Do I contradict myself? Very well, then I contradict myself." Even that weasel-ly self-justification wasn't working.

But the simple fact was: Lakeshore Developments had lots of land, approved plans and, apparently, the money to build this. So, ya bastards, go ahead and build it. Just move it a titch over from my land.

"Jake! Good to see you," Gordon Wellsley said, welcoming me into his cluttered office. Gordon was not one of them crisp corporate lawyers who move, dress, and speak with alarming and studied precision. Rather, he was rotund, rumpled, and bemused, his tie askew, his white hair wispy and wild.

"Come to do your will?" he asked. "There's a way, you know."

"Good one, Gord. No will yet, but I need help with this."

I gave him an abbreviated summary of what had happened so far, then handed him the government package which he scanned with an increasingly furrowing brow.

"Hmmm…," was his first piece of counsel.

"So, is this legit or not?" I asked.

"The Ministry of Health—any ministry—can expropriate private property—by itself or in a public-private partnership—which this is. Usually it's for highways, power lines, mass transit, that sort of thing. It's rare but not unheard of for other reasons. In the legislation, it just says "other interests." It's all based on the concept of public good. And judging from this pack of papers, there are a lot of people who think it's in the public interest. Local council approved it, county approved it. Health approved; Environment approved it."

The aforementioned brow shot up when he found the letter I'd written in support of a nearby nursing home.

"And apparently you approved of it," he said.

"How long's this clown job gonna take?" I asked.

He looked at the government letter again.

"It appears as though they've fast tracked this. Again, rare but not unheard of. You have a month to respond. With a decision to come in another month."

"So, end of the summer. Can we stop it?"

"We?"

"Yeah, we."

"We can appeal. This is Canada; it's an appealing country."

"Good one, Gord. Can we win?"

"I doubt it."

"So the fix is in, you figure?"

"Look, Jake, I'm not going to tell you what to do, but I'm thinking that the technical legal term is: you're screwed."

"That's it?"

"Yes. We delay but I don't think we win."

"So now what?"

"Maybe you can talk the government out of it."

"Sure. Or I can smash my head against that wall over there."

"Well, maybe you can start a petition."

"I *might* be able to get two names."

"Or you can raise holy hell with the media."

"Pissing against the wind. They're all onside with the development."

"Then my advice? If I were you, I'd hold my nose and make nice with the developer. See if you can get him back up to five hundred thousand in exchange for you not delaying construction with an appeal."

I walked out of his office accompanied by the apparent inevitability that I was soon to join the ranks of the homeless and there didn't seem to be a goddamned thing I could do about it. This helplessness led to anger and frustration that led me to the Peterborough gym I was visiting less and less frequently.

Do not, for even a second, imagine that I work out on that variety of medieval torture-looking devices known as modern exercise equipment. "My" gym is a ratty old boxing club mostly attended by young lacrosse and hockey players whose coaches figured they needed boxing training to stay with their teams. Sprinkled among them are older farts like me. We are all watched over by a ratty even older guy named Mac.

If you listen to him, Mac coulda been a contenda. I'm guessing either World War I or Jack Dempsey got in the way. But Mac's a classic example of what you see is not what you get. Despite innumerable shots to the head, Mac is pretty smart, funny, and sly. Twenty years ago, when I first started coming there, Mac would watch me work the bags and spar. Right away, he started calling me Andy. At the time, I assumed it was because Mac couldn't remember anything clearly. No matter how often I corrected him he insisted on calling me Andy. One day, pissed off, I asked why he was being such a dick about my name.

"Like Warhol," he chuckled. "Ya know. Painted tomato cans."

On this day I wanted to hit something or somebody and Mac's place let me do that legally. The heavy bag didn't put up much of a fight. Unlike the eighteen year-old defenceman with whom I stepped into the ring for a sparring session after Mac called out: "Andy! You're up!"

Maybe the kid had daddy or granddaddy issues. As we touched gloves to signify the start of our fight, I could see the angry fire in his eyes, the same fire I had over the prospect of being homeless. But, unlike me, the kid also had youth, talent, and strength.

A regulation referee would've stopped the fight before they finished singing the national anthem. I made the mistake of knocking the kid down with what had to be the luckiest punch I've ever thrown. The kid's surprise and embarrassment at being decked by someone forty years older translated into a truly dizzying flurry of jabs, hooks, and uppercuts that had me in a fetal position on the canvas in no time.

While I was struggling to get up, he was celebrating to the gaggle of bemused onlookers. He shouldn't have done that. I uncorked a haymaker to the side of his head that sent him sprawling.

"Did you hear a fucking bell?" I asked standing over him. "I didn't hear a fucking bell."

Mac intervened, otherwise my real estate problems would've become Halley's, what with her being my next of kin and all.

"Learn your lesson, kid, and move on," Mac growled.

So, I thought, when I was back on the sunny street with my frustration uncured, maybe grease might help. No, not the fucking musical, but the kind you get at Harvey's, the Canadian fast food chain with the best hamburgers in North America. I refuse to count the wave of hipster burger joints springing up everywhere, you know, the ones that charge you fifteen goddamned dollars for about a buck's worth of ground beef on which they put "gourmet" shit like spinach, brie, and/or roasted garlic aioli—whatever the fuck roasted garlic aioli is.

After at least thirty-five years, Harvey's still occupied prime downtown Peterborough real estate at the foot of Water Street by which, coincidentally enough, ran water in the form of the Otonabee River, just as it had when I was a Trent University student here for four glorious years in the mid-70s. In the fall, I'd take my fast food out back and down to the river, get high, eat French fries, and watch summer die. I even wrote a really bad poem whose rhyming scheme you can probably guess.

They assemble the burger right in front of you. While you're conducting them to the aluminum bowls of condiments, getting just the right amount of onions, tomatoes, and pickles laid on, you feel this involuntary Pavlovian salivation going on. I thought it was just me but Beth and later Halley confirmed it.

So my drool and I trundled down the river bank. I hoovered the double burger, fries and onion rings into me, then washed it down with a milkshake. The whole mass felt like a big ol' lump of plutonium in my bloated stomach. I lay back in the grass and started digesting, much the same way, I imagined, the giant anaconda in *Swiss Family Robinson* didn't move for days after swallowing that donkey.

Only, I didn't have that much time to waste—as appealing as lying there, belching, getting fatter, and staring at the clouds was.

I waddled up Water Street to the county's administrative offices that housed the Land Registry department. Might as well find out who had the most to gain.

I'd been there before, twenty years earlier when Beth and I were looking for a place. Once we had settled on the Hovel-by-the-Lake, I wanted to know who owned what and what was zoned for what around us, lest a nuclear waste dump or a Bed Bath and Beyond were being planned next door.

You asked the clerk at the counter for an official map with your lot and parcel number on it. Then you'd ask for all the adjacencies.

The system hadn't changed. Nor had the general sense of unwelcomeness.

I asked for the south-east corner of Mississauga Lake and the clerk kinda huffed and sauntered over to the banks of drawers, slid one open, and sauntered back.

"It's not there," she said.

"What? How can that be? Who took it? What's going on, for Christ's sake?" I demanded with paranoid alarm.

She checked her computer.

"No mystery. We're updating it. Here," she said, swiveling her computer screen to me.

There was me surrounded by a sea of Edgewater Estates marked across the lots around me and up the east shore of the lake.

"Oh…Got the old map?" I asked.

"Somewheres. But it's no good anymore."

"Mind if I see it?"

"I told you; it's being updated."

"Oh, c'mon," I said, staring into her eyes. "Five minutes."

Not exactly cobra and mongoose time, but I knew the longer I stared at her, the tougher the time she'd have extricating herself. Any attempt at wit and charm evaporated into a test of wills as we regarded each other.

"Oh, alright," she said, plainly looking as if it wasn't alright at all.

I spread the old map out on the broad table. There I was, and Carl Breedlove's island. Moving up the east side of the lake, on the old map you could see the original ownership blocks. It looked like about half of them, maybe 800 acres belonged to B. Odell. The kid had moved fast and his 'B' sat on top of a glob of white-out under which was presumably his old man's 'M' initial. Sizeable chunks—I'm talking scores of acres—belonged to Derek Collins, Councilor/septic guy Preston Peterson and a T. Weston. Then there were a number of two-acre lots—maybe twenty of them. The owners' names were unknown to me. Except for E. McQuaig and B. Dugald—Mayor McQuaig and Councilor Dugald. Now that was interesting. I had known they owned land there but in the scheme of things, their holdings weren't exactly vast.

A name I didn't recognize—a G. Grandmaitre—owned a small piece—maybe ten acres—but it was all along the shore, starting just past Isla de Carl and running for about 1500 feet. What also stuck out was the owner's name. I bet it would be the only French-sounding name in that entire bank of maps.

I was about to return the old map to its fierce protector when I looked over at the lots on the other side of me along the south shore. I was surprised—and maybe I shouldn't have been—that a sticker had been added to the lot two west of mine. 'S. Woodson' was covering the name of our recently departed councilor, G. Hill. Ol' Stewie had put his money where his mouth was and bought into the neighbourhood.

I scribbled all the names down with the legal descriptions of the parcels.

"Excuse me, ma'am, could I see the purchase prices for these lots."

"I don't know."

"You don't know if they exist or you don't know if you're going to feel like giving a member of the public some public knowledge?"

"Oh, they exist alright, but not here. Your township tax assessment department. If you hurry…," she said, looking at the standard office-issue wall clock and then turning to me with what could've been her first smile of the day, "…you still won't get there before they close."

Driving back to the lake, past the shuttered township offices in Buckhorn, I considered what I had learned. The answer was not much. I had already known about the majority of bought-out landowners, just not the exact size of their pie slices. The shocking case of political conflict of interest wasn't so shocking anymore as the Mayor and Councilor Dugald hadn't exactly hit the jackpot with their two-acre lots. Councilor/septic pumper Peterson was the only big owner among our political overlords.

Somewhere along the highway outside Peterborough a thought occurred to me. Owing to the rarity of French-Canadian names in the area, I wondered about G. Grandmaitre. Up popped an association of a new fact and an old fact, one that had sat uselessly in some brain fold of mine for perhaps decades. The new fact: Luc Dubois' wife, Giselle— the one who wasn't crazy about her husband's bad English friend— could very well be the G. on the land registry. And that was possible because of the old fact I dusted off: women getting married in Quebec don't legally assume their husbands' names.

At home, I fired up my shitty laptop. Back to the public records. This time in French.

Bingo! Or as they say in French: Bingo!

Luc Dubois and Gisele Grandmaitre were wed in the paroisse of St Sauveur in juin of 1988.

I hate moral quandaries but mostly they're unavoidable. Not big stuff but the little events that take place and usually—with me—involve a simple 'yes I'll do that' or 'no I won't.' Here we had one of those decision points. On one hand, Luc was a friend of mine who had worked hard and was dedicated and decent, and now stood to make some money. But, on the other hand, strictly speaking, he could've had something to do with influencing his ability to make that money by hurrying through the approvals. But on the other other hand, his explanation of how clean the development proposal was convincing.

What to do? What to do?

I decided to let it slide. Good for Luc for having the foresight to buy the lakefront lot years ago. And good for him that he could now finance his Chilean vineyard dream.

None of which got me any closer to solving my own situation.

It sat in my guts—alongside the double burger—but lawyer Wellsley's advice to me was starting to make sense. I took out Stewie's business card and called him.

This time, I swear, I started off more diplomatically than I believed ever would have been possible.

"Let's talk like calm adults, shall we?" I said.

"Excellent idea. Before we start though, I'd like to invite you to the official groundbreaking ceremony next week. Thursday, 2 o'clock."

It was a real effort to choke down the rage bloom in my gut.

"Oh, gee, I can't," I said. "Sorry. I'm re-arranging my fucking sock drawer that day. It's been giving me fits."

"That's a shame. Oh, well…"

"How do you get to have a ceremony?" I asked. "I'm not done with this."

"You will be. It's a formality and you know it."

"If it's a goddamn formality, why did you say that you've stopped the buying process?"

"We do things by the book."

"Then why have all the deeds been transferred to you?"

"They signed; we own. How and when we pay is between us and them."

"Secondly, are you going after Carl's island?"

"No. We dropped the animal sanctuary. Saves us a bunch. Why, we're even saving on your purchase price."

He had to get smarmy, didn't he? And I then had to start to lose it, didn't I? My little rage bloom turned into a giant mushroom cloud.

"How's about saving another bunch of money by leaving me the fuck alone? Really, Stewie, you have to tell me why you've got such a hard-on for my land. Four acres out of, what, fifteen hundred? Way less than point goddamned one percent. Why not just ignore this little point?"

"We've done up the plans."

"It's a fucking drawing! Change the drawing. Put the nursing home somewhere else."

"We're not going to do that. Council approved what they approved. All of our marketing stuff is out there. And besides. Your house… wouldn't be in keeping with the new environment."

"Oh, and Carl's is?"

"We sailed around his island; you can't really see his dump. Yours, on the other hand…"

"On the other hand what?"

"Frankly? Your place is a shithole, a very visible shithole to any of our new owners across the bay."

"Yeah, well, it's *my* shithole. And it's going to stay *my* shithole!"

"We'll see."

And the bastard hung up before I could. Again.

CHAPTER 16

To settle my nerves and maybe to distract myself, I figured my only strategic move was to drink a bunch of tequila and feel sorry for myself as I considered my complete lack of options.

Snookered, euchred, douched—cut it any way—that's what had happened. And all by innocuous, lifeless paper.

That's a bloodless way of settling things these days, leastways in this patch of the planet. Of course, it wasn't always that way. But we don't have range wars between cattlemen and sheep farmers, no murderous union-busting goons with brass knuckles and baseball bats anymore. And that's a good thing. Instead we have the law, the lawyers and the paperwork, mounds of paperwork. Cease and desist letters, restraining orders, peace bonds, all sorts of what are called mechanisms meant to curb the naturally violent or overtly nasty instincts of groups or individuals. Yay for us! We're—mostly—civilized. Personally, I'm glad I can cut my lawn without worrying about invading armies or bands of thieves or the distance to the nearest stockade.

I think we should all take a few moments every week to contemplate how far we've come and how fast.

But there's still a pretty big thumb on the scale. And there always will be because some people will want money and power far in excess of the rest of the people. They believe they deserve all the riches and influence they can acquire and there is not ever such a thing as enough. Their camp followers—lawyers, accountants, and lobbyists—believe exactly the same thing because they are handsomely paid to believe it.

It ain't new. Nor is it a startling revelation courtesy of yours truly. We wouldn't have most of the great art, architecture, or innovation if rich and powerful people hadn't wanted huge buildings and monuments to jerk themselves off over or didn't think it would be kinda cool to have a mural painted on the ceiling of the Sistine Chapel. Or two bands of steel running across a continent that might help nation-building while making them a shit-ton.

"Everybody knows the dice are loaded; everybody knows the good guys lost."

Thanks, Mr. Cohen. No, really, thanks a bunch.

Again, all this shit's been going on forever but the difference now is the style. Not ham-fisted but light-fingered. Deft. A piece of legislation is tinkered with, an electoral district re-drawn, a sketchy medical study bought and paid for.

Yeah, I know. Grumble, grumble.

All this greed and chicanery might make for a lively general conversation but the hard specifics were lonely. Specifically, I now had to wrap my pea brain around the fact that I had no choice but to move. Pack up and abandon the best place I had ever lived in, the place where I wanted to play out the string, where I had planned to be carried out of on a plank when my lucky streak ended.

When you know you're going to lose something, you look at it in a different light. Part nostalgia, part sadness, I actually walked—well, lurched—around the place remembering goofy shit. How Halley had honed her woodworking skills by carving a fairly credible likeness of Snoopy on her bedroom wall logs, the notches I'd put in her doorframe measuring her growth until she abandoned the practice about four inches ago, maybe when she was thirteen. And the short narrow tub Beth had insisted upon because she was short and narrow and liked long baths after a sweaty day mucking about outside.

What the Christ is wrong with sentimentality? Not the maudlin *Ode to Stephen Dowling Bots* kind of diabetes-inducing sentimentality that

Mark Twain mocked in *Huck Finn* but genuine feeling, a simple honest emotion over losing—or gaining—a person, place or thing that means something beyond reason to you and you alone.

Aided and abetted by Cazadores Reposada, I came to the understanding that a very basic principle of mine, a belief I had held for as long as I could remember had just been disassembled. After physical survival, human beings want only two things: for it to be fair and to be left the fuck alone.

This was neither.

And for what? Four hundred thousand dollars in my jeans or a 9% annual return for life? And then what? Go where? With the council approval and Edgewater Estates going full steam ahead, house prices—certainly waterfront house prices—in the 'hood would be skyrocketing—if they hadn't already. I'd have to light out for even more distant territories to afford that if I wanted to stay on water but still be near enough to Toronto and my daughter and an international airport. And I would have to start all over again.

Gee, maybe I could buy a two-bedroom, two-bath lakeside condo from Stewie. How'd that be for irony? And besides which, living in a modern cube stacked among other cubes would violate another rock solid principle of mine: A man should have enough outside space in which he can comfortably pee unseen.

It was mid-June now and I here I was reduced to seeing how far out I could push my looming eviction.

I called Gord Wellsley, told him we were going to appeal the expropriation. Told him to wait until the last possible moment to file the paperwork. When asked, he thought that he could drag this thing out until the end of September, mid-October at the latest. So that might buy me the summer. And then what? Would they show up the next day with the cops and an eviction notice?

Fucking right they would. Knowing Stewie, he'd be driving the bulldozer onto my property at 12:01 AM on the day of.

I went over to Carl's.

"They can do that?" he asked, re-reading my letter.

"Looks like it."

"Fuckers."

"And you get to stay. They don't want your island anymore."

"Don't that beat all?"

"Don't it."

"Hey! You can live here," he said.

"With you?"

"Of course with me. Reasonable rent."

"When the fuck have you ever been reasonable?"

"Arsehole."

"You figure this island's big enough for the both of us?"

He thought about it and I thought about it.

"Nah!" we answered in unison.

"Appreciate the thought, buddy," I told him.

Maybe it was now all coolly academic but I did make the trip to the township office in Buckhorn to look up the purchase prices for the development land.

Sheila Little was the receptionist/office manager/PR guru/customer service queen and any number of other admin jobs as was standard for small municipalities. Her efficiency was legendary. Without her, the township would descend into utter chaos. I could see the bands of bloodthirsty marauders as things fell apart and the centre didn't hold. I envisioned the mere anarchy loosed upon the world of West Kawartha. It would be *Mad Max*-time, only with sensible SUVs—racing down lakeside roads at easily five miles above the speed limit, viciously tipping over empty recycling bins, shouting "Sorry, eh?" at the fearful homeowners.

Sheila knew everyone, was always pleasant and helpful to everyone.

Except to me on that day.

She also knew that legally she couldn't refuse my request to see the tax rolls.

Boy, the assessments—based on recent sales to Lakeshore Developments—had changed big time on the east side of the lake. Odell's land—some 784 acres—was now valued at ten million smackeroos. Derek Collins' chunk was worth two million, about half a million more than Preston Peterson's. Somebody named T. Weston had lucked into a million dollars. Surprising—or maybe not—was the fact that both the Mayor and Councilor Dugald had sold their raw land for $200,000 each for their two acre-lots that weren't even lake-front while similar-sized lots on either side of theirs had gone for 50K. G. Grandmaitre was going to get $800,000 for her parcel. Stewie had forked over 500K for Greta Hill's house and 280 for Drew Bregg's. They'd also paid Jimmy $700,000 for the Angler Arms.

I wrote down and started to add up the purchases.

"Lydon. Could I have a word with you?"

The croaking voice startled me. It was Mayor McQuaig and she'd been looking over my shoulder. Well, not exactly. Even with me sitting down, Her Royal Shortness couldn't manage that. But she was hovering, her head bobbing like a wizened bantam hen's.

"Sure, Mayor. What's up?" I asked, closing my hand over my scribbling.

"In my office."

I felt like I was being sent to the principal's. I followed her down the hall, debating whether or not I should swallow the paper with my list of land sales rather than share with the class.

Once the door was closed, Elsie did not display anything like the friendliness that had got her elected for several eons.

Sitting behind her desk, she lit a cigarette and studied me.

"Can I join you?" I asked reaching for my pack.

"No. You won't be here long enough," she said as she slowly exhaled.

"So how long am I going to be here?"

"Long enough for me to tell you that you better smarten the fuck up and, after that, shut the fuck up and sell to the government."

"I'm appealing the expropriation."

"Don't you even goddamned think about it!"

"Or what…?"

"You've met Ken Larsen, our by-law enforcement officer."

"Kenny? Sure. We go way back."

"Well, you and he are going to have a lot more to do with each other if you don't withdraw your goddamned appeal. If you win—and you might—he's going to crawl so far up your sorry ass for every—and I mean every—goddamned infraction you even *think* of committing."

"Why are you doing this, Mayor? Am I in the way of voting your-self a hefty pay raise or is it just the windfall from your lot inside the development?"

I had to hand it to her; she didn't anger. Her gravel voice just got more gravelly.

"You've been warned," it rasped. "Now get the fuck out of my office."

I had never been intimidated by a small octogenarian before; it was kinda funny and kinda unsettling.

Back at the place, I totaled up the money being doled out for the land by Lakeshore Developments. The company was paying out about seventeen million for its land assembly. Was that a lot? I wondered. Or was it not very much? Or in Goldilockean terms, was it juuuust right?

It wasn't easy trying to get an accurate picture of comparable prices. There were five or six realtors operating in the 'hood, all offering raw land for sale. There was no way of knowing to what extent the inevitability of the development had already jacked prices. And there was no way of knowing if the land for sale was similar unless you drove around to see it. You couldn't go by the MLS listings and the pictures. Stand at the edge of a lake and shoot out at the water and it all looks good. According to their descriptions, every lot had no more than a "gentle slope" down to the water. But judging by some houses around Mississauga Lake, the slope would seem gentle only to a mature mountain goat with nerves of steel.

Even with all those qualifications, it seemed to me that Lakeshore was overpaying, maybe 50%, more than usual for the waterfront lots (including my 'knockdown'). But they were wildly overpaying for the forest. Near as I could tell by looking at vacant land for sale in the area that didn't border water, we're looking at $5-10,000 an acre. Going by the assessments, that meant Lakeshore had paid at least double what the going rate was.

And that struck me as odd. I guess by Toronto prices, it was a bargain.

But this wasn't Toronto. Supposedly sharp real estate guys wouldn't overpay like that. They're used to buying low and selling high. On the other hand, Lakeshore really wanted this thing to take off and once it did, they'd probably be sitting pretty with exploding re-sale prices. So they apparently were willing to pay a premium. But that much?

Like, I said. Odd.

But odd to a reclusive, chain-smoking, alcoholic nerd doesn't mean odd to the rest of the world. Why not go after two birds, I thought, and go to see Mary Ellen Conway, who was both a real estate pro and one of the councilors opposed to Edgewater Estates becoming a reality. She might know what the fuck was going on.

She had a small office in an old brick house on Buckhorn's main street. It was clean and tasteful with IKEA-type blonde wood furniture, beige Berber carpets, and mid-grey walls. Any colour came in the form of inspirational posters on the walls, bold text on vibrant photographs of mountains at sunset or whales jumping or some such shit, all exhorting the reader to overcome all the obstacles which a malevolent universe had put in front of them.

I had time to read them all because Mary Ellen wasn't in her office, although her admin assistant told me she was expected soon.

Mary Ellen bustled into the office, early-thirty-ish, very smartly dressed, a toothy smile ringed by bright red lipstick and crowned with her oft-photographed wide-brimmed hat that was aspiring its way to sombrero status.

As soon as she saw and recognized me, her smile disappeared. As was becoming a depressing trend, she too didn't seem to be all that happy to see me. I was also surprised, figuring she'd believe me to be an ally.

"I'm very busy, Mr. Lydon," she said as I rose to greet her.

"I'm not. But I thought you might be interested in the prices they're getting for the land the development sits on."

"I've already looked them up. Thank you."

"And?"

"And what?"

"Any opinion on how reasonable they are?"

"They're high."

"How high?"

"Anywhere from 50 to 200% more than usual."

"Doesn't that strike you as strange?"

"Not at all. There is nothing usual about Edgewater Estates for this area. It's like…it's like those stories you hear about somebody finding a Monet in their attic. They're about to sell it at a garage sale for twenty dollars and then they take a closer look. As far as Lakeshore Developments, they must've figured all this land was their bargain Monet."

"Yeah, but how'd the landowners know what to ask for?"

"I have no idea. All you needed was one of them to guess how huge this all would be. And then a couple of phone calls to the bigger landowners."

"So is that what happened? The local lads outfoxed the big city developer?"

"I'm sure I don't know, but it does happen. Although I understand there is one local owner intent on fouling everything up."

She was staring rather pointedly at me.

"I know it looks that way," I said. "But all they have to do is move the retirement home. I keep my house—like I'd guess you'd want to keep yours—and everything else is tickety-boo."

Any trace of perkiness had disappeared from her face.

"And if they don't move it to suit you, then what?" she snapped.

"Mary Ellen, why are you so pissed off at me if you're against the development?"

She paused.

"Come into the conference room," she said.

I followed her to a small room with what looked like an IKEA kitchen table, metal chairs and more posters whose headlines told me to Persevere, Arise, Be Strong, and Ride the Wind. I was instantly exhausted just thinking about all that activity. She closed the door. I hoped she wasn't packing heat in what I assumed was her designer knock-off purse/duffel bag.

"Mr. Lydon, can I ask you a question?" she asked, her voice suddenly shaking.

"Sure."

"Do you have any idea how expensive it is to be a single parent of a nine-year old with muscular dystrophy?"

"I'm sorry. I don't."

"Very expensive."

"I imagine it is."

"Since my douchebag of a husband screwed off and has been crying poor ever since, I've been carrying the load for Bobby's care. I *need* Edgewater Estates."

"So, again, why are you on the record as being against it?"

"The development was never going to be stopped at council. Any fool could've seen that. While Woodson was selling inside the development, I intended to get all the sales outside of it. But I don't want to look like a shark, and the people selling out don't want to look like greedy bastards."

"You're going through this charade just to get listings?"

"Mostly."

Mary Ellen paused. I bet she was composing herself after finding herself close to tears.

"There's another thing. When the land sales at Edgewater finally go through, I'll come into a healthy chunk of money. He—the douchebag—is one of the biggest landowners."

I ran through what I'd learned at the tax office. Her ex couldn't be Blair Odell because he'd left the 'hood as a child. It was possible but highly unlikely she would've hooked up with Derek Collins. And Peterson had a wife of longstanding.

"Your former husband is T. Weston," I said.

"Terry. Yes."

"Half a mill would sure help out," I rather pointlessly admitted.

"Yes. And you're the only fly in the ointment."

"If it's any consolation, I'll probably lose."

"You should lose sooner. You delay and we'll be into the fall or maybe early winter and nobody buys or sells in cottage country then. Now if you'll excuse me...."

I felt rotten as I drove back to the hovel, saddened by the big chill that had descended on me. I don't strive to make enemies; it just sort of happens. I genuinely believe that it's easier to go through life at least getting along with the people you run into instead of pissing them off. That's the guideline anyway, now gone horribly awry.

I considered my self-interest versus the weight of a whole region that wanted to see this development happen. Looming large over this quandary was the stunning inevitability that between that day and the end of the universe, somebody was going to build something on that land. And what was worse: I was probably going lose anyway so my resistance was futile, a hollow meaningless gesture.

On the other hand, I'm a big fan of hollow meaningless gestures. I may not go down fighting but I do tend to go down kvetching and grumbling.

CHAPTER 17

The day of the official groundbreaking arrived and I decided to put off my bedeviling sock drawer and attend.

I walked to the main part of the site that started past the highly-prized ribbon of lakefront running alongside Fire Route 162. It was about a mile and a half from my place where the road dead-ended. There was a considerable amount of activity and a bunch of changes since the last time I had wandered in what had been vacant bush. At least a dozen cars were parked on either side of the narrow road, a dozen more on the other side of the low gate across the bulldozed road onto the property. There was a new billboard like the sign by the main road. 'Future home of Edgewater Estates' and in front of it was a wooden stage skirted with bunting—fucking bunting—as decoration. Colourful plastic pennants, more at home ringing used car sales lots, were strung everywhere.

And there was an OPP cruiser. The cop got out of his car and approached me. I won't say his eyes lit up with joy when he recognized me.

"You!" he more or less snarled.

"Constable Dysart, how the heck are you?" I asked, even though I could guess the answer by his scowl.

He was evidently still pissed off over our meeting last summer when he was part of the SWAT team that egregiously and erroneously roughed me up and arrested me. When Lady Justice had her way with the authorities, I got him to deliver the letter dropping all charges against me. He wasn't all that happy with the messenger job. It was

pretty obvious that he hadn't wanted his roughhousing to go to waste
and that he had really, really, hoped that I had been the bad guy in all
the chicanery of last year.

"What are you doing here?" he demanded.

"By here, do you mean at this public event, standing on this public
road?"

"It's private property and it's a construction site. So that's as far as
you're going."

"That's as far as I want to go."

"Good."

"Good."

Having concluded this adult conversation, I stepped aside to see what
was going on. Dysart stepped in front of me.

"Seriously? What are you? Seven?" I asked before giving him a head
and shoulder fake and finding an unobstructed view. I thought I saw
him grin.

Beyond the cop car, in an open area on the other side of the gate, there
were a couple of guys with white construction hats studying plans that
had been unfurled and tacked to a makeshift table. A guy on a bulldozer—I presumed one of Preston's lads—was loudly scraping and
shaping the land to form a winding wide path from the gates. When
the blade hit one of the several billion rocks just under the surface it
made a sound like giant fingernails on an equally huge blackboard.
The crowd winced as one. Unseen in the distance, from somewhere
back in the bush, you could hear at least two chainsaws roaring away
reducing the world's tree population.

There were also another couple of guys just standing around looking
large and nasty. Presumably, they were there as muscle to quell the

fierce demonstration if the considerable police presence failed. One of the monuments was Jerry Glavin. The goons had their own car parked near the road. A crest on the door read Shield Security.

Said fierce demonstration came in the form of Sarah Ruth Evans and several buddies—middle-aged, grey-haired ladies and Drew Bregg, my Volvo-driving, recycling-obsessed arsehole of a neighbour. They all had forlorn expressions that changed to anguish every time they heard the snap then the crash of a felled tree.

Whenever a piece of living lumber smacked the ground, one protester held up a hand-lettered sign (on a 2x2 *wooden* stake) that read: 'WE hear when a tree falls in the forest.'

Near as I could tell, there were maybe four members of the media on hand. They hung together scarfing free coffee and egg salad sandwiches. In the old days—i.e. when I had a job—such a turnout would be considered disastrous and I would have some 'splaining to do. Now, all the media outlets steal and/or share everything so there only needed to be four to ensure blanket radio, TV, and newspaper presence in the area. Depending how you cropped the photos or edited the videotape, any ceremony could be made to look as sizeable as Woodstock or a Black Friday crowd at Best Buy.

On a signal from Stewie, I saw Glavin get on his phone and within seconds the machine noise stopped. And when that din stopped, another one started in the form of a four-piece band of roving musicians sporting a clarinet, trumpet, trombone, and a tuba. I thought it may have been a first in musical history as they played an odd and weirdly compelling fusion of Dixieland jazz and German oom-pah.

All the township council 'yeas' trooped onto the small makeshift stage. The ceremony was about to begin.

Either out of principle or as a form of public punishment, the two living nays to the project—Councilors Phil Vogel and Mary Ellen Conway—were noticeably absent from the stage. The Mayor was last one up and first one to speak. She was barely visible behind the podium. Her brief remarks were cheered by the cheery crowd. Then Stewie addressed the gathering.

As per usual, he was slick and entertaining. He had down pat that lowest common denominator enthusiasm and the cheap jokes of an inveterate game show host.

To the strains of I think a mash-up of *Ein Prosit* and *When the Saints Go Marching In*, the VIPs all filed off the stage and huddled up in front of the gate where Elsie was given a pair of over-sized scissors—well, maybe they were a normal pair that just looked huge in the hands of the undersized mayor. She took a split-second to find me in the crowd and in that moment before a big devious wrinkled grin overtook her face, she looked as though she wanted to take those scissors and force-fully plunge them into my chest.

Cameras and phones clicked as she cut the wide red ribbon strung across the gate. There was much clapping and whistling and cheering and I'm sure, the occasional 'huzzah!'

Then we all milled around for a bit as the very amateur Counts Basies and von Bismarcks struck up the band again. I went up to Phil Vogel who was with his wife, Janice. Both of them, like me, seemed glum and non-celebratory.

"Mayor put you in the penalty box?" I asked.

"Yup," he replied. "Two minutes for interference and a five-minute major for speaking my mind."

"It's a goddamn tragedy, but all least Dr. Hill can't see this," I noted.

Phil stiffened up a bit then turned to Janice.

"Honey," he said to her. "Do you mind asking the Ridleys—they're over there—if they're still coming for drinks on Friday?"

As soon as she'd left, he turned to me and dialed his booming voice way down.

"Why do you keep mentioning Greta?" he whispered. "You got something to say to me?"

"Jesus, Phil, no," I insisted. "You two were on the same side against all this; that's all."

"You sure?"

"Well…to tell you the truth, I've been looking into this whole thing—because of my land—and it strikes me that there are some things that are…confusing about her death."

As Janice rejoined us, Phil's jumpiness subsided while his voice rose to its normal rock concert PA level.

"Of course we should sit down, Jake," he said to me. "We absolutely must take a look at your policy."

They then wandered away as politicians in crowds do—to see and be seen by voters.

Meanwhile, I saw that Stewie, in his own way, was a kind of politician as he looked completely in his element among the crowd, doling out much back-slapping and glad-handing. I, on the other hand, was shunned for the pariah that I was. The closest I came to physical contact was with Derek Collins who offered to punch me in the head for being there. I didn't take him all that seriously because—if it's possible—he sounded like he was being almost playful.

I did manage to make off with an armful of egg salad sandwiches after Stewie briefly accosted me to thank me for coming out.

Walking home, I thought and ate sandwiches. On top of the whole ceremonial clusterfuck, my abiding dislike of both Dixieland jazz and oom-pah "music," and somebody's excessive use of mayonnaise in the egg salad, the thing that got me was Phil's nervousness.

I sent him an e-mail when I got home suggesting that whenever he wanted to drop around to "discuss my policy" he should feel free to do so as I had checked my calendar and I was pretty much open at least until the Leafs won the Cup.

Judging by the e-timestamp, Phil sent his reply some few minutes after he would've gotten home for the supergrand lollapalooza of a ribbon-cutting extravaganza.

"How about 9 tomorrow morning?" he wrote.

When people seem eager to talk to me I get suspicious.

Five minutes before the appointed hour Phil was on my doorstep, looking as spooked as he briefly had the day before.

Coffees in hand we parked ourselves on the deck.

"How do we start this?" I asked.

"You said you were confused about her...death. Why?"

"The overdose doesn't make sense."

"She was in a lot of pain. She took a lot of pills."

"Except fentanyl."

"Fentanyl? I didn't know anything about that!" he said with genuine surprise on his face and in his voice.

"But you knew about the rest?"

"Yeah. I did."

"You guys were involved?"

"....Yeah."

Shit! I thought. Phil was still hurting and I felt for him. Whatever had gone on between the two of them had been way beyond a casual coupling. But I hate this couples stuff! Relationship counseling, along with just about every other form of personal advice, ain't my long suit. Plus, only half of this secret couple was still living.

"Please don't say anything more," I nearly begged. "It's none of my goddamned business."

I could see his sadness doing that slow dance towards anger.

"You think someone did this to Greta?" he demanded.

"I truly don't know. But two councilors within a few months? That's crazy long odds. Was she getting threatened?"

"I wouldn't call it threatened. She was being pressured to either abstain or change her vote. I was too."

"By whom?"

"A bunch of people. The Mayor, Stewie, a fair number of pissed-off voters."

"Anybody stick out?"

He thought for a while.

"No, it's been sort of a blur of angry people."

"Edgewater seems to be bringing out the ugly in people."

He turned to me as he was leaving.

"Janice can't know," he said.

"She won't from me; I swear. What you tell or don't tell your wife is also none of my goddamned business. You think of anything, let me know, OK?"

I didn't suppose Phil was any better off for having talked with me. He seemed relieved that his secret was going to stay that way. But now he could add my suspicion that his lover's death may not have been accidental. And he might pile that onto what I imagined was his frequent twisting in the dark before he went to sleep about his affair and how it had so cruelly ended.

Oh, and he probably considered the nastiness that Edgewater had delivered to his doorstep.

The first of July was approaching. I sent an e-mail to Alex asking if she'd do me a huge favour by calling the Toronto sales office for Edgewater Estates and meeting with them before coming up to the lake, just to see what info she could gather.

She agreed as long as she didn't have to actually buy anything and there was a gallon of chardonnay waiting for her.

I spent most of the next two days cleaning up the place, inside and out. It was a bit exciting because I was doing all this housework in honour of Alexandra's arrival and a bit saddening because I was in full self-pitying drama queen mode considering that all this cleaning would be wasted when Stewie's bulldozer came through the front door in a couple of months.

It all boiled down to the fact that I hate change. It's unofficial but I believe I was the last person in North America to use an ATM or to think that CDs would replace cassettes which I never thought would replace 33 1/3 albums. Here's all you need to know: Mennen used to make a Speed Stick deodorant called musk. However sparingly, it was the only deodorant I'd ever used. When it was apparent they were discontinuing that particular scent, I panicked and started scouring dollar stores and cut-rate consignment stores until I had amassed a hoard of twenty-one musk deodorant dispensers. I estimated that my pile o' of muskiness was gonna last some years but then what? When the stash ran out, I didn't know what the fuck I was going to do. Until I found out you could order it online. But how long was that e-commerce dream gonna last? I wasn't going to chance it. I bought another twenty and was comforted.

I know, right? Not quite *Rain Man* territory but real close.

At any rate, I had more or less lucked into a life I didn't just like, but loved. Bad and/or sad things had happened to be sure, just as bad things and/or sad things happen to everybody. My father fucked off. My mother had died. My wife had died. I did not cause nor could I have prevented what happened to them. It wasn't cosmic cruelty or a pointlessly nasty god. Oh, let's just call it what it actually is: life.

Luckily—and only 'luckily'—I was at a stage and circumstance where I could figure out how to play out the rest of my natural born days at a fairly young age. Most people, I know, don't get or don't take the opportunity at their one and only shot they have to decide how to live.

Even though it ended fifteen years ago, my frenetic corporate existence stood as a reminder that I wanted to, needed to design a different way of living and then protect it lest I wind up back there in the world of white shirts, ties, meetings and, yes, fucking socks. Ironically of course, maybe hypocritically, it was that very corporate life that had financed my ability to chose my life as a series of shrewd—OK, OK, goddamned lucky—investments gave me enough to live on, assuming I don't live a day past eighty. And medical oddsmakers aren't taking that bet that I'll be anywhere close to that age when I kick-off.

Geographically, socially, financially, and emotionally, that business world was a universe away from my current reality. It was as simple as a re-defined phrase. It used to be that the term "wheels up" meant my take-off time for the corporate Gulfstream that was going to jet me somewhere in North America for days of shitty food, anonymous hotel rooms, and frantic, high-pressure PR and investor relations doings which could swing our share value by tens of millions of dollars. Either way.

Today, "wheels up" means I'm about to raise the cutting height on my lawn mower.

But now this. Big-scale commerce had re-entered my life and it was fucking up everything.

And with Alex about to arrive.

I had already determined that I wasn't going to tell her about the shit was going on. Not right away.

The day of her arrival, and despite all my talking to myself to calm the fuck down, I was jittery, powerless to be anything but nervously expectant. And it didn't have anything to do with my housing situation. I tracked her flight, knew when she landed, guessed how long it'd be to clear customs and get her luggage, then the car rental. Another guess for the drive downtown. Because she had the side trip into Toronto, there wasn't a good way to come up with her ETA until after she finished the sales call and was about to fight her way out of Toronto traffic. Assuming she called or texted. Which she didn't.

And that left me pacing back and forth in front of the living room window until I was pretty sure I'd worn the floor varnish off.

When a red Malibu pulled up my driveway I was out the door like an affection-starved Labrador puppy.

Without a word, we hugged and I then hustled her inside, and paused to take stock of the bunch of greatness which had accompanied her. She looked great, smelled great, felt great. And I felt nothing but exceedingly lucky. We were both shaking like human beings as we kissed and held each other and, instantly, she took away the sins of the world.

We barely made it to the bedroom as we went crazy on our respective bodies. There's no crying need for detailed descriptions. C'mon, you know how it goes. And if you don't, words in books won't really cover it, will they?

Exhausted we lay back and, I swear, just giggled. OK, there was a little chortling, maybe some tittering—but we stopped short of guffawing.

"So how have been?" she finally asked.

"Good. You?"

"Good."

"Have a good trip?"

"Yes, thank you."

"We earned us some refreshments," I said as we got up and dressed. I mixed a couple of tequila sunrises and we went out to the deck to watch the sunset.

At first, there wasn't much conversation. Contentment, maybe. Some reverie perhaps and the endless silent fascination of seeing the sun slip away behind the trees on the other side of the lake, the water going to full glitter.

And then the blood-thirsty bugs came out and we went inside to the screened-in porch. That's when I told her that, a few months after her departure back to Boston, I would be leaving for parts unknown as my house was turned into kindling.

After her initial astonishment and my less than charitable explanation of the process by which I was getting fucked out of my home she teared up. I did too, involuntarily copying her the way you do when someone yawns, only with liquid coming out of your eyes.

"Jake, I'm so sorry."

"Me too."

"No way out of this?"

"With all these government approvals and a ton of public support? Not lookin' too good. I'm thinkin' about just selling now and being done with it."

"You can't! You love this place!"

It buoyed this boy to hear her encouragement. But just for a short while. Like seconds. Then reality crept back into the picture. I was fucked and I knew it.

"You know what really bugs the shit out of me? I'm losing to a bunch of shady operators."

"Shady how?"

Without a shred of conclusive evidence, I rattled on about the not completely explained away deaths of two councilors, the glaring conflict of interest for Luc Dubois, the Mayor and Councilors Dugald and Peterson, somebody digging into the backgrounds of both Carl and me, Stewie's odd lack of experience, the speedy approvals, topped off with the possibility of some dubious big money behind the whole thing.

"Maybe this kinda sleaze is what you see in the real estate development all the time. I don't know," she said.

"Speaking of sleaze, how'd the sales pitch go?" I asked.

After landing at Pearson, she'd rented the car, gone downtown to the address I'd given her of the Toronto sales office for her appointment. Apparently, it wasn't in some strip mall as a temporary location with big honkin' roadside signs. Rather it was the fifth floor of a downtown office building. Elegant, quiet. Great big photo displays. An unctuous Stewie-type sales guy.

Alex described the pitch as pretty straightforward. The guy wasn't really high-pressure, more discrete. More 'do you have any idea how fucking lucky you are if I decide to sell to you?' He had qualified her in his mind for a 3500 sq ft 'contemporary' log home between the lake and the 3rd hole.

"Boy, he sure got you right, kiddo."

To her credit, Alex ignored me.

"Really, the only odd thing that stood out," she said, "was when he asked me if I had heard about the place from an American contact."

"What'd you say?"

"The truth. A friend living near here."

"Give my name?"

"No. And he asked twice."

"Did you get any paper?"

"A real thick sales package."

"It'll keep 'til morning."

We fell asleep. And quickly. Some combination of clean air, utter darkness, singing frogs, the odd loon, oh, and being old and exhausted put us under in a matter of seconds.

And under we stayed.

Until the first gunshot.

CHAPTER 18

The shots were nearby and unmistakably coming from the lake. They weren't at all like the distant gunfire you hear during hunting season, but loud, sharp 'pops,' three of them, before I fully came to my senses and rolled with Alex off the bed away from the window.

There were maybe three more shots, fired not as burst but measured. Aimed. I heard them 'thunk' into something close by. Trees? The house?

We're on an elevated point. If the shots came from the lake, the gunman—gunperson?—would be shooting at an upwards angle. I thought—well, hoped—there'd be no way they could hit us through the thick logs below the window frame and the mattress as long as we stayed where we were and they weren't using armour-piercing shells.

We laid there for some seconds, or maybe minutes, the silence broken by our pounding hearts. Until I saw a light come on through the window and then heard two loud booms in quick succession.

"Carl," I said.

We crept outside to see Carl standing on his dock. He was lit up by a small searchlight he has shining across the lake. He was cradling a cracked-open shotgun.

"Carl!" I called out.

"You folks OK?" he yelled back.

"Yup."

"Hang on. Comin' over."

The light was extinguished and in the blackness I could hear the steady splash of a paddle. We beached his boat and he climbed out, shotgun in hand.

"What did you see?" I asked.

"Canoe. Couple of lads making for the far shore. Too far to hit. But they ain't comin' back."

"Sure it was them shooting?"

"Not too many other canoes out at 3 AM."

Alex broke the ensuing silence.

"What the fuck was that? A Canadian drive-by?"

We were all still nervously chuckling as we examined the back of the house after I turned on the exterior lights. We could see no holes, no broken windows.

"They hit something; I heard it," I said.

That's when we saw the marks on my canoe—the red painted wooden one I'd overturned down by the shore. On closer inspection we found five bullet holes.

"How'd he do that in the dark?" I asked.

"Betcha night vision goggles," Carl said. "Popular around here these days for huntin.' How many shots you hear?"

"Six," I said.

"Seven," Alex said.

"I heard seven too," said Carl. "Five hits. That's pretty fancy shooting from a rockin' canoe."

"So at least we know they weren't gunning for us," I said.

"Yet," Carl added.

"Now why'd you have to go and say that?" I said.

"So now what?" Alex asked.

I had this instant vision of assembling the old team, you know, my special ops buddies who had my back in Viet-Nam/ Desert Storm/ Iraqi Freedom. All the guys are still alive and still in superhuman physical condition. There's Yancy whom I suddenly remembered was my best friend. He's the hand-to-hand combat expert. Donny, our demolition pro, and Sparky, the comms guy, rounded out the team. We'll just go shopping at Vince's—he's the weapons guy—and he has this underground private arsenal in Arizona somewhere, There, we'll break out the Sig Sauer MCX and the Beretta GLX 160, mostly for its attached 40 mm grenade launcher. We'd try to talk Donny out of the Belgian-made FN-SCAR-L which he always prefers; I don't know why. We'd sidearm up, likely with good ol' Colt .45 SOCOMs but not the Glock 39 which is inaccurate and underpowered for this kind of wet work. We'd arrive there (wherever 'there' was) and set up a perimeter, wait until dark then go all in, wearing ATN NVG7-3 night vision goggles to establish the suppressing fire zone, pinpoint the bang grenade targets and go straight on to blow the shit out of absolutely everything. Sparky would get in the chest from the return fire. We'd all be sad but before he died he'd reveal the name of the mole at HQ CAMSOV who was trying to sabotage the mission. And then we'd blow the shit out of him.

I was about to lay out the plan, but Alex had already dialed 9-1-1.

The three of us sat on the front steps and waited.

"Carl, you know anybody who's that good a shot?" I asked.

"Pretty well everybody raised around here," he answered. "We all grew up with guns and huntin'—ducks, deer, groundhogs, oh, and rats at the dump. That's where you get good."

We sat some more until Alex pointed out that if and when the local constabulary arrived, seeing Carl with his 12-gauge double-barrel might not provoke the kind of helpful reaction we wanted.

"Don't feel up to an interview anyways," Carl said, heading back to his boat. "Let's not mention my accidental discharge of a firearm, OK?"

"Done," I called after him. "And thank you, sir,"

Without turning or breaking stride, Carl raised his shotgun up above his head in an armed version of 'You're welcome.'

"That was almost brave, what you did when the shots started," Alex said, staring at me with a ton of affection.

"Actually, I was trying to wrestle you between me and the shooter."

"Arsehole."

The hidden sun was lightening up the sky and the local bird population was yelling at the top of their little lungs. And we were still waiting.

We heard a siren and then flashing cop car lights bathed the house. The cruiser braked abruptly sending up a cloud of stone dust.

And who do I see crouched by the window of his open car door pointing his revolver at us in a nifty two-handed grip and yelling at us to stop and put up our hands up but my ol' buddy, ol' pal Constable Dysart.

"Dysart, for fuck's sake, cool your jets, will ya?" I shout.

He looked a little sheepish as he holstered his revolver, reached into the car and turned off the noise and lights.

"Dispatch said shooting," he grumbled as he walked up to us.

"Yeah, of my canoe."

We walked down to the dead vessel. Dysart opened his flashlight and examined the holes.

"That's pretty fancy shooting," he said.

"I've heard that," I said. "Shots came from the lake," and I needlessly gestured to the big fucking body of water only a few feet from where we were standing.

Dysart dutifully stared at the lake before turning to us.

"So, do you want me to head out there?" he said absolutely deadpan. "You know, I could look for boat tracks. Although it'd be better to wait for full daylight."

There's no way I could stop from laughing. Same for Alex. Dysart joined in.

"Look, folks," he said, getting serious. "This probably isn't just punks being punks. Any idea who'd do this?"

"We could maybe narrow it down to the people who are pissed off at me," I said.

"From what I understand, that list would have just about everybody around here on it except you and your neighbor."

"So that's it?"

"No, no. I'll get the crime scene guys here. We'll canvass the neighbours, see if anybody saw or heard anything. But there must be what—fifty cottages around the lake? Never mind that the boat didn't have to come from a cottage; they could've launched it anywhere."

I walked the constable back to his car, filling him in on the vandalized mailbox, the door chopping, and the sabotaged water pump.

"They seem to be escalating," he said.

"If it's the same 'they'."

"Let's bet. It's probably not much consolation, but they weren't trying to hurt you. A shot that good wouldn't miss if he didn't want to."

"You're right....It's not much consolation."

"You want to see if I can get you some protection?" he asked.

"Naw, but thanks." I said. "And thanks for comin' out."

"My job."

He paused.

"Ya know, Mr. Lydon, I'm not a bad guy."

"What a coincidence; I'm not either. And it's Jake."

"Alright. Jake. We just don't take chances anymore."

"Don't blame you."

We shook hands and that was nice.

Back in the house, I decided a little false bravado was in order.

"Mess with me? Mess with my woman?" I proclaimed, pounding my chest. "It's farging war!"

"Somehow I don't feel even a tiny bit safer."

"Alex, seriously, maybe you shouldn't be here. You don't need this shit."

"Forget it, Captain Canada. I've been roughed up by mine pit bosses in Peru. Things got pretty dicey with the some renegade loggers in Mexico. Nope, I'm staying."

"And here I was thinking you were just a bean-counting analyst in a fancy-shmantzy Boston office."

"I do that too, but if I'm recommending these ethical stocks, I need to see what's what because every goddamned company around now claims that they're green or ethical or sustainable."

"You know what bothers me about last night?"

"Your beauty nap got ruined?"

"There was no need to shoot up my canoe. The fucking expropriation letter had already come out. Why keep up the punk ass vandalism?"

"Left hand not knowing what the right was doing?"

"Maybe."

"Getting you out sooner?"

"Maybe."

CHAPTER 19

Odd perhaps, but there's something about being in the midst of an armed assault—to me anyway—that makes you want to forget the whole thing. The crime scene lads showed up by nine, poked around, took pictures and strung that yellow tape around the trees like they were decorating for a fucking garden party. I watched them as they dug out the bullets, heard one tech grumble that they must've been soft points because they'd been reduced to flattened blobs of unrecognizable metal.

But after they left, what were we supposed to do? Shore up our defences? Mine the bay? Plant shit-smeared *pungi* stakes on the perimeter?

Instead, we spent the day diverted by pleasant, mindless outdoorsy things that were fun. We walked, we weeded. We drove around to the more inhabited side of the lake where the cottage association had built a half-assed tennis court upon which Alex beat me stupid. Christ, that lanky woman can cover territory.

Then we showered and did some pleasant, mindless indoorsy things that were also really fun.

All in all, we earned an early cocktail hour.

Setting aside the gunplay, it had been a great day, capped off by sitting on the deck with my lady watching the orange and yellow and reds gather around the sinking sun. We were all quiet and serene and content in the middle of a perfect postcard.

Until I heard the sound of major rustling through the darkening underbrush along my shoreline.

Call me crazy but I think most people don't spend much time rehearsing what they'd do in a situation like this. So the two of us froze before I came up with the bold strategy of shouting out "Who's there? I've got a gun!" Of course, I was hoping the answer wouldn't be: "Just us murderers back to finish the job! And no you don't."

Instead I heard a weak call-out.

"Don't shoot! It's Drew."

I was mightily tempted to call back "Drew who?" just for the fun sound of it. Instead, we waited while my next door neighbor worked his way up to the deck, accompanied by a thick cloud of mosquitoes that he furiously swatted at.

"Jesus, man! Want some Off!?" I offered reaching for the spray can.

"No. DEET is a dreadful chemical," he said.

"Suit yourself," I said as I applied a glistening coat to my forearms. "What can I do for you?" I asked as he watched me slather up with the expression of somebody having a turd waved under his nose.

"Well, after the events of last night, I talked to some people and—" he began.

"—Who?" I interrupted.

"That's not important."

"Of course it is. Who?"

"Just people, OK? And we want to urge you in the strongest terms to accept the offer and leave."

"Why would you possibly care? You took the buy-out, right? You're leaving anyway."

"Yes, but right now, to be frank, the sooner you're gone the better. The gunshots, the police sirens, your presence here constitute an immediate threat."

"Call me kooky, but the immediate threat is the fucker who shot up my canoe."

"We have to consider our families."

"For God's sake, think of the children! That sort of thing?"

"I don't appreciate your sarcasm."

"And I don't appreciate your presence here, so, unless there's anything else…"

In full harrumph, Drew turned quickly and went back into the brush, swatting and thrashing.

"Now, where was I?" I said. "Oh, yeah, getting loaded."

"You may have disqualified yourself from the Good Neighbour awards this year," Alex noted.

"Life's full of disappointments. But, almost seriously, you know what?—and you may learn this, young lady, when you reach my age—"

"You're four months older than I am," Alex pointed out.

"Like I said, when you get older, you may learn that, after the necessities, people want two things: for it to be fair and to be left the fuck alone. And right now, it ain't fair and I'm sure not being left the fuck alone. My tao is seriously fucked up."

"By that guy?"

"That guy is the proverbial last straw."

"Meaning?"

"Meaning I'm going to fight this clusterfuck. Excuse me."

I went inside and called the number for the presentation centre. This is the message I left for Stewie: "It's Jake. I thought about it and the answer's no. I'm gonna let the expropriation play out. Oh, and fuck you."

"What are you thinking, babe?" I asked when I returned.

"About math."

"I beg your pardon."

"Look, let's set aside the possible theory that strangers knocked down your mailbox, burnt out your water pump, axed your door, and took some potshots at you just because you're a dick."

"Yeah but that's a pretty solid theory."

"I realize that, but let's look elsewhere."

"Don't have to look far. I don't want to sell and other people really, *really* want me to."

"OK, but who?"

"Everybody."

"How about we take a step back and look at the whole project. Maybe all this crap falling on you is a lot more organized than we think."

"Grassy knoll time?"

"What kind of numbers are we talking about?"

"Dunno."

"Well, let's find out."

The sun was gone; the mosquitoes were moving up in hordes from the shoreline and we went inside. Alex sat down at the dining room table, opened her laptop and then started assembling all the paper we had from Edgewater Estates. I stood in the doorway to the screened-in porch and smoked.

"I hate math," I said in that winning pouty way I have, stopping just short of stomping a foot or two.

"Well, we have to do some. Like taking castor oil."

"I hate that too. *You* do the math."

"Fine. I will."

"Fine."

"Fine. Says here in the marketing stuff that there'll be a hundred and eighty homes. You could just buy the land, Assume it's a bargain, this "pre-construction" price. Average lot price looks to be about $200,000. Now assume everybody opts for outright land purchase, that's thirty-six million."

"On land they paid less than eighteen for. Sweet deal."

"Yes and no," Alex said. "They've got a sample sales contract here. You only have to put up a 10% down payment right away, and you have to start building within a year after you agree to all sorts of covenants—you know, the square footage, materials, exterior finishes, number of garage spaces and so on. I was told at the sales office that the balance is due when the company has completed at least 75% of the amenities."

"So the 10% down gives them three point six million in the kitty."

"Right, but if the landowners agreed to a staged payment plan by Edgewater, they still would've been paid some millions in total. *And*

Edgewater now has to build everything. Take the club house. How big is that supposed to be?"

"Brochure says 10,000 square feet," I answered.

"Let's assume two hundred bucks a square foot construction cost. So that's about two million right there. What's it cost to build a golf course?"

"Fuck knows. Let's see what the Google say."

Tap-tap-tap.

"Google say two to four million according to the USGA."

"But that's in *real* money, not Canadian dollars."

"So say four mill Canadian."

"Let's just speak in Canadian, eh?"

"OK. Then there's the pool, tennis courts, landscaping, that's gotta be another million. So we're up to eight. All the subcontractors will demand deposits and the full pop when they're done."

"But the big expense is the infrastructure," I said. "They have to pay for water treatment, paved roads, street lighting, miles of wire for the power and pipes for the sewage system."

"So add it all up and that's easy ten mill worth of stuff they have to build *before* the houses even start. That's all cash out the door. Right now."

"Then you have the office in downtown Toronto, the one here, salaries, all the signage, marketing and presentation materials."

"And all the consultants' reports."

"Plus the first year pay-out to the former landowners on the REIT by the end of the year. What's that?"

"The first year pay-out is locked in, based on what they paid. So, upwards of two million."

"That's if everyone bought into the REIT and didn't take the straight cash deal."

"Stewie said they're all in," I said.

"Stewie's full of shit. No way a bunch aren't just taking the money and running. Say half are in."

"Meaning they'd have to come up with about ten million in cash to buy the land outright."

"And they obviously don't have it. Think about it. If they did, they wouldn't have even bothered to set up the REIT."

"OK, but by their own pricing of the lots they're selling, they value the land—right now—at about 36 mill."

"Meaning that the second year they'd have to pay out at least five and half million."

"At least. And maybe double that the third year when everything's built. So that's going against expenses."

"What we're forgetting is the likely sales rate," Alex said. "I've seen big developments like this before. If Edgewater Estates was beside another established development, it might sell quickly because people can see the idea works. But up here, in the middle of nowhere, with nothing to compare with, they likely will be reluctant to dive in. And that makes everything worse as time drags on."

"Of course. And even worser case: say after a year or two, you drive around and see maybe seven or eight houses built. You think it's a ghost town. You turn around and leave."

"Exactly. Meanwhile, they're bleeding cash. And they keep bleeding until the sales rate picks up—if it ever does. And no bank is going to bridge finance that."

"OK but they'll have stuff up and running," I pointed out. "The golf course, the restaurant."

"There's just not that much gravy in operating profit. Golf courses? Real thin margins. Lots are losing money. Restaurants and bars? Most fail in five years. A medical clinic and grocery store with hardly any-one to treat or feed? They're money losers too."

I'll admit it. The torrent of numbers even with dollar signs in front of them had caused me to glaze over.

But not Alex. She was positively humming as she rattled off the numbers.

"Bottom line it for me, will ya?" I asked.

"That's my point. There *is* no bottom line. I just can't see any way they can make a go of it. While they're guaranteeing Madoff-type returns on the REIT in this day and age, they're fucked in the capital budget and fucked in their operating budget."

"God, you're beautiful when you speak accounting."

"And I haven't even figured out the money to build those five blocks of lakefront condos."

"Five?" I said.

"These," She said as she unfolded the map that was part of her sales package. It was mighty familiar, the same map I had originally been sent. Except it wasn't.

"Here," she said, indicating the five beige rectangles, three on the east shoreline and two around the corner on the south shore. On my goddamned land. Where the retirement and nursing homes were supposed to be going. There was a legend. A beige box was marked 'Lakeside Condos.'

I took out my map. The beige legend box was there but only for the three blocks on the east side. The old and the old-old folks buildings were in mauve on my map.

"So they updated the map." Alex said.

"Doubtful. These two blocks—the ones they want my land for—are for a retirement and a government-subsidized nursing home. It's the only basis for expropriation—imminent domain in Yankee terms."

I looked at her package. On the back of the fancy embossed folder, in the top right corner, someone had hand-written "US" in pencil.

"Alex, did you get a pitch on the condos?"

"Yeah."

"Did they call them retirement villas or assisted living or some such shit like that?"

"No, just condos. But they could've just been fudging. Nothing personal and you may find this hard to believe, but not a lot of Americans want to retire to Canada. They might vacation or invest here, but, they're heading south, not north for their sunset years. I mean, do you guys even get sun up here in the winter?"

"As a matter of fact, we don't. Stops our igloos from melting."

Alex returned to running numbers, assuming three blocks of condos, an assisted-living home and a government-subsidized nursing home. She took a conservative occupancy rate of 30% in the first year, 60% in the second. She set up a separate column for the nursing home whose monthly rents were government-controlled and whose costs were higher for nurses, doctors, medical equipment.

While she was doing that calculating, I dozed off on the couch. She gently shook me awake and led me to bed.

"If you believe this deal can make money, then I got some swampland in Florida...." she said as I drifted off again.

I don't dream much. Not that I recall. Except the one and only time when I tried to quit smoking and took Champix. Every night a bunch of very strange movies played in my head—the kind that make *Mars Attacks!* look like a documentary. I gave up trying to give up smoking but I got another prescription for Champix anyway, just to see how my elaborate films ended (p.s. Thanks to me, the aliens lose. You're welcome).

On this night, I dreamt. I was chest deep in brackish marshy water. Reeds all around me, water lilies hanging off me. It was steaming hot. I woke up with a jolt just as I was watching a log float towards me. A log with two eyes and a big mouthful of teeth.

CHAPTER 20

"**S**onofabitch!" I said to the utter darkness.

"What?" Alex said, apparently not all that pleased at being abruptly awakened for the second night in a row.

"Swampland! They are selling swampland!" I said.

"I proved that to you last night. Try to keep up, old man. They just can't make money off this."

"They can if they're selling the same thing twice!"

"Want to let me in on your, for want of a better word, thinking?"

I sat up, completely awake.

"You're right if they were selling then building just one thing," I said. "But what if they're selling the same thing over and over again? Take a lakeside condo. That's one sale, say to an American client. 400 grand, g'day. Now they turn around and sell the same unit to a Canadian. G'day, another 400K. Or they rent it out annually as a retirement villa—you get first and last months."

But why stop there, I thought.

"And then they also start renting it out as a weekly vacation rental. Now look at the houses. Say somebody hires them to build the house. You pay 100% of the land, then at least 30% of the building cost as a deposit with the construction company."

"That they own," Alex added.

"That they own. And at the same time, the same house gets sold to six to ten other people who want in on a fractional ownership deal. And on top of that, you wait a bit—maybe sometime this fall—and you flog the same house as a weekly vacation rental but into a whole different market. Christ, people arrange summer cottage rentals a year or more in advance. They'd snap them up at maybe five or six thousand a week for the log mansions. Hell, while you're at it, why not rent the same prime week for the same house a bunch of times to different people? They'll never know. They're not ever going to see the reservation schedule.

"You rent it on a weekly basis to Joe Schmo looking for a Kawartha family vacation. Before I bought south, I rented houses in Mexico and the DR through VRBO or Flipkey or Airbnb. You have to send in 50% right away to hold your reservation. How many houses?"

"180."

"So say they don't use the big rental companies and list only on their site or take out a few ads. 180 houses times what?—twelve decent weeks of summer—that's more than 2000 weeks."

"2,160," Alex said.

"Show-off! 2,160 available weeks times the deposit you send—half of five thousand a week—...is..."

"Just over $10 million."

"Now, assume you rent the same week for the same house to three different families. That's 30 mill in deposits up front. Meanwhile, you rent the condos the same way. 300 condos times twelve weeks times half of a house rental, let's say two thousand bucks a week rent is... three and half million. And. *And*. They rent that same week say, three times, and you got another ten million."

I'm on a roll now.

"But they can also rake more in on top of multiple sales. Why not organize an investor roadshow to the US, and pitch a select bunch of hedge funds and private equity firms on buying shares in the whole development? You've got deposit cheques, sales contracts; you've got letters of commitment; you've got rental money to show them. And you've even got the goddamned government behind it. A solid investment made even better by the shitty Canadian dollar."

"But think, Jake. Everybody's gonna find out."

"Sure they will. But not for a while. That's the key. Stewie even said they weren't doing any mass marketing. Part of—what he'd call it?—the fuckin' panache. Discrete. Only for high wealth. Any sales guy can buy lists. They can find rich pricks who only invest in healthcare. Or rich pricks who invest in golf courses, or REITs. Retirement age rich pricks. You just have to be sure to keep everybody separate for a while. A few more months at most."

"The fuckers!"

The obvious finally dawned on me.

"What if they don't intend to build anything? Like, ever?" I wondered.

"What?"

"We're all just believing them when they say they're going to do this."

"But aren't they actually working on the roads and the golf course right now?" Alex said.

"Big noisy machinery can make it seem like there's a whole lot going on. But really, how much does it cost to hire a bulldozer and a couple of guys with chainsaws for a few weeks?"

"They got big expenses so far but they're peanuts compared to what they're collecting, say over the next four or five months. They paid for all the consultants' reports to council; they'll pay out the first year REIT; they give you your 10% down payment, office space in Toronto, salaries, legal fees, printing and the rest. What's all that worth?"

"Maybe ten mill?"

"But meanwhile they're going to be taking in cash. Lots of it."

"How much?"

"Millions more than their costs."

It was 5:30 and there was no way we could get back to sleep. We kinda paced for a bit, all nervous until Alex settled us down.

"You make coffee; I'll run some more numbers," Alex said.

I agreed to this fair division of labour. While I was banging around the kitchen I could hear Alex.

"Fuckers!" she said over and over again after she'd been calculating for a while.

"Whaddya got?" I asked.

"Rough guess: the worst case is—if for whatever reason nothing sells all that well—twenty-five million, mainly from the lot sales and vacation rentals."

"And best case?"

"About one twenty-five. *Clear.*"

Alex stared at the screen, shaking her head.

"I don't get it," she said. "It's not like they're doing all this in secret. Everybody knows who's involved. What do they do when it unravels?"

I thought a bit.

"You know, that could be the easiest part," I said. "There can't be that many people who actually know what's going on. All the money is likely getting parked in their mother corp in the Caymans or some other tax haven as it's coming in. When they've hauled in as much as they can then it's just one more expense: a few one-way tickets to Paraguay or another non-extradition country and it's gone, baby, gone."

"So who's going to Paraguay? Stewie?" Alex asked.

"Maybe. But I'm sure he's just the front man. There's gotta be others. For sure, this Stavros."

"I just can't believe the balls it takes to pull this off," said Alex shaking her head again.

"A con only works if it seems real."

"Maybe this is all just too outrageous. Maybe we've talked ourselves into it by running our numbers in a bubble."

"Meaning?"

"Meaning why don't we go check out the progress? Maybe it's all legit."

I grabbed my keys and headed for the door.

"How far is it?" Alex asked.

"A good mile."

"Oh for Christ's sake! How about using your legs?"

"Like a sucker?"

"Like a sucker."

It actually was a nice walk. Warm breeze, all sorts of dappling going on through the canopy of maples, birches, and elms. We even held hands. Like I said, it was nice.

Reaching the site, I saw a bunch of changes had been made over the weeks since the grand opening extravaganza. The stage was gone, along with the fucking bunting, streamers and oom-pah band. A tall chain link fence with a high locked gate had replaced the low cow gate across the driveway. No cops, no polite protesters to be seen.

And no workers or cars either, even though it was after nine. There was a small construction trailer just inside the fence and in the distance there was one of those highway road graders and a bulldozer. Both were yellow, motionless and quiet.

"Look," I said, "unless there's a construction holiday—like Bob the Builder's birthday—I'd say we were right. There's fuck-all going on here."

"Let's go take a look around," Alexandra said.

"At what?"

"Oh, c'mon."

I can barely climb an eight-inch stair so scaling the eight-foot high fence was just not on; although I'm pretty sure Alex could have done it without breaking a sweat. Instead, we plunged into the bush on the side of the security fence hoping to find a gap in the links. But there were no gaps. Because there was no fence. It ended about ten yards into the thick underbrush and we just walked around it.

Standing on the gouged landscape, we were enveloped by an eerie silence. You heard the flapping of the orange plastic streamers tacked to the tops of their surveying stakes. And that's about it. No birds, certainly no sounds of human activity. We checked out the trailer first. Peering in the widows, we could see it was completely empty, nary a desk or chair or even a calendar featuring large breasts.

We trudged towards the yellow machinery. It was impossible not to notice new weedlings growing in the ruts and scraped earth. As we drew up to the grader we saw that it had been freshly spray-painted. All over. Normally black hydraulic lines, a blade which should have been worn silver, even the windows and the ground around it. Everything. All yellow. Same for the bulldozer.

"Well, fuck," Alex said.

"Can I borrow your phone?" I asked.

"Someday, you cheap Canadian bastard, you're going to get your own."

I punched in the number, putting the thing on speaker.

"Stewie! How the fuck are you? It's Jake. Just checking in. Everything going well?"

"Just great!" he said, matching my enthusiasm.

"You're sure now? I'm standing here at about, I think, the 14th tee. I'm no golfer but the course doesn't seem to be quite playable yet."

"That's your fault we had to stop."

"Oh, horseshit it is!"

There was a pause.

"And I understand we've also had a brief delay in some construction financing," he said. "Pretty standard on these big projects. But with us taking over your land, all systems will be go."

"Well, that's a relief to hear, Stewie ol' pal. I was a bit worried that this whole goddamned thing was one big fucking scam and with any luck you're going to spend the next twenty fucking years in jail, you fucking fuck conman fucktard, you! I'm hanging up now. Bye!"

And I punched the Off button as hard as I could.

"You really are a big child, aren't you?" Alex said.

"Am not, ya poopyhead."

"So what now?"

I think we head home and batten down the hatches. I'm no meteorol-ogist—but there's probably a shitstorm a-comin'."

CHAPTER 21

If I'd paid a little more attention to those doomsday prepper shows, I could've mapped out a survival plan. Maybe whipped up a service-able bomb shelter, stocked it with bottled water and rows of dehydrated food pouches. Then I'd surround it with those great spools of razor wire I always kept handy for exactly this kind of end-of-the-world-as-I-know-it scenario.

Instead, we paced around inside and out for a bit.

"Alex, we gotta tell somebody else."

"Who?"

"The cops, for starters. Ontario Securities Commission. Consumer and Corporate Affairs. Somebody."

"And exactly how do you think we prove a crime?" she asked. "My math on a napkin? And even if we could set off alarm bells, how long do you think it'd take to investigate? Months, I bet."

"And meanwhile, Stewie's thumbing his nose at us from his new *finca* outside Montevideo."

There was something truly frustrating about witnessing what amounted to a slow-motion smash and grab, even though we're all getting used to watching governments and companies do it.

"Time to shine a light," I announced.

I dialed Steve. [Technically, of course, that's not accurate as nobody dials anymore. But nobody punches in numbers either]

"I was just about to call you," he said. "I found Stavros!"

"That's great! And…?"

"I found him. That's all you asked."

"What'd you do, punch him on the shoulder and shout 'Tag. You're it!'?"

"More of a light tap."

"Stop fucking around. You swear you found him?"

"Yup."

"Lemme guess—10 Mercer Street."

"Fuck off!"

"Second floor?"

"Ha! Third."

"Did you talk to him?"

"Yes. It took a while to get him to agree to do the interview. He started off by telling me to call his lawyers."

"Traynor-Veitch?"

"That's the guys."

"You could've just walked down the stairs. Their offices are right below his."

"Well, aren't you the smarty trousers?"

"Did you get him to talk?" I asked.

"Well of course I did. That's what I do. I told him I liked any story about a guy making a comeback, rehabbing the ol' reputation with a high-end project. Class all the way, that kind of bullshit. He said he'd think about it. Then he called me back and got all co-operative."

Steve described going to his office in the non-descript brick building on Mercer.

"He insisted he couldn't do it until around eight last night. It was just Stavros and an admin assistant. Nice digs, lots of leather, dark oak, all understated, classy. Group of Seven prints on the wall. Christ, maybe they were originals, how was I supposed to know?"

"Could we skip the local colour?"

"Alright, alright. He was skittish at first, real guarded. But I turned on the Golding charm. Actually, he seemed waaaay impressed by me— what with my book. I saw it on his desk."

"OK, now could we skip the jerking yourself off part?"

"Geez, buzzkill. Anyway, he warmed up and then positively glowed when he got talking about this integrated offering he was spearhead-ing. The wave of the future, he claimed. Rich and semi-rich people setting up their own enclaves. Tasteful, discrete, self-contained, safe, back to nature, blah, blah."

Steve described Stavros' excitement over what he called the business model of the future in retirement living where mid- to high-wealth retirees had access to every lifestyle choice you could imagine. All to fill a need. A need that perpetuated itself as people aged. Big house got to be too much for you? Move to a condo. Health failing? Move out of the condo and into the nursing home.

"You could waltz through the last forty years of your life in the same neighbourhood," I said. "I'm a little surprised that they don't have their own cemetery."

"Oh, I'm sure that's coming," Steve said.

Mirroring this no-fuss aging was a parent company with the slew of subsidiaries I had found. Even though I was positive they were all bogus, they sure looked smart on paper. Separate companies—for the golf course, the restaurant, the rentals, construction, property management, the medical centre, sales. Multiple revenue streams flowing into the main holding company.

"Did you ask to see his financials?" I asked.

"Of course, but he said no. I expected that. Private company and all."

"So did you get anything besides being snowed?"

"Well, all the stuff you sent me, all the company connections, he pretty well confirmed all of it."

"And all on the record?"

"Yup....No, wait. He didn't want me talking about Kawartha Klear. Said he wasn't ready to launch that."

"What the hell is that?"

"Bottled water. He called it craft water"

"Jesus H. Christ! This bastard thought of everything."

I told him about the permit allowing him to draw hundreds of thousands of gallons from the lake supposedly to water the golf course.

"OK, did he talk about setting aside houses or condos for weekly vacation rentals?" I asked.

"No. The closest thing to that was setting up a small system for the fractional ownership to put the few leftover weeks they can't use into a pool."

"But nothing about hundreds of one-off rentals?"

"No."

"See any travel brochures lying around for Paraguay?"

"What?"

"Nuthin', Steve. Oh, except for the fact it's all a scam. Every last fuckin' bit of it. One gigantic elaborate fraud."

I laid it out. As I babbled on, I didn't know how much sense I was making. But that happens a lot these days.

"Holy shit!" Steve said. "This can't happen. What do we do?"

"Hmmm...lemme think. Oh, I know. How about you stop being a fucking celebrity, get your skinny ass off the laurels and go back to being a reporter again?"

"You *are* a dick. But send me what you got."

"Deal."

"Wait a minute! I'm not too sure I should spend a minute chasing something based on your math."

"Alexandra did all the cipherin.' Her, you can trust."

"You know, there's one thing I don't get. If it's all bullshit, why would Stavros even talk to me?"

"You guys belong to Post Media now. He probably guessed this might wind up in the financial section of the *National Post*. He has to double down, not hide. It takes real stones but he needs some reputable positive press so he can get to sell all his so-called 'offerings' as fast as he can. The whole thing hangs on that happening."

"Hit quick and get out."

"In a way, it's genius. Must've taken years to plan out."

"You talked to anybody else?" he asked.

"Sorry, Scoop. Already did an interview with the *Ontario Hinterland Daily*."

"Arsehole."

"Can you keep me out of this?" I asked.

"Oh, sure, I'll tell my editor that the idea of chasing down a land swindle in the fuckin' boonies just hit me like a thunderbolt out of left field. I *gotta* mention you, dude."

"Alright, alright. but I'm counting on you downplay me."

"Pitch it like you're a drunken idiot savant who stumbled onto it? That kind of thing?"

"Exactly! Just like you did last summer. Serious now, give me your best guess—based on you rubbing up against all those nasty people on the crime beat for years: Do you think Stavros is capable of murder?"

"Whoa! You're sure now that those two councilors were whacked?"

"Looks more and more like it. To me, anyway. There's tens of millions of dollars at stake."

"Then you've answered your own question. Push comes to shove, for that kinda cash, just about anybody is capable."

CHAPTER 22

It took hours for Alex to enter everything into spread sheets, all sorts of best case/worst case scenarios for each element of the alleged development. I'd be passed out over the keyboard from boredom and/ or fatigue if I had to puke out all that math. Plus I still haven't figured out how to set up a spreadsheet.

But she was a keener, obviously having entered a new plane of existence, an ethereal place where numbers and dollar signs and 'what ifs' collide to produce model after model of how much the fuckers could be raking in.

As it was, I tired pretty quickly of entering all the connected numbered companies Stavros had set up. I looked up from my raft of post-it notes that laid out the corporate octopus.

"I don't understand why they'd set up all these separate companies, if they were just planning to take the money and run."

Alexandra considered my point.

"It's not that big a deal to register them, maybe an afternoon's work. Then they have this solid-looking structure for anybody who's asking. Plus they can move money around pretty easily because it's all owned by one holding company. And I wouldn't be surprised if they're already shopping shares to private equity investors."

"Makes sense. So whatcha got?" I asked her

"I added in the bottled water scheme and figured as many variables as I could: standard initial uptake, occupancy rates…currency fluctuations, interest rates—"

"—Wind speed, tides, curvature of the earth, yeah, yeah. How much?"

"It's a big range but minimum *net:* 38 million, maximum: 165, give or take."

"Canadian?"

"US….You know what kills me?"

"What?"

"A little modesty, some scaled-back plans, and this development could actually make some money."

"On top of that," I added, "it was real decent looking. It's almost a shame."

Rather than send Steve e-reams of tables Alex summarized the info in a few spreadsheets and I wrote a narrative of sorts that Alex edited the shit out of.

We basked a bit in having the thing done and sent, but then a listlessness set in. This wasn't the instant gratification of painting a room or planting some shrubs. All we had done was set invisible wheels in motion, nothing more. No timetable, no guaranteed outcome.

Around noon, we had a visitor. It was Jerry Glavin, Stewie's bulldog of a site operations and security guy. He was maybe 5 foot 8, in either direction, more than 250 pounds. His bull neck bulged over his tightly buttoned white shirt the way fat rolls spill over a pug's neck. His military-type buzz cut did not do his fleshy face any favours.

"Mr. Woodson would—" he started to say.

"—Who?"

"…Stewie would like to talk to you."

"Pretty sure I don't need to talk to him."

"That's not my concern. My concern is getting you into that car in that driveway," he said, pointing at the dark blue Shield Security Lincoln. "And I like my odds," he added.

I sized him up while he sized me up. I'm taller but I'm blubbery-er and a hell of a lot older. I liked his odds too.

"Just a second," I said.

I went back inside and told Alex I was expected.

"Are you nuts?" she asked.

"Three people—you, me, and Steve—know we're onto something," I whispered. "They can't possibly have a clue. I'm sure Stewie just wants to lean on me a bit more."

"Don't tip your hand."

Looking back, my getting into Glavin's car may have been the height of idiocy. But in my defence: all we had been doing was collecting public information and then applying some private speculation. I figured Stewie was just pulling another good old-fashioned dick-flopping power play that reminded me of my corporate days which were filled with all kinds of palace intrigue and the maneuvering of kids in suits displaying all the dynamics of a nursery school recess.

"Mr. Woodson would like to buy you lunch," Glavin said as we started up.

"I'm not hungry."

"Eat. Don't eat. It's not my concern," Glavin said as we passed the Angler Arms.

"Where are we going?" I asked as nonchalantly as I could while inside I was feeling some panic.

"Buckhorn."

I breathed a silent sigh of relief as we did, indeed, turn south at the main road towards civilization and not north towards coniferous fuck-allness.

We didn't say another word as we drove to the Buckhorn Lodge. It was a glorious day and I wondered—because Stewie was paying—if the restaurant served lobster.

Stewie was on the patio overlooking the water.

"Who the Christ is that guy?" I asked as Glavin receded.

"We hired Shield Security. Standard practice for a big project. Mr. Glavin is extremely useful."

"You could've just called."

"I need your undivided attention."

"For what?"

"Jake, we can't have you going around calling this development—what was the word you used?—a fucking scam."

"I agree. I apologize," I said in full milquetoast mode.

My folding up like origami took Stewie aback.

"Look. I'm not real happy about what you're doing to me," I said. "But I do understand libel and slander laws."

"Good. I'm glad we got that out of the way. But tell me—I'm curious—why did you call it a scam?"

No time to hesitate, Jake. And I didn't, piping up instantly: "Just a word I grabbed. You know, I was angry. I could've just as easily called it a shit show or clown job or clusterfuck or—"

"—Alright, alright. I get the idea," Stewie said, looking mollified. "Let's get back to our current situation, shall we?"

"Let's do have a drink first, shall we?"

As he had originally claimed, Stewie was a patient man. He had a bemused look on his face as I ordered and waited for my double spicy tequila Caesar with a beer.

"To recap," he finally said after my first sip, "Being the lone hold-out you've managed to piss off a lot of people. Once the expropriation goes through—and it will—you'll lose anyway. And all you would've accomplished is to delay us three or four, maybe five months. During that time, money doesn't flow, jobs don't start, and winter'll be coming on. Folks around here aren't going to forget that. If you want to stay in the neighbourhood, I guarantee you your life will not be pleasant."

I hadn't really looked ahead but—damn it—Stewie had.

"Jake, I'm holding all the cards; you know that, right?"

"I do."

"So why don't you do everybody—including yourself—a favour and just sign this? And we can all move on."

Stewie pushed a sheaf of papers across the table.

"You'll see we've upped our offer to 450," Stewie said.

"And I also see you want me out in a week," I said, flipping down to the closing date.

"We can't lose the construction season. We'll put you up here at the Lodge while you look for another place. And we'll pack you up and pay the storage costs for your stuff. It's all in there."

"I'm not signing shit without my lawyer reading it."

"I understand. I'll hear from you in, say, two days?"

"Gimme three," I said as I rose with him and we actually shook hands.

"You've made the right decision," he said.

"I haven't made a decision yet."

Stewie was unflustered. He waved to someone behind me.

"A little added incentive," he said as I turned to see Blair Odell walking up to our table. "You two gentlemen have lots to discuss. Order another beer. Put it on my tab."

Blair and I sat down as Stewie left.

"Well, isn't that just an amazing fucking coincidence that you're here to finish the tag team," I said.

"I'm staying here at the Lodge while all this gets sorted out. Stewie mentioned that he thought you might be receptive to a bit of a bonus."

"How much of a bonus?"

"150,000 dollars."

"That's a bit of a bonus alright. I'd like it in writing."

"Can't," he said without missing a beat. "If the other landowners who just sold get wind of this, we'll have some of the smaller ones up in arms. You have to trust me."

He didn't drop his gaze and I wondered if Sincere Staring 101 was taught at your better law schools.

We lapsed into thoughtful silence as we sipped our beer. Well, I didn't know if Odell was thinking about anything. He and Stewie had pretty well laid all their cards on the table. For all the paper and machinations, it was a simple deal. Sign on the dotted line, get paid, fuck off. I was starting to feel like it was too bad all of it was bullshit. 600K in my jeans and a lot less grief were pretty attractive right about then.

"Well," I announced as I drained my beer. "I've got some thinking and some lawyering to do."

As we shook hands, Blair said with a smile: "I may have mentioned this before, but there isn't much that can't be negotiated as long as the parties remain reasonable."

Jerry Glavin, the boulder with legs, materialized to drive me home.

We didn't chit-chat a lot on the return trip. I may have had something to do with that silence.

"So, Jerry, I understand you've really been driving around up here."

"Lots to see," he said, then turned to me. "Lots to learn," he added, his expression full of something that looked like menace.

Safely back home, I filled Alexandra in on the details of the lunch and my slight disappointment that all the paperwork, the offer, Blair's bonus, everything was all completely counterfeit.

"Do you think one or both of them are in on it?" she asked.

Her question stopped me.

"Ya know," I answered. "I don't think so. If it was all Monopoly money, why were they sort of nickel and diming me? Why didn't they offer something like a gazillion fake dollars to make sure I took the deal and went on my way?"

Steve called, telling us that the spreadsheets had convinced him something real shitty was up.

"Going back at Stavros?" I asked.

"Oh, I will, but not yet. I want to get my head around everything that's going on up there. Want a roommate for a few days? "

"Already got one. A whole lot prettier than you."

"Threesome?"

"You're a pretty classy fella."

"At least ask, will ya?"

Steve showed up the next morning while Alex and I were having coffee on the deck. We heard him long before we saw him.

"Ho-ly sh-it!" he yelled, turning three syllables into about eight.

We ran around to the front to see Steve rooted in his tracks and pointing wildly at the front steps.

"Snake! Big fuckin' snake! Right there!"

"It's harmless," I said. "It was probably more scared than you. If that's even possible."

"You ever heard of the Mississauga rattler? This is Mississauga Lake. See the connection?"

"That's Massassauga rattler, moron."

"Yeah, well. Fuckin' nature. That's all I have to say."

Turns out Steve was as uncomfortable in the wilds of lake country as I had become in the wilds of the city. He had spent a couple of weeks up here last summer, working on his exposé but he had confined himself to the Hovel for most of it, taking a break from writing by either running—ugh—on the roads or strong arming me into going to AA. No, wait, that was me strong arming him. He didn't drink anymore.

We settled Steve into the guest bedroom then we all took a walk to the construction site. Still quiet, still desolate. Steve took some pictures.

"Remember the good ol' days when they'd have to assign a photographer?" I asked.

"Call me fuckin' Karsh."

We had just returned when Carl came over.

We all repaired to our newly-established War Room, democratically located in the screened-in porch because three of the four of us smoked.

I hit the highlights of the scam with Carl. Maybe he was surprised but ol' poker face didn't betray any real reaction.

"Saw Preston Peterson in town. Said they had to take a break while the banks got their shit together. Blamed you too."

We spent the evening drinking and thinking about how to approach the whole she-bang.

It was nice to scan the room and see three of those closest to me all together in the same place. Bonus: they all got along. Alexandra knew Steve from years ago when she was a stock analyst for a big investment house which followed the company I worked for and Steve wrote about. After Alex got in a few chip shots on Steve for being a member of the fake news and he retaliated with a vampire squid reference, everything went swimmingly. And Carl? Well with Carl, all you had to do was make a logical case to him about the inherent weakness of a 3-4 defence in today's NFL—as Alex had—and you've got a friend for life.

"Up here, the only way into this scam is through Stewie," Steve said.

"You're not going to get much of anything from him," I said. "He's a pro at this."

"I'll break him."

"Well, you'll do it by yourself. I can't be there unless you want me to be the Greek chorus singing "Liar, liar, pant's on fire" after every answer."

"I'm doing all the interviews on my own. You can't be around."

"So what do I do?"

"I could use another soda," he said and then turned to Alex. "Do you mind going through all the numbers again?" Steve asked. "Be conservative."

While she was cipherin' away, Carl and I, between us, drew up a master list of all the major and minor players, looking up names, addresses and/or phone numbers and providing background info on the ones we knew.

I reckoned that Steve should hold off calling the obvious cases of conflict of interest—Mayor McQuaig, Councilors Dugald and Peterson and Environment guy Luc Dubois. Those chats should be in-person. But then I gave my head a shake. If we were right, there really might not be a conflict of interest because nobody was actually going to see any coin from their attempted abuse of power.

One by one, Steve called the numbers of the minor landowners we handed to him. Everybody wanted to talk about what a swell thing the Edgewater Estates project was and he scribbled furiously to catch their gushers.

The next morning, Steve was onto the politicians and Luc for interview times. Finally he tried to set up appointments with the four big "lottery winners" as he called them—Blair Odell, Derek Collins, Preston Peterson, and Terry Weston, Mary Ellen Conway's ex-douchebag. They all agreed except Derek Collins who wasn't answering. I realized I didn't know anything about Terry Weston but Carl kicked in that he was an odd jobs kinda guy who spent a fair amount of time either working around or drinking at the Buckhorn Lodge.

Steve then called all various and sundry government bureaucrats and, lastly, the township council—both the pros and the cons. The process went smoothly until he tried to arrange an interview with Mayor McQuaig. Wily politician that she was, she knew a set-up when she smelled one. She slammed the receiver down in Steve's ear.

"Glad I'm professionally trained to understand these non-verbal clues," Steve said with a big grin as he rubbed his ear. "That means she *really* wants to talk to me in person. So I'll just show up."

Over dinner that night—pan-fried rainbow trout, a Carl specialty— we didn't really talk about anything beyond the campaign to blow up the Edgewater scheme.

"What we need is actual proof that they've been double or triple selling," I pointed out. "Otherwise all we've got is a really good guess."

Alex jumped in. "And even then, they can just say: 'Oooops, guess we put a shitty deal together. My bad.' That may be dumb but it isn't a crime."

"For that," Steve said, "we've got to get any sales records. They had to write it all down somewhere."

"10 Mercer. That's the mother lode," Steve said.

"Think you can you get back in?" I asked.

"Maybe. I could go at him with: 'Mr. Stavros, sir, I understand how discrete you want to be, but what would really play with readers are quotes from a couple of happy buyers.' But I can't see him letting me wander around the office stealing paperwork."

"Up here, the records are either in the sales trailer or…"

"Stewie's house. Feel like a little B&E?" Steve asked.

"Sure, I understand that cat burglars reach their prime at sixty-one," I offered.

"You're sixty-one?" Alex said in mock horror. "You never told me that!"

"Daddy issues?" Steve said to her.

"What am I? Four months older than you, witch?" I said.

"So, to summarize: we've got all sorts of facts and figures and supposition that would add up to fuck all in a court of law," Steve said.

Steve's cell rang just then. It was a short conversation, ending with Steve saying "But Mr. Peterson, it's really impor—"

"Councilor Peterson just cancelled our interview," Steve said as he put his phone down.

"The Mayor must've got to him."

"So I guess I just turn up there too."

In a few minutes, P. Bradley Dugald called to nix his interview.

"Alex. Any chance you might be interested in some undercover work?" Steve suddenly asked.

"What did you have in mind?"

"Think you can go back to Toronto, to the sales office? Convince the sales guy that you're serious about buying, wave a cheque around. Tell him you just have to know what kind of people might wind up being your neighbours. Tell him all your rich Boston friends also have to know before they invest."

"And then what?"

"See what you can see. Maps, lot numbers, names, anything that looks like it overlaps."

I was getting all anxious about her being involved and I told him so. I also thought it was a long, long shot. But he was insistent.

"Here's a fact: sellers gotta sell," Steve said. "He won't give a rat's ass about privacy and such. If he thought that giving Alex a few names would help close her, he will."

"I'll do it," Alex announced, looking, shall we say, somewhat peeved at my paternalism.

Carl, who had been watching us, got up.

"Gettin' late, folks. Time to turn in," he said and left.

We called it quits soon after that, although you could tell Steve was still jacked with a reporter's zeal that should be precious to us all.

In bed that night, I repeated my concern to Alex.

"Babe, you don't have to do this."

"Shush. It'll be fun."

"I want to go with you."

"You can't be seen anywhere near this. I'm a hot prospect to them; you're the enemy."

"I'll wait in the car."

"And do exactly what if something is happening inside?"

"I dunno. Be there."

"Relax. What's the guy going to do? Attack me in the office?"

CHAPTER 23

Carl turned up early the next morning. That wasn't real surprising as he often stopped in for coffee before he started on his dizzying list of outdoor jobs for the day. What did catch me off guard was the sheaf of papers he carried.

"Mebbe this'll help," he said as he dumped them all on the table.

I quickly sifted through them. There were maps of sections of the development with lots marked, some shaded as 'Sold,' sales contracts, contact names, and addresses.

"How...?" I asked looking up from treasure trove.

"Couldn't sleep last night so I went explorin' for a bit."

"Where?"

"Sales office."

"But how—"

"Might not know much, I guess, but I do know how cheap them locks are on trailers. Used to live in one. And I know how to run a photocopier."

"I could kiss you!" Steve said.

"You might want to reconsider that," Carl warned.

Alex called to make an appointment in Toronto. I gave her a hard time for using the phone in the Hovel.

"Roaming charges are killing me," she said in her defence.

Steve and I spent the afternoon mapping out the story he'd been given the go-ahead by his editor to write. She insisted, however, that the piece needed a lot more than buyers and politicians. She wanted the "before" picture first, a straight-ahead portrait of the development, its plans, future prospects, reactions from politicians, the landowners, and the 'ol man in the street viewpoint.

The basic idea was that he collect all the local perspective, add in what Stavros had given him, then unravel the scam with our proof and call everybody back for their reaction.

"And if we don't turn up the evidence?" I asked.

"Then we got squat. No choice but to turn it all over to whoever investigates this kind of thing and wait for them to blow it up. All this stuff I got will have to be kept on the backburner until then."

"That could be months," I said. "And meanwhile, they keep scamming and, oh, I lose my house."

"Sorry, dude. What can I tell you? That's the way this whole evidence thing works."

Alex left early the next morning for her appointment at the sales office in Toronto and Steve headed out to start his interviews.

I had the day to myself and I couldn't think of a goddamned thing I wanted to do beyond pacing anxiously.

Alex finally called mid-afternoon.

"Where are you?" I asked. "I was worried."

"Well, don't be," she said and there was a slight but unmistakable hint of annoyance in her voice.

"You're just not used to my particular brand of chauvinism/paternal-ism/sexism, are you?" I said.

"And you should know, I don't ever intend to get used to it either."

"Fair enough. But just to be clear: you oughtta accept the fact that I always want you to be OK all the time."

"Fair enough," she said, her voice getting all warm again. "Just coming up on Buckhorn, babe. Should be there in twenty min—Hold on! There's an idiot—FUCK! —"

There was the sickening shriek of crumpling metal above her cry.

Her phone went dead.

CHAPTER 24

"Accident! South of Buckhorn!" I yelled at the 9-1-1 operator before rushing out the door and fishtailing onto the highway as fast as the Vibe could manage while still keeping all four tires on the road. I blew through the town, laying on my ridiculously meek horn. My heart was pounding but there was little thought beyond "She has to be alright! She has to be alright!"

Rounding a wide bend, I could see the police lights of two cruisers and an ambulance on the right shoulder of the half-mile long causeway dividing two lakes. Alex's red Malibu was in the water to my right, its ass end sticking out at a 45 degree angle, its windshield half-submerged. Farther down the road I saw another cop car parked behind a green sedan.

Massive, massive relief to see Alex wrapped in a blanket standing by the ambulance.

I skidded to a stop, ran to the scene, evaded one cop and hugged her. She was wet and shivering and her eyes were far away.

"I'm fine, Jake. Fine," she said.

"Ma'am, ma'am," a paramedic insisted. "You *have* to go to hospital."

At once, Alex's eyes focused.

"I said I was fine!" she snapped.

"Check her out, buddy," I said. "But I think the lady's right."

"Jake," she whispered. "Get the papers from the car. Front seat."

Reluctantly, I left her as the two EMTs ran through their tests. A cop yelled at me as I was scrambling down the bank and into the water.

"Gotta get the papers! It's a rental!" I shouted over my shoulder, firmly believing—well, hoping—they wouldn't follow or shoot me in the back.

I was waist-deep in no time and slogging through the soft mud of the lake bottom. The driver side door was open but the seats were underwater. I plucked a couple of sheets of paper that were floating above the dash and then reached down to the glove compartment to retrieve the plastic packet from the rental company.

Dripping wet, I rejoined Alex and the first responders just as they were reporting the results of their field tests.

"No sign of shock, blood pressure's fine, no concussion, she's focused, nothing broken," a paramedic said. "But she should see a doctor, get X-rays."

"She will, she will," I answered.

Two cops who had been hovering closed in.

"Just a few questions, ma'am."

"Ma'am! Ma'am! Ma'am! What the fuck ever happened to 'Miss'?" Alex wanted to know and I had to smile.

"Just tell us what happened," the other cop said, notebook at the ready.

Without a trace of hesitancy, Alex recounted the incident. As she came out of a bend, she saw a big, black pick-up on the shoulder of her side of the road. As she slowed and swung out a bit to pass it, the truck had suddenly accelerated and pulled onto the asphalt. Alex was now fully in the opposite lane. She floored it but the truck sped up too, running right alongside her. She looked ahead and saw an oncoming car. She stood on the brakes but the truck's driver had anticipated that and did the same. Trapped on one side and facing a guaranteed-fatal head-on, her only choice was accelerate again, leave the road, and drop the car into the lake.

"Did you get a license number?" one cop asked.

"No."

"Did you see the driver?"

"Not a good look. The truck was all jacked up so I was staring at his door. Young guy, I think. Ball cap, that's about it."

"Make of the truck?"

"No idea."

"Anything else you can tell us about the accident?"

"Accident?" I said. "Broad daylight. Sunny, dry road, and a truck *accidentally* runs Alex into the lake? Are you fucking kidding me?"

"That's enough of that," a policeman cautioned.

"If it wasn't an accident, do you have any idea why someone would want to hurt you?" the other cop asked.

"I'm a tourist. No. No idea at all."

"Mad—I mean Miss—you'll have to come in for a full report," said the other.

"Can it wait? She needs to rest first. OK?" I said.

They relented and let us go, after we took their business cards and swore we'd be at the Apsley OPP detachment before noon the next day.

We didn't say much for a long while as I was carefully driving back to the lake. Alex stared out the window.

"You say 'I told you so' and it's you who's going to the hospital," she said finally. "P.S. I'm not kidding."

"Got it."

She pried apart the sodden papers I'd rescued from the car.

"Motherfucker!" she said. "Can't read most of it!"

"Don't worry about that shit right now, OK?"

"I damn well will worry. All this had better be worth something."

We lapsed into silence again.

"I can remember the names. I got seven of them," she said as we pulled into the driveway.

She declined my drink offer, changed into sweats and went right to bed. I tucked her in after nagging her into vowing that she had no headache, that the bumps and bruises she'd received were hurting less.

Our eyes locked and there was no mistaking the sense of shared relief that she was safe. Shaken up, but safe.

I kissed her on the forehead as I fussed with the blankets.

"Jake. How would anyone know I'd be on that road at that time?" she asked.

"No idea, babe."

"And how would they know what I was driving?"

"Get some sleep."

As I was pulling the curtains closed, she asked one more question.

"Jake. They'll find this guy, right?"

"Of course, they will. They probably already have," I said with the same fake conviction I'd used on Halley when she was a child to assure her the Tooth Fairy was on her way.

"Sleep now."

I got a beer and sat in the kitchen, fully understanding that she—we—had been incredibly lucky.

And that I didn't have the answers to any of her questions.

Steve didn't show up until it was almost dark. He was bubbling with excitement over finishing up his interviews and taking a bunch of pictures to illustrate his piece. I immediately killed his enthusiasm with news of Alex's wreck.

"Holy shit!" he said.

"Shhh, she's sleeping."

"Holy shit," he whispered.

We sat on the deck, watched the last of the sunset in silence. I was angry with Steve for his idea to have Alex spy on the sales office. And he knew it.

"Look, bud. I'm sorry but she agreed to do it," he said.

"Did you ever think that just maybe she agreed because she's nice, because she wanted to help?"

"Yeah, but—"

"—And that just maybe she had no idea of the possible danger?"

Silence again.

"I don't think any of us saw this coming. We're close, Jake. The crash proves we're close."

"Jesus, we better wrap this up soon," I said.

"We will. Lemme tell you about what happened today."

Steve described his interviews starting with Stewie. Likely acting on Stavros' green light, Stewie had slipped into hyper-sales mode and rambled on interminably about the development until it assumed the proportion of Speer's plans for post-war Berlin.

"He didn't seem nervous or anything?" I asked.

"No. Why?"

"What happened to Alex. It happened up here but it must've started down there. And that means they're on to us."

"Who's on to us?" Steve asked.

"I don't know. Doesn't seem like Stewie. From what you said, he sounded way too calm."

"Maybe he's just good at this."

Steve went on to describe how he had ambushed the Mayor in her lair, describing her as reserved and more than a little cranky.

"But she said all the right things," Steve said. "Sometimes using the exact same phrases as Stewie had about the benefits Edgewater Estates would bring."

"Anything odd about your chat?"

Other than threatening me if I wrote a negative piece?"

"Yeah."

"She asked where I was staying."

"And you said…?"

"That I was just up for the day and going back."

"And then she said…?"

"She offered to comp me a room at the Buckhorn Lodge."

"Did you flat out accuse her of conflict of interest?"

"Nary a word. Same with Dugald."

"You saw him?"

"Yeah. He tried to beg off at the front door. I guess he's as afraid of the old grey mayor as much as you are. But I flattered the shit out of him about how great his writing is and he started yakking. And yakking. And yakking."

"Anything of value?"

"Not really, He described his switching votes, took some pride in being the "saviour" of the project, as he saw it. He did 'fess up about owning a slice of land which in his mind only proved he was darn smart. He described his holding as "insubstantial" and then—get this—he invited me to look around his house and then tell him if I thought he was hurting for money."

"What about the big landowners?"

"One for four at the plate. Collins wasn't at his place. But that fuckin' dog was. I didn't spend a lot of time wandering around. Peterson wasn't home either. I talked to one of his boys, said the old man wasn't coming back for a long time, oh, and would I mind getting the fuck off their land. Blair Odell wasn't at the Lodge; he checked out and, I guess, went back to Toronto so I'll catch up with him there. I did talk to Terry Weston."

"And?"

"Like Carl said, he was at the lodge. He's a handyman of sorts. Said he was also a fishing guide—part-time—and I think a more or less a full-time lush."

"Not that there's anything wrong with that."

"Not that there's anything wrong with that. But judging from his thousand-yard stare and all the broken blood vessels in his face and his shaky hands, I'd say he loves the high-test. Oh, and he had three double rum and cokes on me while I talked to him."

"What'd he tell you about his land?"

"Bought it years ago dirt cheap. Always wanted to open a hunting and fishing camp but said he never got around to it. Said he might do it now somewhere else when he got the million bucks from the sale."

"Did he mention his son?"

"No."

"Overall?"

"Put it this way: I was completely surprised when I asked his age for the article and he said twenty-seven. He looks just as torn down as you."

"That bad, huh?"

"That bad. But I think what you see is what you get. If he isn't officially the town drunk yet, he's got a good shot at the next election. But he seemed harmless enough. Not exactly care-free, but he just doesn't appear to give a shit about anything beyond the life he has. And he doesn't seem to care too much about that either. I don't know if I'll use it because it's such a fucking cliché, but the only time he brightened up was when I asked him about his background and all he wanted to talk about were his glory days as the local high school quarterback."

I climbed into bed as quietly as I could. Wordlessly—and perhaps unconsciously—Alex wriggled her back into me. I fell asleep with my arm around her.

When I awoke, she was gone.

I found her in the kitchen, cooking bacon and looking impossibly cheery to a man without a goddamned cup of coffee in his hand.

"How are you, darlin'?" I asked.

"A little sore. No worse than a hot yoga class. Look on the kitchen table," she said after we kissed and after I had the aforementioned goddamned cup of coffee in my hand.

On the table, I found a piece of paper with a hand-written list on it:

Jack and Doreen Wexler, Pittsburgh 4A

Jerry Zimmer, Cleveland 6A?

Bill and Rose Tuckey, Boston 8A

Barbara Bushmill, New Rochele 3B

? and ? Orpen, Bristol 5B

Kurt and Anna Jaeger, Monmouth 6C

Donald and ? Applegate, Columbus 5C

"I picked a lot—4B—and asked who would be around me," she explained. "Salesman didn't even hesitate to cough them up. I could still read bits of their names and a general idea of the map on the soaked paper you rescued."

"You, my dear, are a fucking marvel. Where's the stuff Carl brought?"

"In the living room."

"Well, let's get at it!"

"Already did," she said, looking ridiculously calm.

"And? C'mon, c'mon!"

"Four matches!"

"Four?"

"Four Canadians were sold the same lots. Copies of their sales contracts are right there."

"Good god almighty, we got 'em!"

"Not yet. We have to check them all. Make sure they actually bought and weren't just listed as 'maybes.' But first, we eat."

Over a swell breakfast featuring bacon stacked like cordwood, we planned our day. First, we had to deal with the car rental company. It was just past eight. I cleaned up listening to Alex on my phone as she went medieval on their ass—accidents happen—police report coming—airbag didn't deploy—imagine the lawsuit—never mind the publicity—any way to treat an American tourist?—By tomorrow?—Yes, an upgrade would nice. Mississauga Lake. Address?" she asked turning to me

"Number 18, Fire Route 162," I said and she repeated it into the phone.

A thought occurred to me as she loudly hung up with a big grin on her face.

"That's how they—whoever 'they' is—knew where you'd be yesterday!" I said. "You used that phone to make the appointment—caller ID. They know me so they knew you were staying here. All they had to do was take a peek down the laneway to get the car model, license number."

Our smiles disappeared. Both of us understood how creepy this was getting. This shit was not random; it definitely had been co-ordinated between Toronto and here.

"No more Hardy Boys—" I started to say.

"—or Nancy Drew," Alex added.

"We gotta bring the cops in on this. We have to see them this morning anyway. We should get going."

"What about all this paper?"

"I'll handle it."

I walked down to the guest room and pounded on the solid wood door.

"Get the fuck up, Golding! You got work to do! What, you think this is a fucking summer resort?!"

Steve suffers from the standard disease of most reporters and all rock stars. Morning Aversion Syndrome, more commonly known as Keefititus. They're used to working late and getting up late.

Not today, buddy boy, I thought.

I don't think he understood half of what we said as he sat stunned-looking at the kitchen table while we bombarded him with coffee and proof of Edgewater's double-selling.

He snapped to as he pored over Alex's list of Yankee names.

"Nothing personal, Alex," he said, "but I'm supposed to go on what you *think* you remember?"

"Oh, for fuck's sake," I said as I snatched the list from him. "It's not going to take a lot of digging to find these people. How many Orpens do you figure live in Bristol, Connecticut?"

"OK, OK. I'll track 'em down—LinkedIn, Facebook, 411."

"And Carl got us the Canadian owners. But start with the Yanks. Before they get a chance to warn them off."

"Deal."

Owing to the scarcity of east-west roads in the area, it took almost an hour to get to the Apsley OPP detachment, first by heading south then east then back north so that, in effect, we drove around the bottom of the provincial park. But it was a nice drive as much for the sunny day as for the shared sense that we were coming to an end of all the defrauding in the air.

CHAPTER 25

We were expected. Constable Beckstead who had done the questioning at the scene, ushered Alex into an interview room to fill out her more detailed statement.

Turns out, there's not a lot to do in a police reception area except to sit around and fidget and look guilty of something or other. But then I saw Dysart coming in. I rose to greet him.

"How's your ladyfriend?" he immediately asked.

"Alexandra's fine, thanks. Still a bit shook up. A few aches and pains."

"That's good to hear. You folks are quite the topic of conversation."

"We are?"

"Yup. I talked to Beckstead. He's pretty sure the crash was deliberate. They spoke to the witness at the scene, the guy in the oncoming car. He corroborated her account. Only he thought it was two punks drag racing and what were we going to do about it. Plus, we have the skid marks when they braked—first hers, like she said, and then his starting a bit further."

"So now what?"

"Well, we've got the facts; we just don't have the big questions answered: Who and why?"

"Find the truck and you find the who."

"Well, yeah. But it'll take some time. There's gotta be at least a dozen jacked-up black pick-ups around here, all owned by guys wearing ball caps. That I know of. Likely a whole lot more."

"Seems to me 'likely' is Derek Collins."

"Derek? I know Derek. Rough piece of work, but it's not him."

"Why not?"

"I've had occasion to visit him. And to pull him over. His truck is all jacked-up alright. But it's white."

"I've seen it too. But maybe he got a new one…or borrowed one; fuck, I don't know. But I do know that after Blair Odell, he stood to make the most from selling his land. And I know he's got a temper."

"I'll look into it."

"OK then, I also think I can help with the why," I said, looking around to see if anybody was listening. Dysart picked up on my furtiveness.

"Come with me," he said.

In another interview room, I described what we believed—what we now knew—was going on with Edgewater Estates, the money and people involved. Dysart wrote furiously. I stopped and he studied his notes.

"Why didn't anyone say anything about this yesterday?" he asked.

"We weren't sure. Today we're sure."

"No disrespect but right now, all this is just you talking. Got any proof, anything on paper?"

"At my place."

"This is huge," Dysart said.

"I just reported a crime, didn't I?"

"That you did."

"So now you have to do something, don't you?"

"That we will. I'll start with some calls. This is a whole lot bigger than this station. In the meantime, what are you going to do?"

"What do you mean?"

"They know you're digging around."

"Yeah, but they couldn't possibly know exactly what we found," I said, trusting Carl's assertion that his little B&E had gone undetected, a little B&E I didn't feel bad about not mentioning to the police.

"Sure about that? They were hauling a red Malibu out of the lake this morning."

There wasn't too much I could say to that.

"Look, Jake," Dysart said, "if I were them, why would I stop comin' after you?"

"I had thought about that and I guess I had hoped that with a reporter and now the cops on the case because of the wreck, the bad guys would back off."

"They won't."

"Can I borrow your phone?" I asked.

"What, no cell?"

"Don't start with me."

I called Steve. It went straight to voicemail. On one hand, that wasn't surprising. He had at least fifty calls to make. You hardly ever get someone on the first try, so earlier calls would be returning his message while he was on the line making other calls. On the other hand, what if? What if he'd had unwelcome visitors.?

I left a message for Steve suggesting that he might want to have Carl over for a coffee, maybe invite him to bring a shotgun or two to clean on the front porch.

"Remember when you mentioned police protection a while back?" I said to Dysart after my call.

"We're stretched a bit thin right now, but I'll see what I can do."

The drive back wasn't as leisurely as our trip there. Alex was a tad tense after the report she'd filed. I was a little wound up having set the cops onto this scam. And I didn't know what I was expecting to see when I got home. Maybe a pitched gun battle between Carl and the baddies. Jesus, I'm a drama queen.

I drove slowly up the driveway, hearing no gunshots, finding nothing out of the ordinary. Except there was a giant black Chevy SUV squatting in front of the house.

"Your ride's here," Steve said to Alex from the front porch. "Enterprise dropped it off about an hour ago. Poor bastards."

"Why 'poor bastards'?" she asked.

"Carl met them."

There was a rustling in my overgrown hydrangea bushes off to our left and Carl stood up, cradling a shot gun.

"Afternoon, folks," he said as he casually sauntered up to us.

"Thanks, buddy," I said.

"Need the practice for duck hunting in the fall."

"Yeah, well, I owe you."

"Now that you mention it, I could use a few days' help cuttin' wood before you leave."

"I mean: Steve owes you."

"First week of October or so," Carl said to Steve. "Bring some work clothes."

We traded accounts of our respective mornings. Steve had found all seven American buyers and got six of them to go on record by suggesting quotes which they agreed to, like "wise investment decision" and "glad we got in on the ground floor" and "impressive plans for a beautiful place."

Constable Dysart called to tell us to stick around the place as we could expect to see some heavyweight fraud investigators from Toronto arriving late that afternoon or the next morning.

"They want to see what evidence you've got," he told me. "Right now, they're real interested but all they have is my summary of what you told me. You better not be bullshitting."

"I'm not bullshitting, Constable Dysart," I said, loudly enough to get Steve's attention. "And of course we'll co-operate with the Toronto detectives. Thanks for the heads-up."

As I hung up, I faced a pissed-off journalist.

"We will turn exactly fuck-all over to them!" he said. "I know those guys; they'll hide this thing until they get to claim credit with a showy press conference. No way!"

"Then I suggest you get copying real fast and then, Jack snap, get the fuck out of here."

It took him less than hour to copy down and assemble everything, pack, and skedaddle out of there. As he was set to leave, he turned serious with me.

"You're going to drop a dime on me with the cops, aren't you?"

"Yup. How long do you think it'll take for them to find out—if they haven't already—that you've been nosing around?"

"Then I better pitter-patter. Probably works out better anyway that I'm far away when I call back all the people up here whom I talked to yesterday to let them know they've been fucked and to ask them what they thought about that."

I studied his face

"Admit it," I said. "You're scared of the mayor too."

"Damn straight I am. I woke myself up last night with my own screams as I was dreaming about her reaction."

"Cops can't stop you from publishing, can they?"

"They'll try. But not a chance."

"Stay in touch."

"Sure thing. I gotta get writing so can you run down the Canadian buyers, get some fluff quotes?"

I agreed, and wished him a safe drive.

Notionally, it was swell to be alone with Alex again but practically, I was irritated that instead of hanging out with her, I had some phone sleuthing to do. Alex was a champ, busying herself by telecommuting to her job back in Boston.

I didn't like doing it but I was pretty good at it. In my high tech gig, I had years of practice in wheedling, flattering, and cajoling the company's clients into publicly saying something nice about us.

Three of the four Canadians agreed to be mentioned. The fourth got all huffy about privacy and such. But, I reasoned, we had his signed contract and it was going to be public knowledge anyway as soon as the sale was registered, so tough noogies.

I did feel a tad shitty knowing what I knew and still dutifully copying down their glowing assessments of Edgewater Estates.

Round about cocktail hour(s) we had visitors. Carl provided his armed greeting that was met with drawn pistols and police badges. The investigators from the OPP Organized Crime Enforcement Bureau were more than a little miffed about facing a double-barreled shotgun and their mood didn't improve when we sat down with them.

Detective Holman was the bigger, older, and dishevelleder of the two. Unfair, I know but Holman's considerable girth instantly had me associating it with a police career filled with donuts. On second thought: cruelers; he looked like a crueler man. His grayish blue suit was ill-fitting, although it did match his eyes and hair. His tie knot sat on the portion of his wattled neck exposed when he undid the top button of his wrinkled white shirt. All in all, Holman looked perpetually weary and in possession of absolutely zero fucks to give.

Detective Farisi, on the other hand, was a study in contrasts to his big rumpled partner. Short, trim, moussed black hair, well-dressed. He sported the terribly au courant and apparently now mandatory three-day face stubble. I guessed he achieved this faint bearded look with one of them new electric razors which—I shit you not—are sold as shavers to make you look like you hadn't shaved.

We—mostly Alex—began by going through her financial models that suggested something was way off with Lakeshore's numbers. I explained that their wonky math had convinced us that major crimes were being committed by selling and re-selling the same property. So, naturally, we wanted to confirm it by tracking down some new owners before going to the police.

"How did you obtain all the names of buyers?" asked Detective Holman.

Alex told them how the sales guy in Toronto had offered up a list of American buyers.

"And the Canadian names?" Farisi said.

"I went through the garbage from the sales trailer," I said.

"You did, did you?"

"Yes."

"And what day was that?" Farisi asked.

"I can't remember."

"Do you want to tell us about a reporter who's been interviewing people around here?" Holman said.

"I'm wildly guessing you already know about a reporter who's been interviewing people around here."

"Why don't you tell us about him anyway?" Holman suggested.

I explained that Steve Golding was a friend of mine, a business reporter doing a piece on Edgewater.

"Good friend of yours?" Holman asked.

"Yeah, sure."

"That isn't exactly true, is it, Mr. Lydon?"

"Excuse me?"

"Well, a *good* friend might know that Golding's a crime reporter for the *Sun*, not a business writer."

"Want to start again?" Farisi asked.

Fuck, I thought. Getting caught in a lie I didn't even have to utter. Rookie mistake. I figured I looked like the target of a Mike Wallace *60 Minutes* interview. You know, when the camera zooms in and you see the quivering lip ringed by beads of sweat.

But they let me off, though. A warning shot across the bow. Next one, I figured, would be coming below the water line.

"You related to Lydon in Toronto homicide?" Holman asked, apropos of nothing.

"Yes. My daughter. Know her?"

"Our paths have crossed."

"Fraud and murder often go together," Farisi observed.

The interviewing stretched on into the evening, an extended version of the kind I was accustomed to in my old PR job. These guys were good. Re-phrasing identical questions, circling back to earlier questions, asking out-of-left field questions. And just as with my former PR job I went into a zone that is antithetic to my normal verbal diarrhea way of talking. Short answers, Jake. No speculation, Jake. Repeat and repeat.

"Look, fellas," I finally said. "We're not the bad guys here. I told the police within two hours of us knowing definitively that there's a big scam going on."

"We have to be sure. You understand. These are big-time accusations you're making."

"And we need the paper you've got."

"Photocopies?"

"No. Originals. Chain of evidence. You understand."

I turned over the print-outs of the spreadsheets Alex had done. That was no big deal; we still had them on the computer.

"Now, all the stuff you found in their garbage," Farisi said.

Reluctantly, I handed them the file folders with the sales contracts and contact lists that Alex had neatly prepared.

"Wow, these people really are neat with their trash," Farisi said, staring at me. "Not one piece of paper crumpled up."

At that point, I got red-faced, even when Farisi smiled a bit.

"Notes?" asked Holman.

"Notes?" I echoed.

"C'mon, Mr. Lydon, all this just didn't pop up on Xcel," Farisi said.

I rummaged around, pulled together some of our jottings, my post-it notes, and that seemed to finally satisfy them. They turned to Carl who'd been sitting there the whole time.

"Anything to add, Mr. Breedlove?"

"Nope."

"We'll deal with Golding," Farisi said as they packed up. "Best not warn him."

"Is this the part when you tell me not to leave town?" I asked.

"Maybe you watch too much television," were Holman's last words to me.

After their car disappeared, I called Steve, told him to expect some visitors, and to act dumb and surprised when they did show up.

Maybe an hour after the Fraud Squad left, I saw headlights flash in my driveway. They were way too close to the house for them to be from a car using the driveway to turn around.

"Carl, we've got company."

"Got it," he said, picking up his shotgun and leaving from the back of the house to take up his strategic position in the hydrangea.

Chickenshit that I am, I peeked out the side of the front room window as a figure approached the house. Carl waited until whoever was almost to the front door before approaching him from behind.

It was a very surprised Constable Dysart. In civvies and driving his own car.

"Figured I'd drop by, see how you're doing. Maybe stay a while," he said when he was inside.

"That is darn swell of you."

I thanked Carl, told him he could take the rest of the night off.

"Nice night, maybe I'll sit on the dock for a bit, see how things are on the lake."

"One if by land, two if by sea."

"Somethin' like that."

Dysart went back outside, turned his car around so it was facing towards the road.

I brought him a beer which he declined. I then offered it to me. I accepted.

"Coffee? I asked.

"Not yet."

"Mind if I join you?"

We shot the shit for a while, chatting amiably about his background (Prairie boy—comes to Toronto—goes through cop school—works the streets—gets tired of the guns and gangs and asphalt—joins OPP and transfers to Apsley—here five years—and loving it) and about hockey (a fuckin' Oilers fan!). I actually don't make a big deal of his mystifyingly poor choice of team as it was hard not to notice the gun in his lap.

After I made coffee for him, I turned in. Alex was asleep until I woke her by stumbling around getting out of my clothes. We laid awake, on our backs holding hands and were comforted, not only by the fact that there were good people now selflessly protecting us. It was the sound of a loon starting up that calmed us and told us there was life very much removed from all this complication.

We waited for its cry—or maybe it's a laugh. I never could tell.

CHAPTER 26

The telephone ringing jolted us awake. I could tell by the feeble light from the widow that it was early. Normally, I wouldn't even consider answering in an un-caffeinated state. But these were not normal times.

"Read the *Sun* today?" Steve demanded.

"I did not. Kinda busy, what with hours of interrogation and now being under police protection and all. Why the fuck are you up so early?"

"Stavros is dead."

"What!?"

"Apparently he blew himself away in his office last night."

"The office you were just in?"

"The very one.

"Holy fuck."

"This makes zero sense."

"But you were on to him. Maybe he knew the jig was up".

"I didn't ask one single question that'd lead him to believe I was writing anything but a blow-job. I swear."

"What are the cops saying?"

"Fuck-all beyond finding him at his desk after a night cleaning lady heard a shot and called it in. Massive head wound. 38 on the floor beside him."

"What do you think?" I asked.

"Looks like suicide but…"

"But what?"

"I got nuthin' solid to go on but it stinks to me. Not the facts the cops gave me, but Stavros. Think about it. Here's a guy who scammed a bunch of West Coast Joe Blows out of millions without the slightest trace of guilt, in fact proclaiming his innocence until he disappeared from Vancouver after paying the fine. Rumour had it at the time, he fucked off with a big chunk of those millions that weren't accounted for. He turns up in Toronto, gets a bigger scam going, invites the press in—that would be me—and then suddenly he grows a conscience and offs himself. What, out of guilt? It doesn't fit."

"No, it doesn't. What are you gonna do about it?"

"Well, it sure changes the story. I'll poke around here. Talk to the widow, if I can. Hey, Halley could help."

"Forget it. She barely speaks to me. She sure won't talk to you. You got cop friends of your own."

"Tried 'em already. Got squat."

"So this story dies with Stavros?"

"Fuck no! I'm just getting started."

It felt reassuring to hear Steve's enthusiasm. A smart reporter keen on a story is a thing of beauty to behold. Nothing stops them. The media gets such a kicking these days. For sure, some of it is well-deserved. Over-hyping, clear bias, exaggerated meanings, and worst of all—to me anyway—laziness. All this exists. But here's a fact: no true journalist gets up in the morning and wonders: "How can I benefit a politician or a corporation today?" Put another way, we're fucking lucky to have them. Take them away and you get mouthpieces for dictators or false democracies. And big companies doing absolutely whatever it takes to make their quarterly numbers. Or you get FOX News.

Halley called the next morning.

"Dad, what the fuck are you involved with now?"

"Language, young lady."

"OK. What the fuckitty fuck are involved with now?"

"That's better. And to answer your question: nuthin'. Why do you ask?"

"Nuthin' huh? Golding called me yesterday. Wanted to know about Guy Stavros. Said you put him up to it."

"I did no such thing!" I protested, with truth on my side for once.

Note to self: have a chat with Stephen J. Golding about misrepresentation.

"But while we're on the subject: what'd you tell him?"

"What's the word you just used? Oh, yeah, NUTHIN'! We don't know anything yet, OK?"

"Calm down, sweetie."

As is well-documented, telling somebody to calm down almost always has the opposite effect. Evidently, Halley elected to have some alone time to calm down on her own as she abruptly hung up.

I waited an hour, like we had to do as kids before swimming after eating. I wrote to her instead of risking another phone call.

Daughter dearest, Would you like a motive for Stavros' murder-IFIFIFIF it was murder?

Give. Was all she wrote back.

I'm not sure I should be talking out of school....

The phone rang right quick.

"Dad, stop fucking around. Talk to me."

"Money and lot's of it. That's the motive."

"I got that from Farisi, sort of. But he wasn't big on details."

"Quick question, daughter: what kind of case proceeds more urgently—murder or fraud?"

"You know the answer to that. I repeat: give."

I described what I thought we had uncovered.

"You're sure of all this?"

"Pretty sure. It's gotta be on his servers. You can get access to them, right? Part of any m-u-r-d-e-r investigation."

"Not so easy. Yesterday—about twelve hours after the body was found—Stavros' lawyers already had an injunction stopping us from seizing his records and computers. Some bullshit about proprietary information, impairing the corporation functions, damaging to shareholder value and so on."

"Traynor-Veitch has to be in on it."

"So what am I looking for?"

"Any hint that the same lot, the same rental was sold to more than one person."

I remembered what Steve had said about his interview with Stavros.

"There's an admin assistant," I said.

"We talked to her. She wasn't there. Alibied."

"Best talk to her again. This time about this double-selling. She's gotta know. Threaten the hell out of her. And look, there's no way something this big is being managed by one man with an admin assistant and a law firm."

"We're looking for any other employees. And meanwhile, you talk to your reporter friend about lying to cops."

"What Steve's working on is important, Hal. There's a big scam going on up here."

"I know, dad. Like I said, I got that from Farisi. And by the way, he thinks you're hiding something...and he thinks you might be in danger. Again."

"I think he's wrong."

"I do trust your judgment. I mean, it's always guided you."

"That's right. It has."

"To getting shot. Twice. In one year, for Christ's sakes!" she said, getting all torqued up again.

I'd learned that Halley yelling at me for being a willfully ignorant moron was just her way of expressing love and concern for the old man. And I did appreciate it.

On the other hand, if cops think you're in danger, then you're probably in danger.

CHAPTER 27

Carl, bless him, volunteered to take us in, reasoning that his island was easier to defend than my house on the mainland. Alex and I talked about it.

"Might be a good idea," I suggested. "But you should know that his place makes this place look like Mar-a-Largo."

"Yeah, but at least its owner isn't a dick," Alex pointed out.

We decided to stay put, mainly on my stated belief that the cat was out of the bag, the genie out of the bottle, the horse was out the barn door etc. etc. The cops were on the case now. So were the media. Any offense the bad guys were playing to contain us erstwhile budinskys had broken down.

They were on defence now.

Steve reported in that Detectives Holman and Farisi had paid a visit to the *Sun* newsroom. I could see the cops—looking like cops—Holman all rumply and authoritative, Farisi hip and snappy—marching into the Editor's office. Chances are that the office had floor to ceiling windows looking onto the reporters' cubicles and further chances are that said Editor wouldn't pull the blinds. Reporters love it when they excite police interest. Some nerve's been pressed, somebody's pissed off.

And speaking of pissed off, I got a call from the mayor. Evidently, Steve had yet to call her back with news of the scam. I didn't get the opportunity to tell her. Apparently she alone had figured out that Steve's soft sell on the Edgewater story was bullshit and so was convinced that Steve was setting Edgewater Estates up for a hammer job. I can't recreate the entire one-sided conversation because she was speaking so quickly and so nastily that I was struck dumb. Its highlights included liberal use of the phrases "useless cocksucker", "ignorant motherfucker", "fucking asshole" and my personal favourite, "woebegone son of a bitch". The term "fake news" turned up a time or two.

"She's gonna have to really earn my vote in the next election," I said to Alex who had watched me get the earful.

"If she's this pissed off now, wait until Steve does his call-back," Alex said.

Steve stayed in touch with us, calling after each follow-up interview to let the players know they'd been conned. As per Alex's prediction, Mayor McQuaig was apoplectic, at first refusing to believe it and then, with mounting evidence presented to her, she unleashed a torrent of imaginative invective against Stewie. I actually felt sorry for him if he had to bear the brunt of her storm in person. And, I thought, if I were him, I'd start checking my well water for poison or under my car before I started it.

At the other end of the conversational spectrum, Councilor/septic guy Peterson didn't say a word. Steve said there was a long pause and Peterson just hung up.

Councilor/blowhard Dugald also seemed to have been at a loss for words. Steve told me that he just kept saying "Ruination, ruination."

"I swear he was on the edge of tears," Steve said.

"What about Blair Odell?"

"Actually, he was pretty calm about it. Said he had never counted on the windfall anyway. Now Luc Dubois, there's an excitable boy."

"What'd he say?" I asked.

"No idea. I don't understand French, even when it's yelled, but it didn't sound good."

According to Steve, Terry Weston was completely sanguine at news of the fraud, offering up an "easy come, easy go" to describe his reaction.

I thought about his son and ex-wife.

Steve said that he still hadn't been able to contact Derek Collins.

Steve's story ran as a three-parter. It appeared as though *The Sun* had given him all the space he wanted. He had graphs and charts with circles and arrows on them. He had photos of the abandoned golf course. He had found a picture of Alex's rental car being hauled out of the lake and even a shot of a fucking loon. He had all the interviews of surprised councilors and sheepish and/or furious landowners.

In general, we came off as the pigeons we had been. Presumably the same sort of reaction you have when you publicly admit that you've been long-distanced cheated by a Togo lawyer who wants to give you millions because you have the same name as his dead client. Or you reply to a recruitment pitch for part-time work with a Chinese steel company when your only possible qualification for the job is you like Pittsburgh's NFL team.

Steve couldn't be definitive about the cause of Stavros' death. He implied it was murder most foul by saying "under suspicious circumstances" and "mysterious," but the cops wouldn't confirm or deny.

Just like last summer's shitshow, I did get some credit for "inadvertently" setting the intrepid Golding off on the hunt. And I was fine with that. I didn't need to see my name in print to reinforce my baselessly high opinion of myself.

For balance, Steve had included a quote from Hulk Holman, the OPP Fraud squad detective, saying that it looked like Stavros' "alleged" con had been one of the most elaborate and persuasive swindles he had ever seen. So at least our community had been fucked by the best. He had tried to get somebody from Lakeshore Developments on record but there was no one to comment. Stavros was dead. His wife, M. Stavros, was seen peeking out from the curtains of her house but that's as close as Steve got. Stewie was uncharacteristically tight-lipped, offering up only the absurd "No comment" which always serves as a confession. Steve did track down Leslie Downs, Stavros' admin assistant. Her response was the classic—and tearful—"I just don't believe it. Mr. Stavros was a wonderful man."

There was fall-out. Oh, boy, there was fall-out. The arrests—well-documented by Steve and other reporters—continued over several days following his series. Stewie's was first (which made my day), then Luc Dubois' (which didn't). The net widened to include Mssrs. Traynor and Veitch.

That was big news in Toronto because the lawyers' arrest was taped as they left the Toronto Courthouse. I saw the TV story and swore to myself that Detective Holman was grinning as he slapped on the cuffs, (Steve later confirmed that Holman had tipped off a TV station).

There were new characters—well, new to me—who also found themselves in a perp walk. Holman and Farisi were credited with bringing in Donald Macpherson, the CFO of Lakeshore (and likely Keeper of the Multiple Ledgers) and Fred Sims, Vice President of Development, who would have overseen all the pre-construction elements of the mythical Edgewater Estates.

Their arrests were sensational; the charges not so much. Fraud, conspiracy to commit fraud, breach of trust for the Mayor and Councilors Peterson and Dugald. Under I assume some kind of catch and release program, everybody was charged and then subsequently freed after they put up bail.

They had nothing on Theresa Wright, the marketing rep at the presentation centre up here. Or the sales guy from the Toronto office. Or Leslie Downs, the admin assistant whose only crime appeared to have been blind loyalty to Stavros and loyal blindness to what the business was doing.

Stewie made bail by putting up his house as collateral but was re-arrested several days later on the much more serious charge of conspiracy to commit murder along with Jerry Glavin for setting in motion the attack on Alex. That charge got dropped down to assault pretty quick and Stewie—along with Glavin—made bail again.

Derek, that was another story; he was not ever in custody. He was in the wind and soon the subject of a Canada-wide warrant for being the wheel man in the vehicular assault on Alex.

I did wonder how the cops had built a case against Derek. The motive was there: doing his criminal bit to make sure the sale of his land went through, but I couldn't see how they'd found enough evidence to actually charge him.

Then there was the flock of pigeons—the condo and house buyers and renters who thought they'd acquired their fair share of an alleged paradise. With Edgewater's lawyers being arrested and all, it was a pretty easy job to quash their earlier injunction against release of their dead client's files. The Fraud Squad must've burnt the ol' midnight oil comparing all the transactions on the same property to yield the raft of dupes and duplicates.

Obviously, a number of police forces had to commit major resources to dealing with this bunch. Phones were ringing off the wall—not that anybody puts phones on walls anymore—in police fraud units around the continent as would-be house and condo owners, vacationers and assorted land speculators reported how and for how much they'd been ripped off.

All six American owners whom Alex and Steve had originally found vowed to lawyer up and litigate this until the next century, with two of them—states apart from each other—using the identical phrase: "cheating Canadian sons of bitches." The double-sold Canadians were, to a person, silent.

It'd probably take months to total up the vanished deposits but Holman's estimate as quoted in the media suggested buyers and renters were out least twenty million bucks. Alex figured there were a whole lot more millions which now resided as ones and zeroes in an unreachable offshore bank account

And then, predictably, everything started to die down. There was a brief jump in activity as the *Toronto Star*—note to self: ride Steve's ass about being out-sleuthed—uncovered the extent of the fake sales operation which Messrs. Traynor and Veitch had supervised. At least four separate upper-class boiler room operations had unleashed banks of telemarketers on the rich. Kept separate from each other, they just sold and sold the same properties in duplicate and triplicate all the way up to whatever comes after quintuplicate.

Steve uncovered the rest of it. He did an in-depth piece on Traynor and Veitch who actually came off a bit sympathetic. Career-long partners, both in their late sixties, they had, Doug Traynor said, tried to become entrepreneurial when neither of them actually were. In about the same way Wal-Mart and Costco kill small businesses, the big law firms were getting bigger and squeezing out the smaller ones as corporate clients demanded armies of lawyers, rather than just a battalion or so. Rejecting buy-out offers, Traynor and Veitch decided to grow their firm instead. But they had over-hired and then over-rented in the now-chic 10 Mercer largely, Traynor claimed, based on the potential pay-off of having Stavros as a client. They were in hock up to their eyeballs and watching their retirement plans explode when Stavros started asking them to do more and more things they knew were wrong and illegal.

Steve described Howard Veitch getting all teary-eyed at this point as they laid out how they waded deeper and deeper into unlawful waters.

"We couldn't blow the whistle, we just couldn't," Veitch said. "We had set the whole thing up to begin with, registered all the companies, drew up the sales contracts. Our names were on everything. And Stavros knew that."

I gotta tell you, I was surprised that the legal duo so openly copped to their crimes to a reporter, this at a time when everybody tries to shut the fuck up about legal perils. Maybe it was all artful bullshit ahead of their trial to lay all the blame on Stavros who conveniently wasn't talking much anymore while painting themselves as economic victims, but Steve is pretty good at sniffing out stuff like that.

Steve did another piece that I found fascinating. From Fred Sims who was in charge of the physical development on down to everybody on the construction side of things—the consultants, the landscape architects, the engineering firms hired to lay out the roads, lighting, sewers—none of them had a fucking clue they were working on an utter and complete fiction of a project. Steve surmised that Stavros had been clever enough to convince them all of his dream, that they were working on a long-lasting landmark to be carved out of the Canadian Shield.

Meanwhile up here, I figured there might be a scene at Stewie's place—you know, like the one in *Frankenstein* with the angry mob of townspeople armed with torches, clubs, and pitchforks but that didn't happen.

And then everything went quiet—all wrapped up and nowhere to go until the court dates which would be months away.

On one of his days off, Constable Dysart came by.

"Nice spot you've got here now that I see it in broad daylight," he remarked, drinking the beer I'd given him. "Glad you got to keep it."

"Me too."

"I wanted to let you know how things were progressing. It's all above my pay grade, but I hear things."

"Like…?"

"Like you were right about Derek Collins; he was driving the truck that sent your lady into the lake."

"I see he got charged. How'd you guys find out?"

"Technology and some legwork. Phone records showed the sales guy in Toronto had called Stewie as soon as Alexandra left the office, probably to let him know that he had sold lot 4B. Minutes after that, Glavin called Derek and GPS records put Derek's phone on that stretch of road at that time."

"That's pretty circumstantial, isn't it?

"That's where the field work plays into it. I was part of the unit that went to Derek's place to arrest him. No sign of him or his white truck. What we did find was a big dead dog in the kitchen and a black pickup hidden in the bush. A truck with red paint on the crumpled front fender that probably matches GM red."

"So Stewie ordered it?"

"Not clear. Woodson says he just happened to mention it in passing to Glavin. Glavin claims Stewie told him to hurt her. So, he said/he said at this point."

"What do you think?"

"I'm tending towards believing Stewie. He was pretty convincing describing how Stavros insisted on Shield Security being involved. Which suggested that Glavin might be a plant directly reporting to the head honcho. So they pulled phone records. Reams of calls from Glavin's cell to 10 Mercer, most of them at exactly 9 AM or 6 PM. All of them made to Stavros' private number. He was in deep."

"Any idea where Derek is?"

"Yup. US Customs has him entering the States four days ago at Niagara Falls and, yesterday, leaving the US at Laredo, Texas, heading for, they presume, Monterrey, Mexico or maybe Tampico. He can hide for a while but not forever."

"Yeah but, I could understand if the Mexican government doesn't make it a priority to go after a fugitive from an assault charge."

"I didn't tell you what else we found at Derek's."

"What?"

"A pill factory. Pretty big one."

"Lemme guess: fentanyl was one of his products."

"Yup."

"And you matched it to the batch that killed Greta Hill."

"Not me personally but somebody who works with your daughter did. That puts him on the hook for at least manslaughter."

"So Derek must've figured the jig was up and went on the lam."

"Jake, FYI, nobody says the jig's up anymore or went on the lam."

"Do they still say fuck off?"

Dysart smiled and then went on to describe the elaborate set-up in Derek's Quonset hut. Apparently there was only a tiny bit inventory lying around what looked like a pretty big lab which meant either it was all on the street or, more likely, with Derek.

It wasn't exactly no harm, no foul, but determining damages wasn't going to be easy. What's the redress for embarrassment and the crushed greedy dreams of Derek Collins, or Blair Odell or Terry Weston or Councilor Peterson, never mind the smaller landowners who all went back to owning their acres of bush and rock? How should a hopeful community be compensated? You'd think that somebody had to pay something. I called my lawyer pal Gordon Wellsley to ask about what might happen next.

"Well, for you, not much," he said. "I suppose you could claim pain and suffering for all the inconvenience it created but how much? You could go after Stavros' estate through small claims. Up to $35,000, but did you really lose more than that? And you got to be able to serve somebody. "

"Good one."

"Pardon me?"

"Dylan?....Serve somebody?....Forget it, Gord."

"And, Jake, this ain't Kansas or anywhere in the States. We just don't load up on lawsuits."

"And the other landowners?"

"Odell and Collins and the others, I expect they'll want to file suit but against whom? They have to prove that—based on the sale—they made plans that cost them money. Bought a Mexican villa or a race horse or something."

"Heard about Collins?"

"No."

"Well, he might actually have bought a Mexican villa. But he's not suing anybody. What about everybody going after Stewie for the bull-shit sales?"

"No bad deed goes unpunished either."

"Fuck, you're hot today, Gord-o."

"Woodson has to be proven to have known or co-operated in the criminal case they've got against him. If he gets acquitted then he's probably safe from lawsuits."

"So they plunder Stavros' estate?"

"Maybe. But they'll have to stand in line. Let's bet he stiffed a lot of people. The banks'll get first crack. They always get first crack."

"Are you telling me that nobody gets their pee-pee whacked over all this?"

"Mr. Dubois isn't out of the woods."

"Good bilingual one, but he's been fired."

The fact is, all the landowners still had their land. It would take some time—but not a lot of time—to get the deeds switched back to them. Their acres were assets. Their land wasn't worth near what Stavros had said he'd pay—maybe half or a third of that—but it was still a hell of a lot more than what all of them originally paid for it. True, there might be some stigma attached to it, call it the ghost of Edgewater Estates, but it's not cursed like Carthage after ol' Scipio tore it down and salted the earth.

I did feel bad for the hopes that had been dashed, but I was also a little disappointed that there wasn't a line-up outside my place of the swindlees thanking me for helping to uncover the swindlers, probably for the same reason a kid never thanks anyone who tells them that—spoiler alert!—Santa Claus is bogus.

CHAPTER 28

Alexandra stayed an extra week into August which was wonderful. She admitted to being pleasantly surprised that my Internet connection wasn't dial-up and so could continue to work. Even though she blithely ignored my attempted edict banning her Tom Brady jersey from the property, she is beautiful to me as she tap-tap-taps at the keyboard, her long tanned legs stretched out under the table, her hair spilling around her shoulders like Cohen's "sleepy golden storm." Let me amend that: she's beautiful to anyone with eyes.

And while she was spending the mornings working away at analyzing something or other, I got all charged up about my novel and went back at it with an energy and zeal that surprised her—and me. I mentioned to her that there might be something to this Muse thing. She thought that that something was paying her a 30% royalty.

The afternoons were ours.

Even though I hadn't asked him to, Carl, the big bastard, repaired my shot-up canoe, which I hadn't missed and it wasn't long until I was coerced into paddling around with Alex. I don't want this getting out but it actually wasn't too bad this being out on the water and exerting myself, especially after I rigged up an ashtray on the crosspiece (which for some reason or other is called a thwart, by the by) in front of the stern seat. Although I may have been thwarted in acquiring anything like expertise with a paddle, I actually got to the point where we weren't just going around in circles.

For some strange reason, I am compelled to point out that our weeks together for the first time were not some unbroken string of unimaginable bliss. There was friction as there had to be because humans living with each other—especially ones who have been alone for years—are bound to rub up against each other and not in a good way. Personal habits and idiosyncrasies have to be accommodated. So there was a lot of give and take, mostly her giving me shit and me taking it.

For example, I like to think of myself as a fearless, early-stage eco-warrior championing the conservation of our most precious resource: water. Did I get credit for that? No, siree. No, I did not. What I got instead was "How about you flush the toilet once in a while?" or "Do you think you could shave and shower?"

This kind of thing mattered more to her than me, so I cleaned up my act. Benefits accrued because none too surprisingly, I was irresistible as hell. After a union bargaining session's worth of concessions, life at the lake became as I once had and wanted again. Ease, grace, comfort, kindness. And hanky-panky and a lot of laughs. What the hell else do you want out of your stay on the planet?

But as we slipped into August, a sadness descended on us. Alex had been an absolute champ for staying longer, for putting up with me—with or without threatening land scams. For caring. But I knew she had to go back to Boston, if for no other reason than to end the suspension of her life for her involvement in mine.

I watched her pack. We both were quiet and sad.

"Alex, you gotta be getting sick of Boston winters, what with your age and all."

"Carl's right, you know," she said. "And Steve. You really are an arsehole."

"Come to the DR this winter for more than a couple of weeks. What about a couple of months?"

"We'll see."

"I mean, you should be dialing back the workload right about now."

"What with my age and all?"

"Exactly!"

"Arsehole."

We kissed. We were doing a lot of that.

"You do know," I said. "that if anything happens, about the very last thing you said to me will have been calling me an arsehole."

She paused.

"I'm OK with that," she said. And that wonderful smile.

And then she was gone and for days I did not feel my customary contentment with solitude* (*occasionally getting tangled up in brew with Carl aside). What I felt was antsy, lost. What I felt was the same feeling I had had when Beth would be away on business or family stuff. Some kind of emptiness, some kind of longing. Oh, what the fuck. I was pretty sure this was what you'd call love.

We hadn't said the "L" word out loud to each other. We'd typed it to sign off e-mails. But other than that, we'd danced around anything that verged on talking about our feelings towards each other. And that was fine for a while. I guessed we were figuring out how to deal with our emotions and with each other. But that time was past. For me, anyway.

I wrote to her:

How about I stop bullshitting myself – and you?

I love you.

I was nervous as hell hitting "Send." And nervouser still as I checked my e-mail every ten minutes for a response, awash in school boy waves cresting and troughing with that 'she loves me, she loves me not' jivin' around.

Two fucking hours passed and she replied:

Appears as though I'm willing to overlook your arseholiness.

I love you too.

Holy shit! Holy shit!

After the happiness tsunami rolled right over me, I considered next steps. I mean, now what? Call her? And say what? Write her again? And say what? Send a big blue 'thumbs up' or a happy face?

Whoa the fuck down, Jake. The shadow box understanding we had had was now replaced with a different understanding, a different fact. And it would be a fact until it wasn't. Nothing to do, nothing to say.

Just be happier and more filled up than I'd been in years.

Alex and writing had consumed my days while she was up here. Now, she was gone and my writing turned to shit—my customary trickle of nonsensical randomness. I had time on my hands. Time to get at all those mindless, pesky outdoor jobs that I tell myself every fucking year should get done. But this time, I did them while either remembering swell moments I'd shared with Alex or imagining future swell moments.

And there was somebody I wanted to see.

A "Sold" sticker was plastered over Kelly Anne Conway's picture on the real estate sign in front of Luc Dubois' cottage. He and Gisele were packing up.

"Sorry for the way this all happened," I said.

"Not your fault, *mon ami.*"

"How's the charge against you?"

"Gone. They dropped out."

"Going back to Quebec?"

"I not go there, me."

"So where?"

"There are many of the vineyards in Chile I have dreamed about. My degree is horticulture."

"Good for you. Look, before you go, drop over to my place for a gin and tonic."

I saw Gisele grimace as she rather loudly tore off a strip of tape to seal a box.

"*Et peut-etre, madame, un petite verre du vin rouge?*" I said to her.

I can't say she smiled at my pandering in my high school French but she dialed down the glowering. Little victories.

With no partner, the Ministry of Health withdrew the expropriation notice and actually apologized to me for "any inconvenience it *may* have caused."

Jimmy rescinded my ban at the Angler's Arms.

Wanna know how instantly good my life had become again? Preston Peterson came by, greasy ball cap literally in hand, to tell me he was available to pump out my septic holding tank in the fall.

All around me, the roiled sea calmed and life in the 'hood returned to its quiet, non-dramatic pace, free of the hoopla, lather, tizzy, pettifoggery and fooferaw of the last six months. Once the mobile sales office and signage by the highway had been removed there wasn't a public trace left of the conmen in our midst.

I walked—yes, I walked!—to the out of sight/out of mind fake construction site. Someone had rolled up and carted away the fencing, along with the gate, the trailer and the bogus yellow grader and bulldozer. Even though we had had a dry summer, the weeds were doing what weeds always do: being green and growing like crazy. In a matter of weeks, there now remained only a slight suggestion of the roadways gouged out of the landscape. I even trudged back to where the real forest began where the very temporary workers had been chainsawing away. The felled trees had been removed too, their stumps the only reminder of activity.

But the billboard announcing Edgewater Estates was still standing, peeling and faded, now a bitter irony to anyone who cared to make their way up the east side of the lake.

I imagined that the people around here would torture themselves with the 'what ifs' for quite some time to come.

But that was it.

Except.

Except the deaths of three people who had been involved seemed to have been discounted into oblivion. In Toronto, a shady developer who was the brains behind the attempted scam had those self-same brains blown out. Also in Toronto, months earlier, the city recorded its 300th and some odd fatal drug overdose. And up here, a drunk councilor had taken a giant misstep into a wood chipper.

Case(s) closed.

I wanted to feel relieved that this whole affair was all done with; I really did.

But I didn't believe it.

What no one was offering up was anything that looked like a completely plausible explanation for two apparent fatal accidents suffered by municipal councilors and the probable murder/less probable suicide of the mastermind behind the whole shitshow.

I talked to Alex. That's not something we did a lot when we were apart. Leave it to former two English majors to prefer writing to phone conversation.

"There something that's not settled, Alex."

"You're not letting this go, are you?"

"For Christ's sake, there are three bodies and somehow they're connected."

"Jake, take a minute to try and figure out why you think you have to keep chasing this thing when everybody else has stopped."

Sound advice, I thought while I was sitting on the deck that evening. I didn't need the whole minute for introspection.

I knew exactly why I was going to dig deeper into the deaths of Stavros, Dr. Hill, and Maynard Odell. For me, it's the best reason of all:

Just cuz.

Cuz I felt I should.

CHAPTER 29

I sent Halley a note asking her about the Stavros case. This e-mailing sounds impersonal but I'd rather think of it as me—yet again—being considerate by letting her reply when she had the time. A parent phoning a child is always more insistent, more demanding.

So, of course, when I hadn't heard from her in two hours, I called, determined to badger the hell out of her with the "Can we have a pool, dad; can we have a pool, dad?" persistence of Lisa and Bart.

"Halley, you still working on Stavros?"

"Yes."

"What can you tell me?"

"I like the Leafs defence this season."

"You really don't know shit about hockey, do you? C'mon, daughter dearest."

"Dad, you know I can't."

"Was it murder? Just tell me that. It was, wasn't it?"

"Remember when I was a kid?...Don't say another word...."

Followed by a long, long silence. And then she hung up.

I was a little puzzled at first. It took me a while to figure out what she was trying to tell me. But then I remembered. When she was young,

Halley had the very odd habit of simply clamming up whenever she was cornered about toddler crimes like boosting a cookie before dinner or being the only human in the room with a recently broken lamp. Our friends at the time would tell us that their kids would either provide wildly suspect reasoning or just lie like rugs when apprehended. Halley didn't or couldn't. She'd look up at you with those big baby blues and her jaw would set—not in defiance—but sort of steeling herself to the admission of guilt she was about to offer by not saying anything.

So murder it was!

A few minutes later, I got an e-mail from her.

If you tell Golding, you are dead to me.

A threat like that from a homicide detective is not to be taken lightly.

I called her.

"I swear I won't tell Steve but you have to tell me how you found out."

"GSR. There wasn't enough residue around the wound to indicate that he'd pressed the barrel against his head, the way it's usually done. The gun was at least a foot and half from his temple."

I mimicked the distance with my cocked and loaded index finger.

"I could still do that."

"You maybe, but not Stavros. That's what took so long. On the face of it, I never bought the suicide. Guys like that are sorry for exactly shit. But the distance between barrel and his skull was doable, even though it's not normal. Until we found out from his wife he had really bad arthritis. He couldn't possibly raise his arm to get the gun that far away."

"Suspects?"

"There's long list, starting with all the people he screwed out west. And all the characters where you are. I'll stay in touch."

"So you're saying you got nuthin'?"

"We got nuthin'. But it's early."

So. One murder for sure. There was still no link to Dr. Hill's OD and Maynard Odell's wood chipper mangling. And maybe there was none. One murder, two accidents. Or two murders, one accident.

Or maybe three murders.

I have a winter friend in the DR named Arturo Diaz. That's Chief Inspector Arturo Diaz to you, 'Arty' to me. He's the cop who saved my life the previous winter. He once said something to me that described the way he investigated crimes. His one-liner had stuck with me.

"We must start with the possible things and, because many, many things are possible, we must throw them away one at a time until we are left with the likely things."

Could you make the connection between the three deaths—a murder, a drug overdose and an industrial accident? Yes. You *possibly* could. But was it *likely*? Three deaths—two in Toronto, one up here. Now, unnatural early deaths are rare compared to the march of time and disease, so that made it more possible. But unnatural deaths among three people who were linked by the circumstances of the same big league land scam were inescapable. The creator of the scam, the local politician who opposed it and the man who was to benefit the most from it were all dead. In my mind, that moved it from possible to likely. Maybe even OJ likely.

But even if Stavros had arranged the murders of Odell and Dr. Hill, somebody had actually carried them out as I doubted he personally had even a passing familiarity with how to feed fentanyl to the doctor or Maynard to a wood chipper. And then somebody had turned around and killed him. The who and why were wide open.

There was a pretty healthy list of local candidates, never mind a blast—as it were—from Stavros' larcenous past. And that's not counting thems with motives not money-related. Pissed-off wife, pissed-off mistress, pissed-off offspring?

I couldn't do much about either the personal or the historical reasons that could've been behind why Stavros was murdered. But I knew—or thought I knew—the actors in the West Mississauga summer theatre fiasco.

Let's start with the primo suspect up here—Derek Collins. It played. Almost. By character, he had some affection for violence and a quick temper. He was also no dummy, having had the chops to set up a DIY pharmaceutical lab, a lab that had produced the opioid that had killed Greta Hill. The same Greta Hill that was opposing the development and, by extension, Derek's big pay day. And then suppose he had somehow found out about the fraud—I mean, after all, we did. He could easily have become pissed off enough to pay Guy Stavros a late night visit at 10 Mercer. And then he had fucked off to Mexico, ahead of—perhaps—a couple of murder charges and for sure the assault on Alex and manslaughter charges for the other fentanyl overdoses. So there was a fit there. And it was mighty easy to try and convict a bad guy in absentia.

Except.

Except for Maynard Odell. Why kill a fellow landowner? One he had worked alongside. As a favour to his pal, Blair Odell? Maybe. I like Steve and Carl but not so much that I'd be up for whacking people on their behalf. Of course, Derek could have negotiated a fee for service with Blair, some amount from Blair's proceeds that'd give him enough incentive to commit murder.

It made sense. But so did other possibilities.

Stewie still had to be on the list. Maybe under all that spit and polish there was just spit. Maybe he wanted so badly for Edgewater Estates to succeed that he had resorted to homicide to silence Dr. Hill and cinch the vote. And then maybe—as with Collins—he discovered the swindle, went apeshit, and blew away Stavros. But again, why Maynard Odell? What possible difference did it make to him whether Edgewater pretended to pay Maynard or pretended to pay his son?

Again, *almost* a fit.

Next up in the most likely batter's box—at least as far as motive went—was Blair Odell.

And what did we know about him? Fuck-all really. A Toronto lawyer. Along with his mother, he had had a tough childhood at the hands of Maynard Odell. That's it.

Oh, and as far as he knew, he stood to make a shit-ton of money if Edgewater Estates had been real.

Let's find out about Blair Odell, shall we.

My potential perp list-making was interrupted by yet another fucking knock on my door. I peered through the screen door looking at the cross-hatched version of my summer's nemesis.

"Yes?" I asked.

"I'd like to talk," Stewie said.

"So talk."

"Can I come in?"

I hesitated.

"…Please."

He actually looked human and decent and needful. I was encouraged.

"Go around back," I told him. "Beer?"

"That'd be nice."

Beer in hand, we settled into the deck chairs.

"I gotta tell you," I said, "I'm a little surprised that a) you're at large and b) you thought hanging around this neighbourhood was a good idea."

"Bail's pretty low on white collar charges. And I'm going back to Toronto."

"I saw the sold sign on your house. Sure gonna miss you as a neighbour."

"I'm coming back for the trial. Maybe we can lunch."

"First off, lunch isn't a fucking verb and, secondly, I don't think I ever want to be that hungry."

I'm sorry, but I just couldn't bring myself to indulge in any 'Hail, fellow, well met, let bygones be bygones' bullshit and was determined to be as wary as the feisty mongoose around the cobra. This was a guy as persuasive as any of the thousands of TV ads Peyton Manning has starred in. After all, Stewie had successfully snowed a whole bunch of us. But I had to find out as much as I could, even though presumably he was gonna be just as careful, worried that anything he said could and would be used in a court of law.

"Stewie, what do you know about Blair Odell?"

"Nothing."

"Sure?"

"Beyond the fact that he was walking into millions? No, nothing."

"You two looked pretty cozy at the Lodge."

"He was a client; I'm not going to apologize for taking a client out to lunch."

"So you weren't behind his offer to sweeten the pot if I sold?"

"I'm also not going to apologize for offering you more money on the side either."

"Then why are you here?"

"I just wanted to say that I am sorry for all the other stuff that happened."

"Sorry how?"

"I swear I didn't know about the scam, all the fake plans."

"Cops think different."

"I'll prove them wrong in court. Look, do you really think I would've bought that house over there if I was planning to take the money and run? Edgewater was going to be my big score, worth millions. And instead, I got zero—less than zero—because I was mainly on commission, had to pay my own expenses for the last three months up here. *And* I just lost $30,000 re-selling the house!"

That stopped me. And he could see that it had.

"You never got paid?" I asked him.

"A couple of partial payments on buying the land but they stopped months ago."

"How did you get involved in the first place?"

"Stavros brought me in less than a year ago," he continued. "I had worked with him a bit on a shopping mall project he had a small hand in. I guess he liked my style. I thought it was all straight. He gave me the plans. He footed the bill for everything. Set up the subsidiaries. Did up all the marketing stuff. Commissioned all the reports. And he paid the bills—on time and in full. At first, anyway. What the hell was I supposed to think? He supplied the list of landowners, told me who to go after, how to squeeze. All I had to do was work the council, buy the land and then start selling."

"No matter if it was real or not?"

"Look, it was my job."

One of Mellencamp's many great lines sprang to mind:

"Hey, calling it your job, ol' hoss, sure don't make it right; But if you want me to I'll say a prayer for your soul tonight," I half-sang.

"All that is after the fact, Jake. I didn't know. You didn't know."

"And all the damaged shit? Wreck my mail box, puncture my canoe, really? Block the intake valve for the water pump to burn out the motor. Chop my door, for fuck's sake."

"I didn't do any of that. I swear!"

"But you hoped somebody would. That's why you leaked that Carl and I were holding out. And how about what you put me through? Or Alex, or Carl?"

"It was just business."

"Business! Your business almost got my lady killed!"

"I didn't do that either."

"You should probably go now," I said, feeling myself getting all angry again.

"But…my beer," he said holding up the mostly full bottle.

"Take it with you. You might finish it by the time you get to the main road. Huck the bottle into the empty lot where the sales trailer was.

Everybody else has."

"But…."

"Don't you understand? There is no fucking 'but'!" I said. "As the lawyers say: you either knew or should have known that when you dangle
a pisspot full of money at poor people—at anybody—they just might
do some crazy things."

You could see Stewie was working himself up to some explanation,
some rationalization. What'd I expect? St. Paul on the fucking road to
Damascus? Stewie was gonna be Stewie and me getting all upset about
it was a pointless as shitting on a frog for hopping.

So I stood up and Stewie did the same. I walked with him to his car
and opened the driver side door as he was still protesting.

"But…but if you look at from my perspec-" he started.

That's when I got to go full Clint.

"Get…off…my… fucking…lawn."

This time it worked.

I walked back to the house, feeling a little self-satisfied with the send-
off I'd given him and more than a little mystified. As much as I wanted to discount *everything* coming out of Stewie's mouth, he was probably telling the truth about having had nothing to do with setting up
the scam.

Near as I could tell, Stewie was the only one who had actually lost
real money. Beyond his wasted and mostly free energies to get the
project going, he had taken a hit on selling the house he just bought.
No choice but to drop him down the list of possible Stavros, Hill and
Odell killers.

So back to think-think-thinking about Blair Odell. There needed to be someone who had motive enough to whack all three in this scenario. The only guy I could immediately think of—and he had a lot of skin in the game—was Blair Odell. By general consensus, he was a smart kid and a lawyer. He knew the area, knew the players, seemed like a rational guy. He had badly wanted the deal to go through and why not? He stood to make the most from it in the early stages.

I remembered he had given me his business card. I dug it out of my worn wallet where it was wedged between a restaurant receipt from four years earlier and a losing lottery ticket from three years ago.

First, onto Wilson, Scharf and Arpell's website for a little background. Not that I spend a lot of time reading lawyers' websites, but I did know that legal firms like to provide profiles of their lawyers, not just to note their areas of practice but also their street cred experience and usually a capsule of their volunteer work and some hint as to their outside interests, hobbies, and family situation.

I suppose this lends some humanity to the proceedings, although the cynic in me has often thought that if you could clear two thousand bucks for a morning's work, you had better do some kind of charity work, sort of like imposing a community service sentence on yourself.

The simple rule with these websites is: The younger the lawyer, the shorter the profile. The older senior partners get reams of description about their long-term wonderfulness. The newest attorneys have to scramble to claim qualifications, stopping just short of mentioning their selection as Grade 3 Hall Monitor as an accomplishment and long walks on the beach as a hobby.

Blair Odell's bio was of the briefer variety, padded out by his interests. Twenty-seven years old, he'd been with the firm—coming over from another one—just about a year ago. Specialized in wills and estate planning. Degree from U of T with distinction. Apparently he was "passionate" (why does everybody have to be passionate about fuck-ing everything these days?) about the Boys and Girls Club and—well, well, well, what do we have here?—canoeing. And—well, well, well, *well*—running. More to the point: marathon running. And even pointier, marathon running with the Toronto Olympic Club.

Dr. Greta Hill's outfit of choice.

As excited with this tidbit as I wanted to be, all that actually proved I told myself is that they were likely familiar with each other. Not exactly an indictable offense.

If young Blair was "bent wrong," as Carl would say, maybe he'd fucked up before. On to the searchable database of the Law Society of Upper Canada. Nope. Nothing there. No disciplinary action ever taken against him, no complaints lodged. I glanced at his bar association profile, pretty much a copy from his firm's website. The main difference between the two: it listed his employer previous to Wilson, Scharf and Arpell.

Cue sound of screeching mental brakes.

He had started his legal career with Traynor-Veitch.

CHAPTER 30

What are the fucking odds that these two tidbits didn't add up to a sizeable morsel of illegality? The pieces were locking in. He had the motive, three of them—eliminating a really shitty father to move himself from next in line for a land bonanza, erasing Hill's "no" vote against the development, and, assuming he'd uncovered the fraud, opening a can of Fuck You Up on Stavros. And with jack-of-all forms of violence Derek Collins as a buddy, he had the method. Let the cops figure out exactly how he did it.

I called Halley.

"I got the name of your top suspect. #1 with a bullet—as it were."

"Suspect for what?"

"Guy Stavros' murder."

Halley wasn't exactly dumbfounded at my revelation.

"Well, of course, we're taking a look at Blair Odell. So far, we know he was up there at the time, registered at the Lodge. We're trying to account for five, maybe six hours on the night of Stavros' death because that's how long it'd take to drive down here, do the nasty on Stavros, and drive back."

"Did I mention that he used to work for Traynor-Veitch? And that he knew Greta Hill through running?"

"Now *that* I did not know."

"All the deaths are linked, daughter dearest."

"Maybe. But I need whole lot more on Greta Hill's death to re-open. And as far as Maynard Odell, I'm pretty sure the OPP won't listen to a Toronto cop."

"Jurisdictional pissing match?"

"No, Dad. Collegial respect. Their case for an accident is solid. Sorry."

"You had Blair in for questioning?"

"Not yet. We want some more info first."

"So that's it?"

"Yes, dad. For now, that's it; we're on it. You should leave this alone."

Uh-oh. There was my trigger word again. *Should.*

I felt some private investigatin' coming on. Who knows? Maybe some sleuthin' too.

I reasoned—if you could call it that—that there was no point in duplicating the police efforts to fill in Blair Odell's dance card on the night Stavros died. For one thing, it wasn't going to be easy. Everybody up here is either asleep or passed out by 10 p.m. There was no surveillance camera at the Buckhorn Lodge. That I checked. At 10 p.m. on the Tuesday night in question, Blair probably wouldn't have seen a single car until he was at least an hour away and pulling onto the 401, the main highway going into Toronto.

Two days later, Halley sent me a note, one that I was not expecting to get.

Dad, FYI, (because I KNOW you're not letting this go!) we're dropping the investigation into Blair Odell for now. We had him in. He swears he was asleep that night. We've got two witnesses (night clerk at the lodge and a passerby) who say they saw Blair's Porsche 911 late on the night of parked at the hotel. We've got nothing else.

Well, fuck.

You know when you absolutely believe something despite apparently overwhelming evidence to the contrary—say, the Beatles sucked and the Stones were the real geniuses? Actually, that's a bad example; the Stones *were* the real geniuses. OK, try the Leafs at the start of every fucking season for the last fifty having a legitimate shot at the Cup. That's what I felt like.

There's a reason my Grade 5 teacher had written "For e'en though vanquished, he could argue still" under my yearbook photo.

I wrote back: *Thanks, daughter dear, but I think that's a mistake. Odell is involved. I just know it!!!*

I cringed at my use of multiple exclamation points but I sent it anyway. To her credit, Halley wasn't going to let my questioning of her judgment—or my stuttering exclamation points—just slide on by.

Dad - It's been a while since we tried the "I feel it in my bones" prosecution but who knows? Maybe it could work!!!! she wrote.

I couldn't help but notice she'd one-upped me in the punctuation count, the little witch.

It was in the on-line news the next day that the Toronto police had changed their determination from suicide to murder in the Guy Stavros case. No suspects, some leads. Nerd that I am, I checked the story filing times. Steve beat everybody by at least an hour.

Steve called that morning.

"Old news. I already knew," I said when I answered.

"Dick! And that's not why I'm calling."

"Then what?"

"I know something you don't know," he half-sang in that annoying childhood taunt.

"It's absolutely astonishing how quickly you become tiresome."

"This story has legs…and a bunch of arms."

"What the fuck are you talking about?"

"Did some digging. Actually, did a lot of digging into Stavros' dealings on the west coast. Press didn't really cover them at the time but there was a bunch of victim impact statements at the trial. They're all in the court records. You're not going to believe who one of them was."

"Who?"

"I said you weren't going to believe it, so there's no point in telling you."

"Fuck off! Who?"

"One P. Bradley Dugald."

"Holy shit!"

"That's what I said. Holy shit! is right."

"Did he get hurt badly?"

"He got cleaned out. According to his impact statement, P. Bradley put everything he had into Stavros' scheme. Mortgaged his Granville Island condo, took his pension in a discounted lump sum, the works. Lost it all."

"So he comes back here, licking his wounds," I said.

"And up pops Stavros again. Wouldn't that just piss you right off?"

"Wait a minute. He must've put at least 200,000 into his house renos. Where'd he get the money if he was broke?"

"Mortgaged to the hilt, I bet."

"And counting on the land sale to recoup most of that."

"Say he somehow finds out that Stavros is behind Edgewater. I mean you did, for Christ's sake."

"'Ruination.' Isn't that what he said?"

"Want another fact?"

"Sure."

"Alexander the Great's horse was named Bucephalus."

"Got anything a little more relevant?"

"Jerry Glavin was with Stavros in BC."

"This keeps getting better and better."

"I ain't finished….They sort of found Derek Collins."

"Whaddya mean 'sort of'?"

"They found his head. By the side of the road in the hills outside Tampico."

"Jesus, that's nasty."

"His mouth was stuffed with about 100 fentanyl pills," Steve added.

"Looks like either Los Zetas or the Gulf Cartel took exception to Derek trying to open up a new supply chain."

"Do the cops know all this?"

"They know about Glavin and Collins. I don't think they have anything about Dugald."

"So what's it all mean?"

"I applied my years of experience in business journalism and crime reporting, my analytic skills, and my in-depth knowledge of what's going on up there to come up with the one and only sane conclusion."

"Which is?"

"Fucked if I know."

"Thanks, buddy."

"Don't mention it."

"No, really, than—"

"—Did I not just fucking tell you not to mention it?" And he hung up.

A cold beer and myself went out to the deck to consider this new information.

With Halley having rained on my belief parade that Blair Odell was the murderous culprit, I inserted another two names into my suspect list.

With what Steve had just told me, P. Bradley was worth a look. A brief one. He had the most obvious reason to permanently fuck up Guy Stavros. Fool me once and all that. To find out that he had been majorly conned twice by the same guy could easily snap his suspenders. And he really needed the development to at least make a dent in the losses he had experienced in BC. But, I thought, *because* he really needed the land sale why cap Maynard? Never mind the fact that age-wise of course, he didn't have the chops to personally load Maynard into the wood chipper. So that meant finding some less than savoury soul. And he maybe could've. But not likely.

Jerry Glavin, thug for hire, also demanded some attention. What'd we know about the menacing bulldog? If Stewie's innocence was to be believed, then Glavin was most likely the villain who had set in motion the four truck wheels that had targeted Alex. He was digging up dirt on Carl and me. He had more or less threatened me into meeting with Stewie. *And* he had worked for Stavros before.

But that last fact disqualified him for Stavros' murder. He would've known from the get-go that Stavros had returned to his scamming ways. So why kill him? Could it have been for some stupendously simple reason like a money dispute, perhaps with a touch of blackmail? Maybe. But that didn't let him off the hook for the demise of Dr. Hill and/or Maynard Odell. Yet again it was a stretch. Why off Odell if he was being fleeced anyway *and* he was in favour of the development? Maybe he killed Greta Hill because she was an Edgewater enemy but the means struck me as a little too subtle for Glavin. I couldn't see the brute enforcer somehow finessing Dr. Hill into unwittingly swallowing fentanyl. But that didn't mean that, for sure, he didn't. Nor did it mean he hadn't dispatched Odell or even Stavros for reasons completely unfathomable to me. Or for no reason at all beyond psycho rabies.

Or take Terry "I don't give a shit about my life" Weston, for example. We had written him off almost immediately as an unambitious paralytic drunk. Could the prospect of a million bucks from the land sale have removed the rum-induced sugar sheen from his eyes and cause him to act? Of course it could. To ensure the vote by killing Dr. Hill and the retribution murder of Guy Stavros for completely pissing on his dream of a fishing camp and a new start. But again, why Maynard?

On a minor scale, Terry, as a general handyman and outdoorsy guy when he wasn't shitfaced, could have easily visited my place by land or sea for some good ol' fashioned vandalism. He'd know how to burn out my water pump, was probably an expert paddler and good shot when he controlled his DTs, could swing both an axe and a baseball bat with athletic ease.

At this point, my thoughts were as scattered as a blind duck hunter.

Back up, Jake. What's the premise you're working with?

Haven't you been following along, Jake? All three deaths were murders.

And....?

How about you stop being so fucking coy, Jake?

Alrighty then, Jake. You're assuming that all three deaths were murders committed by one person or one cabal. What if they're totally separate?

Sure, Jake. Three people connected to a major crime just coincidentally die.

Why not? They were months apart and cities apart.

As happens way too often these days, I was totally confused again. And it wasn't just the beer.

I gave up my pathetic attempts at unraveling the knots I'd tied myself up in and stared at the lake. And soon, as usually happens, all thoughts disappear and I scan and re-scan the waterscape looking for a fish breaking the surface, a bird landing or taking off, the ripples from a distant boat. Shit like that.

I went back inside and took a deep breath. With the same grim determination that I used to apply to untangling the inevitable mess of a fifty-foot string of Christmas lights, I went at it again. Only with tunes. I loaded five CDs (quaint, huh?) in the changer, not one recorded after Jimmy Carter's election.

Beside the names of the deceased I wrote all the possible causers.

Guy Stavros – Dugald, Stewie, Blair Odell, Derek, Terry Weston (all for revenge), Glavin, (fuck knows why)

Greta Hill – Accident. Blair Odell, Derek, Stewie, Glavin, Terry (all to cancel her vote)

Maynard Odell – Accident. Blair Odell (money, revenge), Derek (money), Glavin, (fuck knows why)

The Eagles' *Desperado* was playing as I blankly looked at the list.

"We're gonna hit the road for one last time; We can walk right in and steal 'em blind."

So Blair and Derek—separately or in some combination—made the "Most Likely to Take a Life" category for all three victims, but I knew there were other names that could be added. If Steve's and my hunch was right, the kind of money involved might push someone else involved with the development to do the dirty work.

Joplin's *Pearl* kicked in. And my theories became wilder and wilder.

Why not Preston Peterson to cancel Greta Hill's vote? Why not his son Billy to save his old man's business? Why not Jimmy, AA's glowering owner? Maybe he really, *really* wanted to cash out? Oh what the hell? Let's hang it all on Mayor Elsie McQuaig.

With my written list and baseless speculation, I briefly visualized each one of them doing the deeds, adding some pretty convincing dialogue and riveting cinematography. I will admit that ancient and wizened Mayor Elsie tossing 220 pounds of Maynard Odell into the wood chipper required some suspension of disbelief and a nifty little bit of CGI.

I let the music take over from my mental rambling as it often does. Not just music in general but specific songs. In this case, *Me and Bobby McGee*. The Janis version not the Kris version which I think is every bit as good.

By the by, for all you grammar freaks out there, isn't it odd that we forgive music lyrics their Strunk and White trespasses? I mean "Bobby McGee and I" just doesn't have the same ring to it, does it? Years ago, when Beth and I actually were somewhere near Salinas, lord, we'd gone loudly and badly all acapella as we aimed for Monterey.

I cannot hear that song—especially when Janis cranks up the "Na-na-na-nas" near the end—and not think what a goddamned tragedy that Ms. Joplin had died so young. At about the same time and at exactly the same age as Jimi and Jim. Fuck of a bad twelve-month stretch. And all just twenty-seven years old.

Twenty-seven. A few intra-cranial tumblers locked into place. Twenty-seven. The same age as Preston Peterson said his son Billy was.

The same age—as reported by Steve—that Terry Weston was.

I went back to Odell's bio on the law firm's website to confirm what I thought I had read.

Yup. Blair Odell was twenty-seven.

This I know to be true: people from away—particularly if "away" is a big city—don't fully understand the bonds—or the feuds for that matter—that are forged among country folks who grow up—and remain—together for much of their lives.

Slow down, Jake. So all three grew up together, so what? Like Carl said: "Everybody knows everybody around here."

True, Jake but they're all the exact same age which means they went all through primary and high school together. Blair left the 'hood ten years ago so he would've probably been in Grade 12.

If the group dynamics of a no doubt small country high school were anything like my big city version, you stayed in your own lane, rarely if ever fraternizing with kids from other grades.

I repeat, Jake: so all three grew up together, so what?

Well, Jake, real good friends often do real bad things together on dares, to help each other out, any number of reasons to do with loyalty and the human need to belong to tribes that defend—or attack—together.

Is there a way to find out just how close to each other they were? Of course, I simply could ask around—but I guessed that it'd be more efficient to visit the one and only high school in the area because all schools are repositories for yearbooks and long-serving chatty teachers. Watch any interviews after yet another school mass shooting as they dig up childhood witnesses. There's always a teacher or two. "He was a quiet boy, didn't have a lot of friends but was pleasant etc."

Late August and I figured teachers would be showing up, getting their classrooms prepped for the horde of eager learners about to descend on the school after Labour Day.

I drove west to Highlands Secondary in Fenelon Falls. As I arrived, I saw it'd taken me just over a half an hour. I imagined the trip from Buckhorn on a school bus. With all its stops along country roads, as well as likely obeying the speed limits, the ride in the yellow Blue Bird bus would have been at least an hour. Lots of time for the three teenagers to get into hijinks and to bond.

Sitting in the guest parking lot at the school, I rehearsed my story, a bullshit tale about being a writer ("See; here's a copy of my latest book.") who was researching a new book. It was to be a comparative study between us boomers when we were young and stupid and the next couple of generations when they were equally youthful and dumb.

The matronly woman on the front desk was a pro, hiding her wonderment and admiration for me as she listened to my pitch. She sent me to the library to look for a librarian named Harvey. I assumed that the lone figure stocking shelves was the guy I wanted.

Harvey gave me the visual once-over and was clearly not impressed, even though the purple and orange Hawaiian number I wore that day went quite well I thought with the purple and orange 1970sish soft seating we sat on. I admit that I presented a sharp contrast to his starched white shirt partially covered by an argyle-patterned wool vest.

I have some practice in getting people to overcome their initial reaction to me and it was clear Harvey wanted to talk. We shot the shit for a bit about my book which he offered to place on a shelf somewhere. He congratulated me for opposing the development, then for helping to uncover the scam. With a connection made, he wanted to help as librarians the world over want to help inquiring minds.

In no time he came up with stacks of yearbooks, maybe forty of them in total. He sat beside me and talked—in his practiced hushed tones—about what he had seen and what he thought about kids these days and in days of yore. He'd spent thirty-five years in this library and his conclusion? I'll net it out for you: Kids are kids are kids regardless of their time.

As he softly rattled on about the similarities among generations, it struck me that ol' Harvey had earned the right to his observations because, unlike most of us, he had daily contact with the same-age kids over entire decades. It also struck me that I had better settle in because I was about to hear—and agree with—every one of those observations. Time to improvise.

Like picking a card, any card from a deck, I drew out various editions of *Vox Studentiam* and leafed through them, drawing attention to clubs and events that had disappeared over the years. No home ec group, the chess club seems to have been mated, no computer programming clubs in the 60s, (although stage crews throughout the years looking remarkably similar with their short-sleeved plaid shirts); and so on.

Harvey wasn't budging from his position that, although interests—and clothes and hair styles—might be different, kids, for all time, were basically the same. Students still exhibited the same tribal traits and were still driven by the need to fit in. Today, Harvey contended, cliques continued to be formed, petty jealousies still existed. True, he allowed, girls were a little more forthright, guys were a little less Neanderthal but, basically, they were all busy being attracted to and/ or repelled by each other, just as they had thirty-five years ago when he first took up his position beside the wooden trays of Dewey's index cards.

After five or six selections, I picked out the 2009 yearbook and went looking for Terry Weston. I flipped to the sports section where I stopped at the photo of the Highland Hurricanes, the school's football team. On the same page were a couple of blurry action shots and another shot of three helmetless players linked arm in arm. They'd obviously just played a game in the rain. Their ratty uniforms were mud-covered, their hair plastered to their heads. All three had exuberant, mile-wide smiles. There was no identifying caption, just the words 'The Three Amigos.' But I recognized them.

Blair Odell, Terry Weston, and Billy Peterson.

"Take these guys," I said. "Was their friendship as strong as it looks?"

"Stronger than most actually," Harvey answered. "Terry was the quarterback, Blair the running back and Billy was the pulling guard. They were thick as thieves."

"Odd metaphor."

"Simile."

"Sorry."

"But it's accurate. That trio got into a fair amount of trouble. Nothing serious. They'd light garbage can fires, hide roadkill in lockers, pull fire alarms, pranks like that. But I can pick any one of those books and point to another group from another year that was just as close and who did exactly the same sorts of things."

"So these three were real rapscallions."

"Now there's a word you never hear anymore. It's exactly right. It wasn't just football that drew them together. All three had...issues."

"Such as?"

"Poverty. That not unusual around here but all their parents were poor as dirt."

Harvey looked up from the book.

"Odd, isn't it, that three were united again over the development?" he mused.

"That's what I was just thinking!" I agreed. "While we're on the subject: you must've known Derek Collins. How'd he figure into it?"

"He was two years ahead. Now he was real trouble."

"How so?"

"He was different from the Three Amigos there. His family was well-off; his father was the only dentist around. Derek didn't even try to fit in; it was as though he was just marking time in school. Always mouthing off to teachers—he even hit one—routinely getting into fights. Terrible marks. He just didn't care."

Harvey was shaking his head and clucking.

"What?" I asked.

"A real pity too," he continued. "Derek was exceptionally smart, especially in the sciences. But all he seemed to want to do was live off his father's money. As if it would last forever. That's another shame."

"What is?"

"A couple of years after he dropped out, his parents were killed in a traffic accident."

"That's terrible. What happened to Derek?"

"I have no idea. You may find this hard to believe but not many students return to talk to their school librarian."

I thanked him and left, pondering my next move. It made sense to me that I needed a better picture of who these three amigos really were. Billy Peterson wasn't exactly a Chatty Cathy. Blair had gone back to Toronto, so Terry Weston would be my starting point. What's more, I sort of reasoned, a town drunk is probably a town observer. Bonus: some drinking would probably be involved. I didn't think that any standard police operating procedure manual recommended getting shit-faced with a suspect but, back in my corporate days, this approach was both fun and instructive with reporters.

CHAPTER 31

I drove to the Buckhorn Lodge, took a table on the deck and ordered a beer. Why, lo and behold, there sat Mr. Weston by his lonesome at another table. I waved him over. He had more thirst than suspicion so he and the remnants of his last rum and coke joined me.

"Another one…on me?" I asked, as the waitress came over.

"Sure. Why not?"

We didn't say a word until our order came. As he wrapped a hand around his glass, Weston seemed to come to life.

"Dunno why I'm even sittin' here," he groused. "You wanted to kill the fuckin' development."

I wanted to point out that free booze might have had something to do with his seat selection but I fought the urge.

"I didn't," I said instead. "I just wanted a small change to the plans,"

"Same diff."

"But I helped uncover the scam. Did you want to keep getting conned?"

"S'pose not," he said.

Time to change topics. The fake land sale wasn't exactly cheering him up.

"Ran into Harvey, the librarian from Highland," I started out. "He said you were quite the Hurricane."

That perked him up, put at least a spark in his booze-coated gaze.

"Man, I could fuckin' throw," he said. "But fuckin' Coach stuck to running plays, power sweep left, power sweep right. Fuck."

A soon as he mentioned them, those plays came back to me. In high school, I had been a mediocre corner linebacker with a simple job against the typical run offences of the day. Take two steps up at the snap and wait to be steamrolled by at least one pulling guard.

"Fuckin' Billy could lay on a block," Weston said. "When he hit you, you stayed hit."

"Nasty piece of work?"

"Billy? Nah. Always been a fuckin' lamb. But when fuckin' Coach told him to do something, he fuckin' did it."

"And Blair?"

"Not too fast, but, man, he was fuckin' smooth. Always found the hole and—bam!—he'd be through. Shit through a goose."

"What about Derek Collins?"

"What about Derek?" Weston asked, his eyes narrowing even further. "What's he got to do with anything? He didn't play."

"Oh. Sorry. I guess Harvey was wrong."

"Fuckin' Harvey," Weston offered by way of editorial comment.

The drinks kept coming. He had a head start on me—Christ, he had almost lapped me—but as long as I stuck with beer, I figured I could go him as his glory days remembrances tumbled out. He might not have recalled what he did yesterday but I must have heard about every game he quarterbacked, the final score, the key plays, even the god-damned weather that day. The tone changed during the recitation. He had started out happy, awash in the warmth of those memories but gradually a bitterness, a regret seeped in with the booze.

Time, I thought, to wind this up before the sadness changed to rage. He hadn't given me anything useful besides some background and it was too late to cross-examine him at the moment. I'd have to re-convene.

We stumbled to the parking lot. If I was hammered; Terry Weston was pile-driven. We stood shakily between the Vibe and his wheels, a fif-teen year-old Chev Cavalier, beige and battered, the driver side mirror duct-taped on, rust streaming from every edge and weld.

He offered to take me home. I declined. Weston was that type of drunk at that stage of tying one on when everything could easily turn into a source of anger. This I know because, for months after Beth died, I was exactly that type of drunk.

"Wass the matter? My fuckin' car not good enough for you?" he asked, almost begging me to agree.

"No. Fuck no," I said.

"Well, you know what? She run's great. I don't give a fuck what you think. You hear me?"

"I believe—" I started to say but Weston was on a runaway express train of a single thought.

"—Fuck you, old man. She runs great, I said!" And he pounded the hood. "Runs better than that piece of shit Porsche Odell owns. How about that?"

"European piece of shit," I echoed.

"Fuckin' right! What car do you think Blair wanted when his piece of shit wouldn't start? Mine! That's what car."

"He borrowed it?"

"Fuckin' right he did! Embarrassed the shit out of him too. Paid me to shut the fuck up about it. And I did. Even to the po—"

Weston came to stop. Somewhere through his booze haze he realized that he had no longer shut the fuck up about lending his car to Blair Odell.

"So fuck you, old man!" he said by way of a good-bye.

I tried to get the keys out of his hands but he still had a few football moves. He juked me and was in his sorry-ass car before I could stop him. As the engine roared to life at about 10,000 RPM, all I could do is lean in the driver-side window and beg him not to drive.

I damn near lost an arm as he threw it into reverse and tore away. Slamming it into drive, he fish-tailed out of the gravel parking lot, narrowly missing the stop sign he ripped past.

Suddenly a whole lot more sober than minutes before, I realized that I should have memorized his plate number. Although, really, what did it matter? How many beige shitboxes with duct-taped mirrors registered to Terence Weston were in downtown Toronto on the night Guy Stavros became extinct? What did matter was whether or not there was a closed circuit TV camera operating along the block of Mercer. A CCTV picking the car up anywhere else wouldn't prove much. Terry would claim he was driving. And who was to say different? And if somehow we could prove that Blair was driving, again, so what? That would put him in the general vicinity: Toronto. Along with about three million other people.

I gave myself an hour to sober up. Me, my smokes and my new information went down to a public bench by the lake to work some things out.

I could call Halley—and I swore I would—and let her untangle it, but a relatively sober Terry had already survived one round of questioning by steadfastly denying everything. He'd do it again, as would Blair. She could commit all sorts of time and money to painstakingly finding and reviewing any possible tapes from that night. If they even existed. And on what basis would she be undertaking this expensive and time-gobbling new avenue of investigation? Why, on the strength of a drunk blathering to another drunk who happened to be her father. Not exactly the solid foundation for an air-tight case.

Nope, I figured a more direct approach was in order. I needed to have a chat with Billy Peterson, and while I was less hopeful about getting anything useful from him as I was with Terry, I had to try. He was the last of the Three Amigos in the 'hood.

Buddies share secrets. And Terry switching cars with Blair one murderous night was a helluva secret.

The Peterson compound looked the same as it had on my previous visit. The array of heavy equipment, the piles of stone and earth. The only addition I could see was a giant heap of mulch beside an industrial-looking wood chipper.

As I left my car and walked across the yard, I could hear something different. Silence. I could see all three lads but they weren't laughing and joking.

Billy abandoned the truck engine he was working on and approached me.

"What do you want?" he demanded, with the same kind of "Geez, I really want to shoot the messenger" expression that Terry Weston had initially displayed. "My old man ain't here. He's in town talking to the fuckin' bank."

"How's he doing?"

"Whaddya think?" he said then seemed to catch himself for his abruptness. "Not too good. He was really counting on the job. We all were."

"I know, Billy, I know…. I see you're getting into the mulch business."

"Might be something there," he allowed.

"Well, you can put me down for five yards."

That seemed to cheer him up a bit but he soon defaulted back into a sort of robotic gloom.

"You worked at the site?" I asked.

"Yeah, I ran the dozer. Man, when I was cutting the roads, I could see the whole thing, laid out and done. Like the plans said. And then it all went to shit. Good money while it lasted."

"You must've been really pissed when it all turned out to be bullshit."

"That why you came here today? To rub it in?"

"Fuck, no, Billy! I swear."

"Then why?"

"I don't know. I guess just to see how you all were doing."

Billy let his gaze play over the yard before turning to me.

"You know when something seems real, real enough to touch," he said. "And then it all gets yanked away?"

"Yeah, I do, Billy. If it matters at all, I feel for you folks."

"Just a shame. A goddamn shame. Screwed over a lot of people."

"Blair's gotta be pretty messed up," I ventured. "He lost the most."

"He lost fuck-all!" Billy said, suddenly getting agitated. "He's a fuckin' lawyer! He lost nuthin' but extra gravy. He drives a Porsche!"

"Yeah, well from what I hear that car of his isn't running so well."

"What the Christ are you talking about?"

"Nuthin' really. Terry—I ran into him in Buckhorn—and he said he had to loan Blair his car."

"I didn't hear anything about that. We haven't exactly been hanging out a lot lately."

"You pissed at him?"

Billy paused, calmed down a bit.

"At Blair? Yeah…a little, I guess. He started all this. Because of his old man's land. He just waltzes in here after all these years and gets it all going."

"Think he knew?"

"No. He was some upset when that newspaper guy ran the story. I seen him."

"How upset?"

"Whaddya mean?"

"Think he did anything about it?"

"What could he do? He was as fucked as the rest of us."

I can't say I actually studied Billy's face but a quick glance told me that Billy was confused, frustrated by my questions that didn't make any sense at all to him. For sure, he wasn't what you'd call looking guilty or suspicious or devious.

A swing and a miss with Billy, I thought as I drove away. That left one Amigo left to talk to.

Yes, Blair was a lawyer but he wasn't a completely hardened criminal. It's not like I was expecting him to break down with a tearful confession. But maybe the right kind of questions might just yield the tip-off, the clue, something that would undo him.

I didn't want to underestimate him. Blair was different than the rest of the trio. He wasn't a drunk and he wasn't guileless.

To put him at ease, get him to confide, maybe slip up, I needed a convincing approach. While I'm not a member of the Subtlety Hall of Fame, I knew I had to play it that way, rather than just jumping out of the bushes and yelling "J'accuse!" (That was my Plan B).

A bunch of think-think-thinking later, I came up with a role-play scenario that I thought might work. Besides drinking beer and smoking, it's one of the few things I'm actually good at: imagining elaborate, scenarios that weren't quite feature film-length but that had a beginning, middle, and end, and made some kind of sense.

I started out with a comment my financially-astute Alex had offered. Edgewater Estates was actually a good idea. Their golf club cart to hearse approach to retirement living was appealing to an aging population with money and a desire to live in communities of similar people who had lots of interests, including an emphasis on healthy living. While I'm morally opposed to all these things, the fact was: If you didn't overpay for the land, and if you eased off all the luxuries, you could make a pretty solid business case for that kind of development on that land.

Now, all I had to do was convince Blair that it was a pretty swell idea. Even though my envisioned Edgewater Part Deux would be as fictitious as the original, it would make sense to Blair that I approach him first. He already owned the main block of land, 784 acres with direct access to the road; Of course, we'd start there. So, no money out the door to buy land. And no money going to plan the thing because somewhere lay all the drawings, all the specifications for the infrastructure. That was huge. And perhaps huger, all the reports and approvals were also in hand.

I'd tell him that we wouldn't need a developer; we'd *be* the developer, hiring sub-contractors as we needed them, initially paying them from the loans we'd take out on our land, then later from the sales proceeds. There was a shit-ton to make.

I wasn't exactly a land baron but I could prove that I had some marketing chops. And Alex had a ton o' business acumen and she knew a passel of rich folks. On paper at least, we were a solid team. I just had to convince Blair that he should revive an equally solid business opportunity with us.

I called Alex and bounced the idea off her.

"You're not letting this go, are you?" she said.

"Dog with a bone."

"This isn't a very good idea, pal. If you're right, he's killed two people, maybe three. For Christ's sake, let the police handle it."

"All they know is Stavros was murdered. They got no suspects, they cleared Blair, and they're writing off Hill and old man Odell as accidents."

"Maybe they were."

"No. I just don't buy it."

"So it's all up to you?"

"It would seem so."

"I may love you but, Jesus, you might think about learning some humility."

"Will you help?"

"I can't believe I'm saying this, but of course I'll help. What do you need?"

"Some math about how a shrunken version of Edgewater could work. Figure on a development about a quarter the size. And with a lot fewer frills."

"No problem. I'll re-work the spread sheets."

"Thanks, darlin'."

I dug out his business card again and called Blair at Wilson, Scharf and Arpell.

Stilted pleasantries out of the way, I jumped in.

"Ya know, Blair," I said. "It seems like a real waste to me to see all that prep work for Edgewater get flushed down the pissoir."

"It's dead."

"But it doesn't have to be. We scale back everything. Instead of offering the moon, we start out small. We make the connections ourselves, get a local builder, tone down the luxury and we can make a real go of it."

"It's dead," he said again.

Without really thinking about it, I launched a last-ditch pitch.

"Look, Blair, the land didn't disappear. Sooner or later, it's gonna be developed. Why not sooner? And why not us? We start out with your land."

"I've got just about no shoreline," he pointed out.

"So I put up my prime lakefront, I can get Carl to sell. Bit by bit, we buy the rest of the land from your chunk to the lake. We already know that the owners want to sell. Luc and Gisele Dubois, for sure. Terry Weston'd be in, Peterson too. Think of all the groundwork that's already been done. All the consultants reports, all the approvals. Just drop the retirement villa—or move it—and there's something there. Even Dubois' environmental approvals are likely still good. The government went out of its way to insist in the media that they'd whacked Luc over his conflict of interest but the approvals he'd OKed were solid. On top of all that, there was no opposition to the Development. And it'd be the kind of "something good out of nothing" story the media—believe me—fuckin' loves."

Silence at the other end.

"What's in it for you?" he asked.

"A gig working with you. I'm so fucking bored. All appearances to the contrary, I used to be a pretty fair PR and marketing guy. Christ, I'll even cut my hair!"

"Council won't touch it. Even if it is legit."

"Leave that to me. I know these guys. I can spin it to them. Help them overcome the stink."

(Note: Unless it has to do with a washing machine cycle, I fucking hate the word 'spin.' But it's accepted by most people as a description of what PR folks do. And I suppose it's more presentable than the verb "bullshit").

Silence on the line again which I took to be a good sign. He was thinking.

"Legally, the Stavros estate shouldn't be a problem," he finally said. "The deposits they paid aren't refundable. All the deeds have reverted to the original owners so none of the creditors can have any claim. I'm pretty sure I can get all his materials—the contacts, the artwork."

"Of course you can. There's gotta be people you know at Traynor-Veitch that can lay hands on all that stuff."

Blair went quiet again.

"My lady's one of the sharpest financial minds you'll ever meet," I piped up. "She says it could work."

"I'll think about it."

"Look, why don't you come on up here this weekend? We'll walk the land, you know, get a feel for what could be done."

After some hemming and hawing, he agreed.

"Oh, and Jake, let's keep this quiet, OK?" he cautioned. "Word gets out and the land prices will go back through the roof."

"Deal. Let's meet at my place first," I suggested. "Do a little planning before we go out there."

CHAPTER 32

I got off the phone feeling uneasy. I played back our conversation in my mind. His last comment about keeping this revived Edgewater to ourselves struck me as odd. Was he so naïve about business that he couldn't see the landowners weren't in any position to haggle much?

I debated whether or not to involve Carl. Bless him, but Carl's idea of subtlety and finesse is switching to a smaller gauge shotgun.

I did, however, tell him about it. He offered to accompany me.

"It's pretty quiet up there," he said. "Just ask Maynard. 'Cept you can't."

"Thanks but I'll be fine. We're just going to be walking and talking."

As promised, Alex sent her cipherin.' As I studied her financial projections and the assumptions she'd made, I had to smile. Damn, that woman was good. She had me convinced it was a good deal.

Saturday dawned overcast and just before noon the sky carried out its threat of rain, not a downpour but a steady warm drizzle. Isn't that fucking great? I thought. Wandering the sodden bush wasn't even close to my idea of a swell time.

I answered the knock on my door a few minutes after twelve.

"Ready?" Blair asked.

"Let's chat a bit in here before we head over. It's miserable out there."

Blair refused my offer to take his damp windbreaker as I ushered him into the screened-in porch. But he did take the beer I handed him. We sat down across from each other at my card table. I had spread out the Edgewater map and marketing materials.

I reckoned that I wouldn't get very far with Odell unless I could get him emotional. In my limited dealings with him, he struck me as deliberate, in control, and calm. I needed to see if he was flappable.

"Before we start," I said, "let me tell you, it's a real shame about Derek. I know you were close."

"Like you give a shit," he said tensing up.

"Well, he made his choices but it's still a shame to end up that way."

"If it wasn't for you, he wouldn't have."

"What?"

"All you had to do was sell and leave."

"But it was all a scam!"

He went quiet. I mean, facts are facts.

"But what we could do is real," I said trying a tenuous little segue. "Very real."

"Show me."

I had to amp myself up with a jolt of fake enthusiasm as I threw myself into the pitch. I started with golf course, explaining we should scale it down to a nifty little executive 9-holer and a much smaller club house. He nodded. We'd keep the marina as is but scratch the idea of supplying free kayaks and Hobie Cats. Again, just a nod from him. We'd also drop the store and clinic and forget any notion of taking over the Angler Arms. He sat there, arms crossed, barely attentive.

I didn't think my attempted visualizations were working with him so I switched to the numbers and spreadsheets Alex had done and I had studied. I hit the highlights, embellishing more than a writhing soccer player faking an injury about how rich we were going to be, how'd we be able to easily pay for bogus Phase 2 with only a portion of what fictional Phase 1 would bring in.

Again, Blair did not seem at all that enthusiastic.

"So can you see it?" I asked trying to get some reaction.

Again, nothing beyond a weak "Maybe."

Time to grasp at some straws.

"You know what would be handy? You giving me some background on the original shitshow," I said.

"Why not? I've got some time to kill," he said with something of a smile. "What do you want to know?"

"You articled at Traynor-Veitch. You must've known what was going on."

"No, I did not. I was just a kid. They were the founding senior partners; they didn't tell me or, as far as I knew, any of the other juniors anything."

"So it was just a crazy coincidence that they got involved with your father's land?"

"Not at all. Almost two years ago, the partners at Traynor-Veitch mentioned they had a client looking to do a big vacation development. They knew I was from around here. When I told them that dear old dad had a big chunk of land, they became real interested. I did a little research, found out who owned the rest. They took it to Stavros and he loved it."

"The lawyers in on it?"

"Not at first. They just thought it was going to be a ton of business for them. They said they were fine with my family making some money. There was going to be more than enough for everybody. About a year ago, they even had me join another firm to avoid any appearance of conflict."

"But the real reason was to get you far away from what they now knew was a swindle."

Blair nodded.

"What did you have to do?" I asked.

"Help out with things up here, behind the scenes. Most of it trying to make sure the sales happened and council approved it."

"You turned Dugald."

"Yes. Stavros told me he had done some research on the landowners and that Dugald was in financial trouble and needed to move his lot. I brokered that exorbitant price for him plus the promise of another 100K after the deal was done."

"Why did you have such a hard-on for my land?"

"Taking all the shoreline from yours to the bar almost doubled the amount of waterfront we could offer. And, don't let it go to your head, but you had a name for being a contrarian bastard. We figured it'd better if you went away."

"Gosh, I'm flattered. So, when I didn't take the offer, Derek decided to start vandalizing."

"He thought you were a pussy and would turtle."

"To mix animal metaphors."

In the conversation so far, Blair had very carefully not indicted himself for anything other than unwittingly repping what eventually turned out to be a fraud and the knowledge of some petty vandalism.

I convinced myself that the ante had to be raised.

"Blair, I really would like to get the whole picture. I need to know about who I might be getting into business with."

"Understood. What do you want to know?"

Here goes, I thought.

"It's been bugging me that you just happened to know Greta Hill through running. She was against the development and she winds up dead."

"Yes. I mean, no. I did know her through the Olympic Club. But I had nothing to do with her death."

"Not quite sure I believe you."

"I had nothing to do with that."

"Well, then Derek did."

"No."

"It was his fentanyl."

"He had people selling for him. She could have bought it from anybody."

Then our eyes locked. And a fact occurred to me: everybody lies. And everybody else usually knows how to recognize it as it's happening, But most people don't call bullshit. It stays at the charade level and, for the most part, society is allowed to function. But they know.

Just the way I knew and just the way he knew in that instant our eyes met.

"How'd you get onto me?" I quietly asked.

"Why would you believe I knew people at Traynor-Veitch unless you'd found out I had worked there? Which meant you were digging into me. And just now. You knew Hill and I ran out of the Olympic Club."

And with that, he drew a black snub-nosed revolver from his windbreaker.

"Well, fuck," I said as that seemed like the only completely appropriate thing to say.

"You didn't have to get involved," he said.

"Yeah, I did," I said, my eyes riveted on the ugly gun. "It was my home at stake."

"And now here we are."

Blair was back to being his cool self again, I presumed because he was drawing on the comfort a loaded gun might bring. Oddly perhaps, but a kind of calm descended on me too. I had been here before. Twice in the last year. On the verge of being shot and the only thought that occurred to me those two times and again at that moment was "Oh, what the fuck?"

"You murdered your own father." I said.

"No. I killed a cockroach. I killed a fucking prick who beat on me, beat on my mom. I killed a...a monster!"

"Outta hate?"

"Not entirely. That just made it easier."

"Then why?"

"Why? Are you fucking kidding me? The land."

"You're the only child; you'd get it anyway."

He snorted.

"When? Dear ol' Dad was just fifty-five. So twenty-five years from now? Longer? And you better believe there wouldn't be a fucking dime left. No. He owed me now."

"But your own father?"

"Oh, fucking spare me!" Blair said. "You weren't there. Nobody was there to see the shit he did to us. Nobody saw us leaving in the middle of the night with just the clothes on our back. Or living in dumps in Toronto—dive fucking rooming houses—or to see my mother working two shit jobs, then me working two shit jobs to make ends meet, to get through university and not a fucking penny from him. Nothing. Just contempt. And still my mother wouldn't divorce the son of a bitch….That fucker haunted me my whole life."

"How did you do it? With Derek, I presume."

"It was actually pretty easy," Blair said, looking as if he were recalling a pleasant memory. "We took the canoe over to the land because we knew he was working there. It wasn't exactly a tearful reunion but the old man didn't suspect anything because Derek was there and dad liked him. Derek's a handy guy. Really, he's quite smart. He came up with the idea of injecting my old man with ethanol. Did you know that ethanol is what shows up in a toxicology panel? He did the math on the dosage so that daddy would show he was about double the legal limit when they found him. I held him. Derek shot him up. He was out in seconds."

"Pretty easy to feed him into the chipper."

"I was set. It was working out perfectly."

"But then you found out the whole thing was a con."

"All I had done, all the planning, all the work. For nothing!"

"How'd you find out? From Stewie?"

"Sort of. But he really didn't know shit. He had a job to do; he did it. I had a pretty good idea of all the moving parts in Toronto and up here. Things were going really well; the money was pouring in. But then Stewie started moaning about not being paid and that made no sense. Why piss off your main sales guy? I found out about the others. Peterson, the engineering consultants, even the goddamned oom-pah band. A little research into Stavros' history and the conclusion was obvious."

"So you borrowed Terry's car and went to see Stavros…."

"I still had a key to the Mercer Street building. I knew that he was there most of the time. Even that was easy. He liked me, I think. I told him I just wanted to go over some papers, I'd brought. I stood beside him while he read them and bang!"

"And now you figure on getting away with three—wait a minute—soon to be four murders."

"Two murders. And yours. That's three. Jesus Christ, you're thick! For the last time. It wasn't me or Derek who killed Hill."

"So how you gonna try to make *this* look like a suicide?" I asked. "What, nobody saw your Porsche in my driveway and I just shot myself four times in the back?"

Pause.

"Oh, I'm not going to fake anything," he said quietly. "I couldn't give a shit anymore. If you know, the cops know. It's all over for me. My practice, the land, everything."

Fuck! I thought again. Hadn't counted on that.

"So me, then you?" I ask.

"Yes."

"How about you go first? Just throwin' it out there. Think about it."

"Funny guy," he said and then there was that unfunny click of the revolver being cocked. I remembered thinking it was remarkably loud.

But not nearly as loud as the shot that followed.

CHAPTER 33

The gun blast caught Odell dead centre in the chest, flung him up against the log wall like an unstrung puppet.

Stunned, I turned to look behind me.

"Sorry 'bout the screen," Carl said, as he climbed through the window frame, not taking his eyes off Blair Odell's lifeless body.

Carl sounded casual but he wasn't. You could see it in his eyes. And he was shaking as he gently put down the gun and we stood briefly looking at Blair. Odell's eyes were open, his head jammed up against the log wall, lolling to one side, his shirt and jacket in bloody shreds, his chest deeply lacerated and glistening with different shades of red.

"'Scuse me," Carl said and went back outside. I could hear him throwing up.

I phoned the police, not 9-1-1 because any emergency was long past, and was connected to Dysart. I told him Blair Odell's body was splayed out in my screened porch, gave him the highlights of our conversation.

"Don't touch a thing. We'll be right there."

I assumed not touching a thing didn't include beer. Carl and I sat silently on the deck and drank.

I thought about—but did not say out loud—the summing up line from Clint's William Munny in *Unforgiven*.

"It's a hell of a thing, killing a man. Take away all he's got and all he's

ever gonna have."

What I did say was this:

"Carl, I brought him up here. I provoked him."

"And I killed him."

"Saving my life, for Christ's sake!"

"And I killed him," he said again.

We lapsed back into silence.

At that moment, it didn't—and perhaps it never would—matter that it a clear case of him or me and I, for one, was pretty glad it wasn't me. Or that Odell had killed two people so there was some kind of visceral eye-for-an-eye shit going on. In time, I supposed that justifications in the brain would submerse this immediate feeling, this dreadful moment. But that was a ways away—if it came at all. For now, the moment was alive and insistent and not going anywhere.

Over the past year, I had been around more dead humans than I ever wanted to be. Humans that had died violently and, in at least four cases, humans who were dead because of me. It had helped—a lot—that three of the dead guys were stone cold killers. It wasn't a big stretch to see karma bloodily at work. The fourth death—of a good-natured and completely innocent young Haitian—was on me as I had promised him something that was not mine to promise. His death haunted me and I expected it always would.

Two cars of police showed up, led by Dysart. He was all business as he took my statement.

"The fact is, Jake, all of this is you claiming what happened," Dysart said when I'd finished. "He might take a different view of events if he were alive," Dysart said, motioning towards the body.

"Well he ain't," Carl said. "But I am and I heard it all. For once, Jake's not bullshitting."

It, of course, wasn't as simple as Dysart going "Oh, OK then. That's good enough for us. Have a nice day."

There was a lot of official stuff that took days. Probably a lot more attention was paid than usual because this was the second time in a year when there was a prematurely dead guy in my house. "Fool me once" and all that.

As Dysart suggested: "Some folks are a little concerned that this is becoming an annual event with you."

The police did all the forensics to prove what we'd told them. Everything from GSR on the torn screen window, to matching Carl's thumbprint on the spent casing, to where Odell had to be sitting the nano-second before he got plastered onto my log cabin wall. I'm thinkin' the cocked revolver they had to pry from Odell's cold dead hand was what you'd call a fairly conclusive mitigating circumstance.

Farther afield, it took the cops less than a minute and a half to sweat Terry Weston into a confession about lending Blair his car on the night Stavros was whacked and then lying to police afterwards. That bit of recanting was backed up by a surveillance camera next door at 12 Mercer showing his shitbox Cavalier on the street minutes before Stavros skedaddled into oblivion. They widened their search to look more closely at Derek Collins' stuff that they had had no reason to analyze before, including his impounded canoe where they found traces of ethanol. They then combed the property on the east side of the lake, didn't find anything because of the faux construction activity but they did come up with old man Odell's DNA in a blood sample taken from the disposable syringe floating by the shore where Blair and Derek had beached their canoe.

During all this investigation, neither Carl nor I were incarcerated so that was bonus.

I could obsess about the details and reasons how we all came to be where we were—and of course, I did—but there was nothing approaching clarity. Greed. Revenge. It was just that simple. What's a whole lot more complicated is why Blair had acted on his desire for revenge, why did his greed compel him to commit murder(s).

What's a motive for some people wouldn't ever even cross the minds of most people.

Most people don't steal Salvation Army Christmas kettles.

Most people don't pull a gun on a minimum wage-earning teenager at a fast food chain restaurant because the kitchen ran out of a new menu item.

Most people don't murder their own children in a bitter custody dispute.

Most people don't stalk and strangle an ex-girlfriend who dumped them.

Most people don't beat a motorist to death with a tire iron during a fit of road rage.

And on and on.

All these fuckers—with "spooky poetry" in their heads as Vonnegut called it—have a motive, a completely understandable—to them alone—explanation for doing what they did. But in all these horrible events, I continue to believe there was at least an instant, immediately before, during or after the bad act, that the bad actor says to himself—and I'm paraphrasing here—"You know what, buddy? This is just wrong and you fuckin' know it."

The fact that Maynard Odell was a nasty wife-abusing, child-traumatizing prick and that Guy Stavros was a heartless, greedy conman might someday lessen the impact. Someday. But these rationalizations would never, not ever change the fact that everything they may have done to make life unpleasant, even unbearable for other humans didn't amount to offences that were punishable by death.

Halley called. She had kept tabs on all the police work that had corroborated the shit out of what Carl and I had testified.

"Aren't you going to say it, Dad?" she asked.

"Say what?"

"I told you so."

"Halley, Halley, Halley, it's a true fact that if you have to say it, you come off as a real self-righteous asshole."

"That's never bothered you before."

"Point. OK, try this: it's more fun *not* saying it."

"Dad, do you ever get tired of having your ass saved by somebody else?"

"I'm worth it."

"To who?"

"Whom. It's 'to whom'."

"Alright. To whom?"

"Well, me for openers."

"I'm just glad that it's all over and it all turned out."

"Except it isn't over."

"Dad, let it go."

"Alright, alright I will."

"Liar."

"Look, Halley, someone made that pill and we know that was Derek Collins—the recently departed Derek Collins—and someone took that pill. That was Dr. Greta Hill. But someone sold her that pill and we don't know who did that. And that person needs to get caught."

"Let the Peterborough police handle it."

"I said I will."

She was clearly not convinced, probably because I was clearly lying.

CHAPTER 34

It's entirely possible that most people have sound reasons for doing what they do. They think about things, figure out a logical course of action then take it. I even do it from time to time, mostly when it involves planning for my finances to expire a week or so after I do. For just about everything else, I do something because I either just want to or I feel I ought to. This 'ought to' category used to perplex me. It does no longer. I hate myself for using it, but the best analogy is a techie one: Somewhere in my wee brain is a background operating system that sets my rules. I don't care at all when, how or by whom the lines of code were written. It's not quite right to call it a hunch or intuition. It's because I have to.

And right then, I believed I had to have a hand in finding the guy who sold Greta Hill the pill that killed her.

This opioid shit is finally getting the press and the attention it deserves. Out of nowhere, it now kills more people than breast cancer. Over twenty years of involvement in Viet-Nam, 47,000 Americans died in combat. That's the same number of lives as were lost to opioid ODs in the US. In 2017 alone. Most of them were kids. Kids who were mostly looking for a cheap rush then numbness. Most of them were not looking to die.

Now I can—and do—rant about Big Phucking Pharma's role in all this and a bunch of other dark practices just so they get to maintain the highest overall profit margins of any industry, but in this case it was Derek's DIY chemistry at the root of it. And sure as hell, there was going to be another amateur chemist pop up in the neighbourhood looking to fill the void now that Derek had moved to a void of his own.

You will have noticed that this steaming pile of hypocrisy is brought to you by a pharmaceutically-dependent diabetic *and* a cigarette smoker. In my pitiable defence: Companies have been making bank on metformin, my go-to protection against slipping into a sugar-induced coma, for half a century in Canada; I'm bettin' they've recovered the development costs.

And there isn't a smoker alive—albeit temporarily—that doesn't know the danger. But we accept the risk because it's usually a forty or fifty-year process, not the forty or fifty seconds it can take to kill you with a pinch of salt's worth of the fake heroin. And we also know what chemicals are in our white tubular death and disease devices— all 4,000 of them. Those kids don't have clue who cut their pills with what.

So my two-facedness aside, I planned to find the goddamn pusher man.

First off, I figured that me looking like an old hippie might finally have a practical use. No doubt I appeared as though I was either high or wanting to get high. I couldn't imagine anyone getting suspicious if I started asking around, looking for my connection.

But ask who? I'd start with Billy Peterson. He had been chummy enough with Derek to go drinking with him at AA. I'd seen together them at the best cottage country bar in the world™ at the start of the summer. I also reckoned that Terry Weston might be pretty well acquainted with the local illegal pharmaceutical representatives. If he wasn't a customer himself, he'd probably know who was.

I'd also have to somehow involve the Peterborough police. Dysart might help get me a peek at the files they had on the three ODs but I doubted it; he was definitely a by-the-book guy. Failing that, I'd get re-acquainted with Detective Sergeant Les Macgregor at the OPP detachment in Peterborough. Sure as hell, even though she'd seen the files, Halley wasn't going to help out.

More than likely, there would have to be some fawning, some

wheedling, a bit of cajoling to get Les to give. I stopped just short of writing out the obsequious script I planned to use.

Turns out, I could have spent this prep time doing something else. Like getting at that fucking sock drawer.

Preston Peterson showed up one morning, as he always did this time of year, to pump out my septic holding tank.

We chatted amiably for a bit as though nothing had happened over the summer. But I could see something was bothering him.

"Are you alright, Preston?" I asked. "Diabetes getting to you? You gotta see a doctor. You *know* that."

"It ain't that. It's…nuthin'."

"Bullshit. Just say. Who knows? I might be able to help."

"It's my boy."

"Billy?"

"Yeah."

"What about Billy?"

"He's done some things."

"What things?"

"I… found some pills in his room. Maybe fifty in a baggie."

"What'd he say?" I asked.

"He broke down. He started cryin'and carryin' on. Tore me right up."

"He was taking them or selling them?" I asked.

"Selling. Derek—that no good bastard—set him up."

"That no good *dead* bastard," I pointed out. "How did he do it?"

"Billy, he'd get to talking with my customers on his rounds. Mostly their kids."

"And Greta Hill was one of those customers."

"Yeah....He saw her one day at her place. She was in a lotta pain. Billy said he had somethin'."

Preston's voice trailed off then came roaring back.

"He's a good boy! He knows he did wrong."

"So now what?"

"You were in my place, what would you do?"

"It's not up to me to say, Preston. But people got hurt. People died. He's got to face it."

"It don't make it better, but he swears he only sold to my customers up here, never down in Peterborough or where the others died. I believe him. He said he's been doin' it for a year. Hadn't spent a penny. He was goin' to give me all of it. For the business. He showed me. Almost nine thousand dollars."

Preston was crying now. Great sobs shook him. All I could think to do was rest my hand on his meaty shoulder.

"It'll be hard on him for a while," I said. "For years maybe. But that's how it works."

"I know, I know. The right thing."

"The right thing."

"Thank you, Jake."

"Thank me? I didn't do anything. You already knew the answer. But more important, I bet Billy knows the answer."

Billy turned himself in the next day. On their evening news, CHEX showed him—with his father—at the police station, grim-faced, neatly-dressed, and silent. They also had a lawyer and I was glad I had had time to call Gordon Wellsley for the name of a decent criminal defence attorney. Preston was wildly grateful for my offer to pay for the services of Barry Viner, rewarding me with free shit-pumping for life (although we never established if his death or mine would define the upper limit). Paying that legal bill was another thing I figured I ought to do. I also figured it wasn't going to break my modest bank because I bet myself that Billy would plead guilty.

He did. He got a year, I read on-line when I was down south after all the court stuff was over.

I could tie myself in knots wrestling over whether Billy had been hit with too much jail time or not enough. On balance, I fall on the side believing that grown adult customers of illegal shit they know could kill them have to bear most of the responsibility. Put another way, I ain't ever joining any class action against the tobacco companies.

It hadn't been a bad batch that Derek mixed up. That came out during the trial. The pills that Derek manufactured and Billy sold to Greta Hill, the pills that killed her and others, were what they were advertised to be: pure fentanyl coated with harmless baby powder.

And that, of course is the scary as hell part about all this.

CHAPTER 35

By the end of September the first stirrings of real change come. The afternoon light becomes clearer, gone is the July haze. The garden has exhausted itself, the geraniums blooms are smaller, less frequent. Petunias dry out, their branches withered and beyond revival by water. On the plus side, with the occasional threat of frost, we have seen the last of those fucking flying insect vampires.

But to keep the cosmic ledger balanced, sitting outside in a bug-free environment isn't exactly a time to luxuriate because, before you know it, it gets dark by 6:30 and when the sun goes down, a chill arrives. And fucking socks must be worn.

The neighbourhood hummingbirds have already come and gone, having zipped among the canna lilies' red blooms, stoking up for their trip to the Gulf of Mexico. The lake falls silent, no longer troubled by summer vacationers roaring around on those goddamned jet skis during the day or the loud plaintiveness of the loons during the night.

Finally, the Canada geese come and go.

There was a pleasant interruption to this fall's natural cycles. Steve showed up to say goodbye and hang out for a few days. And to repay Carl for his sentry duties. I, of course, owed Carl a whole bunch more so we both pitched in for two days helping him cut firewood to sell. For two guys who basically spend their lives with their heads up their own asses thinking about things, it was a study in contrasts to be bouncing along in Carl's battered F150 through what was to be Edgewater Estates up to his woodlot. We hauled, split, and stacked a mountain of hardwood Carl had felled a year ago until we were sweating under our grungy work clothes and we ached all over.

That wasn't the pleasant part. The post-labour drinking was. Steve watched Carl and I tuck into a case of Ex while he nursed his flavoured soda water. Finally—and nervously—he asked if he could join us. I didn't rejoice. My friend had quit booze years ago and if he had decided it was a problem, then it was a problem.

I asked "Are you sure?" enough times that I became more tiresome than usual. I told him that we'd be watching—sort of like the medical supervision Aldous Huxley arranged for himself when he experimentally dropped mescaline for the material to write *Doors of Perception*.

"Just don't be stupid," I said. "Forever and all time, don't be stupid."

And he wasn't. We laughed like hell.

Round about mid-October I know the end is nigh for my stay in Canada. That's when we have Thanksgiving. No doubt the main reason we are thankful is because we don't have to have the holiday in the third week of fucking November like the States. By that time up here, snow, sleet, ice, and grumpiness cover the land.

As with other holidays, I don't celebrate it anymore, not since Beth died. I sometimes miss the repeated memories of Christmas, Easter, and Thanksgiving—particularly the sights and smells of big meal preparations. Beth buzzing around the kitchen with her game face on. The sound of sheets of aluminum foil being ripped to cover pies and vegetables and turkey—yards of it, enough to clad a stealth fighter or make the hats for a 9/11 conspiracy convention. Hours of preparation, a fire bucket brigade of dishes heading to the table where the feast is gobbled down in no time accompanied by the loud clatter of real silverware and louder conversation, to be followed by satisfaction, drowsiness, and flatulence.

I think about the future of my holidays now that Alex is part of my life. I have no idea if such things matter to her—yet another thing I don't know but want to discover.

By the third week of October I too am ready to fuck off south. I do like to hang around long enough to see the leaves change colour. For a couple of weeks, all the fiery yellows, oranges and reds lining the lake impress the shit out of me and apparently hundreds of thousands of other people across eastern North America who sit in long traffic jams just to watch the leaves change in the hills of New England or the Laurentians in Quebec.

And then, it seems almost overnight, the leaves are gone and the drabness and cold and rain set in. Show's over, folks; nuthin' to see here. Move along.

One of my many, many rituals is to play *Urge for Goin,*' the Tom Rush version of Joni's song. For years and years, that sad last line—"I get the urge for goin,' but I never seem to go."—was an accusation, a jibe, a fantasy.

Well, now I go.

And before I do, I have all sorts of things to do, some of which I actually like doing because they're my punctuation marks, my way of putting a period on summer in Canada. Leaf raking and burning (still illegal), raccoon-proofing my storage shed with chicken wire so the lumbering little bastards can't squeeze under it and gnaw through the floor like they did a few winters back. I crawl around in the aptly-named crawl space under the house vainly using wads of steel wool to plug any possible holes the mice find to invade—sort of like the little Dutch boy at the dyke, only with infuriating vermin.

I dig up the canna, calla, and dahlia bulbs, hose them down, box them with crumpled newspaper, and then barge them over to Carl's where they'll spend the winter in a spare bedroom.

Then I have to suspend things—my car insurance, cable, phone, Internet. All that saves a surprisingly large whack of money that I turn around and cheerfully invest in the Presidente beer company in the DR.

My second last act of winterizing my place is boating over my ridiculously big TV and hooking it up for Carl.

The final act is getting rid of all alcohol-based liquids lest they fall into the wrong hands, i.e. those marauding teens on snowmobiles. Carl shares my civic-mindedness and pitches in to help. We get royally bent and usually trash-talk each other about the NFL because this face-to-face chirping will have to hold us all the way to Super Bowl. We've gone through close to half the regular season at this point so we're usually primed to say heartlessly cruel things to each other about our favourite teams. Fucking Cowboys.

This time, there was some of that, but mostly we re-capped the summer. We usually do that too, but in years past it was to laugh again at all the stupid shit we did. We could not find a lot of yuks over the past five months.

"I forever owe you, buddy." I told him.

"Fuck off, will ya? You'd do the same for me."

"No I wouldn't."

"Arsehole."

"You OK?" I ask.

"I suppose."

But he had a faraway look in his eyes. Like me, he was probably thinking back to the instant he fired that shotgun. In that instant, a lot had changed for him—not as much as it had for Blair Odell—but pretty dramatically for him nonetheless.

I suppose that would have been the moment for me to offer up a patently obvious cliché about time healing all. But I didn't. Saying something like that to a 75-year old who's lived a full and hard life is a fucking insult.

Instead I got him a beer.

We weren't exactly chatty as Carl drove me to Pearson Airport, but then again we never are. Carl was grimly focused on driving in the big city and I was grimly focused on hoping we made my flight rather than dying in a flaming wreck on the 401.

There were two different things about our trip this year. Carl had to look for the Delta Airlines section and not WestJet at Terminal 3. That's because I was heading to Boston for a week with Alex, a week I planned to spend enjoying myself and her while freezing my ass off. A week in which I would resume haranguing her about coming to the DR for a big chunk of the winter.

The other different thing happened when Carl and me and the Vibe stopped at the terminal. I got out with my shitty laptop and trusty bowling bag. Carl got out. So far, so normal. But instead of rather formally shaking hands as we usually do, we spontaneously hugged. Just a bit. Briefly but firmly. It was an affectionate bridge too far and we both knew it.

But it felt good.

"Have a shitty winter, bud," Carl said.

"You too, my friend."

ACKNOWLEDGEMENTS

I want and need to thank some recurring characters in my book-scribbling enterprise.

Once more, Glenn Torresan is responsible for the cover design, photography, and lay-out of the book. Fun fact: *Bushwhacked* also marks the third cover where Glenn has made an appearance—well, parts of him. There may not be enough blue agave in Mexico to truly express my gratitude.

Big appreciation is due Ron Corbett, a dear friend and a dear publishing dude. His determination in birthing and raising Ottawa Press and Publishing is downright inspirational. My deep thanks for his thoughts on writing and on getting that writing out there.

And to Maggie: Thanks, babe, for your encouragement and help. And for caring.

I may have taken some geographic liberties with the shape of Jake's lake. Forgive me my cartographic sins. Every other mistake you find is also mine. Although, if I made it deliberately then it's not a mistake, is it?

If anything in this book offends you—Jake's foul mouth, his views on anything, his looseness with the English language—well, gosh, I'm sorry.

John Owens has written three books in the Jake Lydon mystery series with a fourth Lydon book—*Jackpot*—well underway.

Owens is also the author of two works of historical fiction. *On the Rails*, a cross-Canada Great Depression-era saga and *The Sixth String*, the story of a flamenco guitarist caught up in Hitler's Germany.

He lives in Morrisburg, Ontario and Indian Rocks Beach, Florida with his ridiculously patient wife, Maggie. There's also now a dog involved but the less said about Buster, the better.

You can find out more about the books at johnowens.ca or on Facebook. You can also go to ottawapressandpublishing.ca

Four of his novels—*Connecdead*, *Machete*, and *Bushwhacked*, as well as *On the Rails*—are available on Amazon.ca, .com, and .uk as e-books or print copies. Purchasing Hint: type in both the book title and the writer's name. Otherwise, you'll likely find yourself scrolling through the works of 17th-century English Puritan theologian John Owen who evidently was not a barrel of laughs, although both *The Mortification of Sin* and *Temptation: Resisted and Repulsed* had their lighter moments.